KILL SHOT

SALLY RIGBY

TOP
DRAWER
PRESS
CRIME FICTION BOOKS

GET ANOTHER BOOK FOR FREE!

To instantly receive the free novella, **The Night Shift**, featuring Whitney when she was a Detective Sergeant, ten years ago, sign up for Sally Rigby's free author newsletter at www.sallyrigby.com

Detective Chief Inspector Whitney Walker stared open-mouthed at her daughter Tiffany, not quite believing the words that she'd uttered.

'Could you repeat that?'

This couldn't be happening. It was a joke. She'd misheard … anything … but not …

'You're going to be a granny.'

Whitney glanced across at the forensic psychologist, Dr Georgina Cavendish, her friend and colleague, whose stunned expression replicated her own.

'How?' She diverted her attention back to her daughter and Lachlan, the boy she'd returned home with after a year travelling in Australia, having taken time out of university. Whitney hadn't been ecstatic about her leaving, but knew Tiffany had to follow her own path.

'I don't think I need to spell that out, Mum,' Tiffany said, as she exchanged a knowing glance with Lachlan and grinned.

But Whitney couldn't return the smile. This was going to change her daughter's life forever. She was too young to tie herself down when there was so much more out there for her to experience and enjoy.

'Didn't you learn anything from my mistake?' She rested her hands on the table, jagged breaths catching in her throat.

'What are you saying? That you regret having me?' Tiffany asked, her voice tinged with hurt.

Whitney swung around to where her daughter was standing next to Lachlan. 'Of course not. From the day you were born, you were the best thing in my life. But that doesn't mean getting pregnant at such a young age was the right thing to do. Surely you must see that?'

There had been so many obstacles for Whitney to overcome. But she'd never shared that with Tiffany. She didn't want her growing up thinking that she was the cause of any problems.

'I'm not seventeen. I know what I'm doing.' She turned to Lachlan. '*We* know what we're doing.'

'Do you? Do you really? Then how did you let yourself get pregnant?' She turned to Lachlan, who'd remained silent. 'Have you told your parents?'

'They're cool about it,' he said, shrugging.

She glared at him, wanting to knock his laid-back, surfer-dude attitude into the middle of next week. Surely she couldn't be the only one to see the awful mess this was? She also hated that his parents knew before she did.

'What do you think, George?' she said remembering her friend was standing close by.

'It isn't for me to comment. It's a family issue.'

A typical George remark.

'You're like family. Without you, Tiffany wouldn't even be here,' Whitney said, referring to the time George had been instrumental in saving her daughter's life when she'd been kidnapped by a serial killer.

'I'm leaving now so you can continue your discussion in private. Welcome home, Tiffany,' George said as she made her way out of the kitchen.

'What about the pizza?' Whitney called out, glancing down at the box on the kitchen table which they'd brought home with them, unaware that Tiffany had returned. The front door slammed. 'She doesn't want any,' she muttered returning her gaze to her daughter. 'It looks like it's just the three of us. I'll get some plates.'

'Not for me, thanks. We ate at the airport,' Tiffany said.

'I'll have some,' Lachlan said.

Whitney pulled out two plates from the cupboard, using the time to try to relax. She wanted to come across as acting rationally, even though her insides were going crazy.

'I can't believe your reaction. I thought you'd be happy for us,' Tiffany said as they all sat around the table.

Was her daughter really that naïve?

'My happiness doesn't come into it. I know how hard it is for someone with their whole future ahead of them to be saddled with a child.'

'Is that how you thought of me? That you were *saddled*.'

Damn. She hadn't meant to say that. Not least because it wasn't true.

'No. Look, we all loved you. Me, your granny, grand-dad, Uncle Rob. But that doesn't change things. What you decide to do now is going to affect you forever.' She looked at the boyfriend who was wolfing down his pizza, seeming totally oblivious to the conversation going on around him. 'You do know this, don't you, Lachlan?'

'Yeah, sure.' But his eyes told a different story.

'So what are your plans? Are you going to live here with me?'

She'd need to have a clear out in the spare bedroom if

it was to become a nursery. Maybe that wouldn't be a bad thing. She'd been hoarding stuff in there for years.

'Initially, if that's all right, as we've got plenty of space,' Tiffany said.

Plenty was a slight exaggeration, but she'd rather they were here than anywhere else so she could keep an eye on things.

'That's fine. Have you thought about work?'

'I'll find a job,' Lachlan said.

'Have you got any qualifications?'

'Not exactly,' he said shrugging.

'Can you be more specific?'

'Mum,' Tiffany interrupted. 'This isn't a police interview.'

'It's okay, babe,' Lachlan said.

Babe? Seriously?

'Sorry. I was curious, that's all,' she said, trying to play it down. They were kids and had no idea of what it was like to be in the real world. But they would do soon enough.

'I dropped out of uni because I wanted to have more free time to enjoy myself,' Lachlan said.

'And you think this is going to give you more free time?' She threw up both hands in despair.

'It'll be cool. We love each other.' He leant across the table and placed his hand over Tiffany's.

Until the novelty wore off. But she wasn't going to say that now. She'd already upset her daughter, which she hated doing.

'Have you got any money?' she asked, taking a more practical approach.

'A little,' Tiffany said. 'There's bound to be a bar job Lachlan can apply for and I can work until I have the baby. I'd get a bar job too, if it wasn't for the fact that the smell of beer is turning my stomach at the moment. I'll apply to work in a shop. You don't need to worry, we'll pay for ourselves.'

'I'm your mum, of course I'm going to worry.' Her eyes filled with tears, but she quickly looked down at her plate, not wanting Tiffany to see, and blinked them away.

'Mum, I get that you don't think this is ideal, but what's the alternative? Surely you don't want me to get rid of the baby. I could never do that. You didn't.'

Should she tell her the truth?

'It was something I'd considered, and Granny and Granddad said it was my decision, and they'd stand by me, whatever I did.'

'But you went ahead and had me.'

'Yes, because I knew it was the right thing to do.'

'And this is the right thing for me to do, too.'

Whitney sighed. 'I understand. You telling me like that was such a shock. I'm sorry, I didn't mean to go off on one. You know, it's not going to be easy.'

'We'll survive, just like you did. In fact, you more than survived, you made a huge success of your life. You're my role model.'

Whitney allowed herself a smile. Maybe she'd overreacted and it would be all right after all.

Chapter 2

Three months later

Whitney stood in the doorway of the lounge and stared at her daughter, Tiffany, sitting on the sofa reading a magazine having just finished her breakfast, even though it was almost lunchtime. It seemed like only yesterday when Tiffany was a tiny baby and yet here she was, her hands resting on her heavily pregnant tummy, the baby due in only twelve weeks. It had been three months since the bombshell Tiffany and her now ex-boyfriend had dropped, and Whitney had finally got used to the idea of becoming a grandmother. Despite declaring in no uncertain terms that no way would she be called grandma, nanny, granny, or anything remotely similar as it would make her feel a lot older than her *thirty-nine going on forty*.

Lachlan hadn't stayed in Lenchester long, and after a few weeks, had returned home to Australia as he couldn't get used to being in the UK. He didn't give it much of a chance and had spent most of the time sitting on the sofa watching telly, moaning about how cold it was. Whitney had been glad to see him go, although she realised that even with support, which Tiffany would have in bucket-loads from her, the enormity of having sole responsibility for another human being wasn't going to be easy.

'Can I get you anything?' she asked.

'No thanks, Mum. Come and sit with me.' Tiffany patted the space next to her.

Whitney wandered over and dropped down on the sofa.

'How are you feeling today?'

For the last few weeks the baby had been putting pressure on Tiffany's sciatic nerve and had caused her a great deal of discomfort, especially when she'd been at work, as her job in a department store in the city had involved being on her feet for many hours at a time.

'Okay, thanks. The pain isn't so bad today, so hopefully the midwife was right when she said that it will go away of its own accord within a few weeks.'

'Fingers crossed,' Whitney said, rubbing her daughter's leg. 'Have you heard anything from Lachlan recently?'

She hadn't asked for a while because she didn't want to upset Tiffany, but she was curious to know how it was going to work out.

'No but I don't mind. It was ridiculous of me to think we had something long-lasting. Once the reality of being stuck here in Lenchester hit him, being away from the ocean, the good weather, and his friends, he changed. I still like him as a person, but he wasn't the settling down type, and it's a good job I found out sooner rather than later.'

Amen to that.

Tiffany was strong, sensible and courageous and Whitney couldn't be any more proud of the way she'd approached being pregnant and her plans for the future. She'd intended on working until the end of her pregnancy, but what with the morning sickness, which hadn't eased and still lasted most of the day, and the sciatica, Whitney had suggested that she handed in her notice. Her last shift was the day before yesterday and they gave her a leaving present of a voucher to spend in the store. They'd also offered her a job after the baby was born if she wanted to go back.

Whitney didn't mind Tiffany not working, she'd rather her daughter rested, and it wasn't like they were financially strapped for cash. They might not have as much money as George, but they had more than enough to cover all expenses and have some left over for non-essentials.

'I'll be here to help you with the baby every step of the way. Although I might leave the throwing up to you.' Whitney could face most things, but the sounds and smells created by someone being sick, even a tiny baby, turned her stomach.

'Oh.' Tiffany gasped. 'The baby's just kicked. Feel it.'

Whitney put a hand on her stomach as the baby moved again, warmth flooding through her. 'I can't wait to be your grandmother, little one,' she whispered.

'You don't look old enough to be one.'

'Thanks,' she said, giving her daughter a hug. 'I've got to admit I feel it sometimes. Just remember, you're not facing this alone. I'll be here for you whenever you need me.'

'Apart from when work calls.'

'Trust me, it will all fit in. I've done it before when I had you, and your grandparents were there to help.'

Whitney's dad had died twelve years ago, and her mum was in a care home because she had dementia, so they wouldn't be around to pitch in, which Whitney was sad about. Whitney's brother, Rob, was getting excited about the new baby. He too was in a care home after a savage attack when he was a teenager left him brain-damaged.

'Thanks, Mum,' Tiffany said.

Whitney sucked in a breath. Was now a good time to, once again, broach the subject with Tiffany of her father, Martin?

'I wanted to ask you about Martin. Have you decided yet whether you'd like to meet him?'

When Tiffany had arrived back from Australia, Whitney had explained that she'd recently been in contact with her father. Tiffany took it well, but at the time wasn't sure about getting to know him. Understandably, as Whitney had always maintained that at aged seventeen she'd had a drunken one-night stand with a waster. Tiffany had accepted the explanation without questioning her further. It was only when Whitney had met Martin at a school reunion that she realised what had actually happened was nothing like she'd played out in her mind over the last twenty-two years.

'I've been thinking about it a lot, especially as I've got so much time on my hands. I think maybe I will, but not quite yet. I'll let you know once I'm ready.'

'He's definitely keen for you to get together.'

He hadn't been pressuring Whitney, he wasn't that type of man, but he'd made it clear he'd be willing to do what-ever it took to connect with his daughter. For years he'd believed that he couldn't father children, so when he'd learnt about Tiffany he was thrilled. Whitney had told him about the baby, and he was almost as excited as she was.

'It's been hard to come to terms with after all those years of not knowing who, or where, he was.'

Whitney grimaced. 'I know, and I'm sorry about that, but I genuinely thought it was just a drunken night. What I hadn't realised was that I'd given him a hard time and actually ignored him despite him wanting us to be together. It was all very complicated, as everything was at that age.

But he would really like to see you and I'd like for you to get to know him. He's a decent guy.'

'It never bothered me before. I was happy with it being just you and me, Granny, Granddad and Uncle Rob. But now I've got this little lump,' – she patted her stomach – 'I feel differently about it. Obviously, I'm going to have to tell the baby about Lachlan when the time comes.'

'He might want to come back over here once it's been born.'

'I doubt it. He seemed happy to get away from here. I'll let him know after the birth, then he can decide if he wants to be a part of our lives.'

'Well, whatever happens we'll deal with it, and—' Whitney's phone rang and she glanced at the screen. It was work. 'What now? Sorry, I'd better get this. So much for having a day off.' An exasperated sigh escaped her lips.

'No problem,' Tiffany said, waving a hand. 'I'm used to it.'

'Walker?'

'Guv, it's Brian,' DS Chapman, who'd recently joined the team, said. 'We've just had notification that Ryan Armstrong has been found dead in the car park next to the snooker club he owns. Suspected shooting.' Her heart sank. Not another murder. She'd scream if it turned out to be a serial killer, which seemed to be what usually happened in Lenchester. It was like they had a sign at the entrance of the city saying *Serial Killers Welcome Here*.

'Crap. The media won't give us a moment's peace once they find out. We need to get onto this pronto. Text me the club's address and I'll head out to the scene. Meet me there.'

Ryan Armstrong was more than just a famous snooker player. He was Lenchester's biggest celebrity and most people in the area were aware of who he was. Whitney knew nothing about snooker, but she knew of him. His face was always on the telly, as so many companies used him to advertise and endorse their products. He was also known for the charity work he did locally.

She turned to Tiffany. 'I'm really sorry, love, but something's come up and I've got to go out.'

'I realised that from listening to your side of the conversation. Don't worry about me, I'm going to sit here and relax. And probably eat my body weight in Mars Bars as that's all I seem to be doing recently. I don't know how I'm going to get rid of the extra pounds afterwards.' She grabbed hold of her tummy and wobbled it.

'It will soon drop off because you'll be running around after the baby. I'll try not to be too long, but you know what these things are like.'

'Another murder?'

'It looks like it. Ryan Armstrong, the snooker player.'

'Oh, no,' Tiffany said, raising her hand to her mouth. 'That's awful. He was at the uni a couple of years ago doing a show. He did some awesome trick shots. What happened?'

'This is between us, obviously, he was shot in a car park next to the snooker club he owned. I'm going to call George to see if she's around and can meet me there. Contact me if anything urgent happens. I've no idea when I'll be back. I'll try not to wake you if it's late.'

As Whitney left the house to get into her car, her phone pinged with the address.

She hit speed dial for George.

'We've got a murder,' she said once her friend had answered. 'Can you meet me at the scene? It's' – she paused while opening the message – 'the Palace Snooker Club in Fletcher Street. The body was found in the car park next door. The victim's a professional snooker player and local celebrity, so this will be high profile. I'll need you on it from the start.'

'You're lucky to catch me. If I hadn't come home to collect a book I'd forgotten, I'd have been at Ross's and it would have taken me a while to get to you. I'll be with you in twenty minutes at the most.'

'Great. By the way, what do you know about snooker?'

'Nothing.'

'That makes two of us.'

Chapter 3

George drove down Fletcher Street, stopping when she reached the police cars and a cordon across the entrance to a car park. She parked on the other side of the road and got out of her car, scanning the area to see if Whitney had arrived, but there was no sign of her. Claire Dexter, the pathologist, was there, as evidenced by her car, an immaculate MGC which George coveted each time she set eyes on it. She was about to go over to take a look when Whitney pulled up behind, so instead she went to meet the officer.

'I see Claire's here,' Whitney said, nodding at the car.

'Yes, but I haven't spoken to her.'

They crossed the road and went over to Whitney's sergeant, Brian, who was standing close to the two uniformed officers stationed by the entrance to the cordoned off area.

'Is SOCO here yet?' she asked him.

'They're on their way. Dr Dexter arrived about ten minutes ago and headed straight for the body, which is in the silver Lexus parked down there in the corner.' He pointed down the short drive which ran along the side of the building housing the snooker club.

'Who found the victim?'

'Molly Arthur, who works at the club, when she arrived for work about forty-five minutes ago. She's in a state of shock and is in a police car with one of the PCs.' He nodded in the direction of a police car stationed close by. George could see the shadow of two people on the back seat.

'We'll check out the body before we speak to her.' Whitney took the log from the officer by the cordon and signed herself, Brian and George in.

They headed down the entrance of the disused piece of land that was used for parking and turned left as it went behind the red-brick building. Claire was on the far side, standing next to the car which was facing the back wall, its door open, pointing her camera inside.

'Hello,' Whitney called out as they approached.

'Don't come any further I haven't finished,' Claire shouted, not even bothering to look up and acknowledge them. Typical Claire behaviour, and what they'd all become used to.

George strained to see inside the car. The man was against the door, his head slightly to one side. There were some blood splatters on the windscreen, but not enough to bother her. She'd mainly got over her blood aversion, thanks to hours of hypnotherapy, but occasionally when faced with large amounts it still affected her.

'Was he shot?' Whitney asked.

'Yes, but I won't know whether that was the cause of death until he's on the table at the morgue,' Claire said.

'Time of death?'

'Sometime between 11 p.m. and 4 a.m.'

'We'll come and see you for the post-mortem. Do you recognise him?' Whitney asked.

'Of course, I do. I don't live on the ark. He's Ryan Armstrong the snooker player.'

Claire knew about snooker? George wasn't one to prejudge, but she certainly hadn't expected that.

'You're a snooker fan?' Whitney said, shaking her head, most likely thinking the same as George.

'In last year's world championship, our man here' – Claire waved her hand in the direction of the victim – 'played one of the best shots I've ever seen at a time when the pressure and stakes couldn't be higher. The white ball headed towards the corner pocket and it hit the edge at a tight angle and then came back and hit the red, which was halfway up the table on the opposite side. It was the turning point of the match and he went on to make a 147, maximum break. Extraordinary play. The man was a genius.'

Fascinating. Perhaps she should look more into the intricacies of the sport.

'I'll take your word for it. I know nothing about snooker,' Whitney said. 'Nor does George. But irrespective of that, this investigation will be under public scrutiny as he's one of the country's top sportsmen and a local celebrity. It's an extremely high-profile case, and once the media hears what's happened they'll be on our backs the entire time. You might want to be on your guard because, no doubt, you'll be scrutinised, too.'

'They can try,' Claire said, giving a frustrated sigh. 'Despite who the victim is, I really didn't want to be here on a Sunday. Ralph and I had plans.'

Whitney glanced at George. No doubt she'd have something to say about Claire sharing her private life with them once they were alone.

'Weren't you on duty?' George asked, surprised Claire was complaining as she should have expected the possibility of being called out to deal with a suspicious death.

'I wasn't meant to be, but it turned out the person on duty was ill, so I was called in at the last minute. Typical. They assume that I'll stand in however little notice they give.'

'You know you enjoy it,' Whitney said, raising an eyebrow. 'And at least it wasn't first thing this morning. I know how you love early call outs.'

If the pathologist had her way, all deaths would happen in the afternoon. She was even more cantankerous than usual when called out to a crime scene before noon, as George and Whitney had witnessed on many occasions.

'True. But I still had plans that had to be cancelled, which was irritating, to say the least. Now, if you could all leave, I'd like to get on.'

Having been dismissed, they headed back the way they'd come.

'Brian, I want you to go into the snooker club and interview the staff. After George and I have spoken to the member of staff who found him, we're going to the victim's house, as his family needs to be informed. We'll meet you back at the station later.'

'Yes, guv,' he said, striding on ahead of them.

'What's with Claire and all the personal details?' Whitney said, after they were out of earshot of both the pathologist and Brian. 'And she's a snooker fan, as well. In a million years, I'd never have guessed that. It's like we've been dropped onto another planet.'

Whitney's propensity for hyperbole was often a source of amusement to George.

'I suspected you would mention her disclosures—'

'Sorry if I'm so predictable, but you have to agree that

16

it's weird when half the time she acts as if she hardly knows us, even though she does, and then suddenly we get some insight into life with her new husband, plus learn about her snooker addiction.'

'Discovering that she enjoyed snooker was most unexpected. Although I'd hardly categorise her enjoyment of the game as an addiction.'

'You would say that. Come on, let's have a word with Molly Arthur. Hopefully, she's calmed down enough to help.'

They headed up to the officers standing by the cordon. 'Jade, which officer is with the woman who found the body?'

'PC Brigstock, guv. They're over there.' She pointed to one of the police cars.

They headed over and the officer got out.

'Guv,' he said. 'I'm with Molly Arthur.'

'Is she calm enough to talk to us?'

'Yes, I think so. Do you want to sit in the car with her?'

'Yes, that's easiest. You stay out here, we don't want to overcrowd her.'

Whitney got into the back seat next to the woman, and George sat in the front. 'Hello, Molly, I'm DCI Walker and this is Dr Cavendish. How are you doing?'

'Okay, I think,' she said sniffing. 'I keep seeing his face, and the blood and … It was … just …'

'Are you up to explaining exactly what happened when you arrived for work this morning?' Whitney asked gently.

The woman tensed and gave a sharp nod.

'I-I start at ten-thirty on a Sunday and drove into the car park, as usual, noticing that Ryan's car was there. I was surprised because I knew he was having his monthly *boys' night* at his house last night and that he hadn't intended coming in to the club today.'

'Would he often tell you his social plans?'

'No, but we all knew about the monthly get-together with his friends.'

'What happened after you noticed his car.'

'I could see a shadow in there, so I went to take a look, thinking it might be him. I got up close and saw his body leant against the door, and his head tipped back, with his eyes open, staring into space. There was blood on his clothes. I screamed.' Her hands were in tight balls in her lap.

'Did you open the car door?'

'No. I phoned 999. The operator told me not to do anything and wait for the police, which I did. But I saw him more clearly when they opened the passenger door. His face ... it was ...' She leant forward, her face in her hands, and began sobbing.

Whitney rested her arm around the woman's shoulder. 'We'll leave it for now. Thank you for your help. We do require a statement from you at the station, but that can wait until you're feeling a bit better.'

George and Whitney left the car.

'Arrange for someone to take Ms Arthur home, please,' Whitney said to PC Brigstock who was standing close by.

'Yes, guv.'

'Come on George, we'll go to see the family.'

Chapter 4

'Marsden House, Pennington Grove,' Whitney said, as George drove them to the victim's house. 'Snooker must be extremely lucrative to live in a mansion like this.'

'Technically, a house is only classed a mansion if it's over eight thousand square feet. Which I'm unsure whether this is. Regarding his income, he most likely makes his money from advertising and promotional events, like other sportspeople,' George said, driving through the open wrought-iron gates and up to the front of the house where an old Toyota Corolla was parked.

'Stop nitpicking. He's clearly loaded.'

Whitney sucked in a breath as they headed to the front door. However many times she went through the process of informing a family of their loved one's death, it never got any easier. If anything, she found it harder now because she could anticipate their response.

She used the brass knocker and tapped it against the door several times.

After a few minutes a woman in her fifties, wearing an apron, answered.

'I'm Detective Chief Inspector Whitney Walker and this is Dr Cavendish.' She held out her warrant card for the woman to check. 'Is Mrs Armstrong home?'

'No, she isn't. She and Sienna, that's her daughter, stayed the night with her mum and dad to keep out of the way because Mr Armstrong had his friends round. She hasn't arrived back yet. I don't know where Mr Armstrong is. I was expecting him to be here when I arrived.'

'And you are?'

'Chelsea Caswell. I'm their cleaner. Well, more than a cleaner. I do lots of jobs for them when they need me to.' A proud expression crossed her face.

'You work Sundays?' Whitney asked.

'Not usually, but when Naomi, Mrs Armstrong, asked me I said yes because we need the money. My husband lost his job recently, so we only have one wage coming in. She told me to come in at eleven-thirty to clear up because Mr Armstrong's friends usually made a mess, and she didn't want to deal with it herself.'

'What did you do when you found Mr Armstrong wasn't here?'

'I went into the kitchen to start washing the glasses, which had been put by the sink on the draining board. Mrs Armstrong doesn't like them going into the dishwasher because she says that it ruins them.'

'Were you surprised at seeing the glasses there? You mentioned Mr Armstrong and his friends always left the place in a mess.' George said.

'That was Mrs Armstrong's view but I don't agree. Mr Armstrong and his friends are nothing like my husband and his mates. They'd have left bottles and glasses all over the place. Mr Armstrong always brings the glasses and plates up from the games room in the basement after his friends have been here.'

'Were there no plates this time?' George asked.

'No. They must still be in the basement. To be honest, I haven't been downstairs yet.'

Had Armstrong been interrupted by someone, or something, and he'd gone out to meet someone in the car park?

'May we come inside to see the games room?' Whitney asked.

'Has something happened?'

'We're not at liberty to discuss this with you, but if you could show us the games room, it would be a great help.'

'Um … Okay.' She opened the white door, and they entered, going through the porch and into a large, square entrance hall. 'I hope Mrs Armstrong won't mind.'

'We'll explain it all to her. I'm sure it will be fine,' Whitney said, wanting to reassure the woman.

'It's in the basement,' Chelsea said, taking them across the hall to an open door with stairs going down.

'You stay here, we'll go on our own,' Whitney said.

'I'll wait here for you.' Chelsea stepped to one side so they could pass.

'Wow,' Whitney said as they reached the bottom. 'This is some games room.'

It was huge and had two full-sized snooker tables, two fruit machines and a table tennis table. Along the walls were dark red sofas with low tables in front of them.

'He must have begun clearing up and was interrupted,' George said, nodding at the plates stacked up on one of the tables.

'If that's the case, why? And by whom? We need his phone so we can trace any calls. Claire might have it at the morgue.'

After having a quick look around, they returned upstairs to where the cleaner was waiting.

'Thank you, Chelsea. Do you have the address for Mrs Armstrong's parents?'

'Yeah. I helped at a party they had last year. They live at 160 Windsor Close.'

'I know the area. Please, can you let me have your contact details, as we may wish to speak to you again.' Whitney pulled out her notepad and pen from her pocket and handed it to her. 'I'd also like you to go home now and stop cleaning.'

'B-but Mrs Armstrong won't want it to be messy.'

'I'll let her know we sent you home. We'll see ourselves out.'

Once they'd returned to the car, George keyed the address into the satnav. 'Do you think Chelsea will contact Mrs Armstrong and let her know we've been?'

'She doesn't know about Ryan's death so, it won't be a problem.'

The parents' house, in Windsor Close, was only a ten-minute drive and when they arrived Whitney knocked on the door. An older man answered.

'We're looking for Naomi Armstrong. I'm Detective Chief Inspector Walker and this is Dr Cavendish.' She held out her warrant card. 'Is she here?'

'Yes. I'm Bruce Dixon, her dad.'

'We'd like to come in and speak to Naomi.'

His body tensed, and his grip tightened around the edge of the door. 'Has something happened?'

'We'll explain to Naomi when we come in.'

He opened the door and ushered them inside. 'Cheryl,' he called, urgency in his voice. A woman in her fifties scurried into the hall. 'This is my wife. It's the police, do you know where Naomi is?'

'She's in the day room playing with Sienna. What is it?' Her panicked tone hung in the air.

'Is there someone who could stay with Sienna?' Whitney asked, her voice sounded calm, but the lines around her eyes were pulling tight.

'I will.' Mrs Dixon turned to her husband. 'Take the officers into the front room and I'll send Naomi in.'

They followed Mr Dixon and stood in the centre of the room beside a white marble fireplace. After a few seconds a young woman, who looked to be in her late twenties rushed in.

'What is it? Mum said you want to speak to me.'

'Let's sit down,' Whitney said, gently.

'I can't. Please, just tell me.'

Whitney glanced at Mr Dixon, who headed over and stood by his daughter's side.

'I'm sorry to have to tell you, but there's been an incident and Ryan has died.'

Naomi gasped, and Mr Dixon reached out to steady her. 'An incident? What do you mean?'

'His body was found this morning, by one of his staff, in the car park next to the snooker club.'

'What happened?' Naomi asked.

'We're waiting for confirmation from the pathologist.'

'What was he doing there? I don't understand. He should've been at home. He—' a sob escaped her lips.

'Sit down, love,' Mr Dixon said, guiding his daughter to the sofa. He sat down beside her, his arm protectively around her heaving shoulders.

'He was with his friends last night. Were they with him, when you found him?' Mr Dixon asked, while his daughter sat beside him, shaking.

'No one else was at the scene.'

'Oh, my God. I can't believe this is happening. What am I going to do?' Naomi said, as tears rolled down her cheeks.

'We're really sorry for your loss. Do you think you'd be able to answer some questions at the moment?' Whitney asked.

'Don't be ridiculous,' the father said, waving his hand. 'Look at the state of her, of course she can't.'

'It's all right, Dad,' Naomi said, sniffing and brushing aside her tears with the back of her hand. 'What do you want to know?'

'Do you know who was at your house last night with Ryan?'

'I expect the usual crowd, Scott Marshall, Tyrone Butler, Kurt Kastrati and Rory Clarke.'

Whitney pulled out her notebook from her pocket and jotted down the names.

'Did they get together often?'

'Once a month, sometimes less. It depended on whether Ryan was away at a tournament or doing a promotional event.'

'Are they all professional snooker players?'

'Scott Marshall is, but not at Ryan's level. The others play but not as a job.'

'What time did you arrive here last night?'

'I'm not sure, maybe around five, in time for tea.'

'Did you go out at all?'

'No. I was up most of the night with Sienna as she wasn't well. She'd eaten something that had disagreed with her.'

'Can you confirm that, Mr Dixon?'

'I wasn't awake all night, if that's what you mean. But I resent you asking the question. Surely you don't believe that my daughter had anything to do with this.'

'It's a standard question in order to eliminate people from our enquiries. What about your wife, was she up during this time?'

'I doubt it. Once she's taken her sleeping tablet, she's dead to the world until morning.' He glanced at his daughter. 'Sorry. Bad choice of word.'

'Naomi, can you think of anyone who might have held a grudge against Ryan and wanted to harm him?' Whitney asked.

'Everyone liked him. He didn't rub anyone up the wrong way. Oh … There was a woman who stalked him for a long time, and he ended up taking out an injunction against her. He didn't want to, but after we saw her in the garden taking photos of me and Sienna, he said she'd gone too far and he had to do something about it.'

'Do you know her name?'

'Um … Deborah … I can't remember her surname.' She leant into her father and let out a deep groan.

'Enough now. Surely you'll have this on your records,' Mr Dixon said, pulling Naomi closer to him.

'Yes, of course. We'll go now, but we will need to speak to you again.'

The partner of a victim was always high on the list of suspects. However, Whitney was prepared to leave it for the moment, as the woman was in no state to help.

'Thank you,' Mr Dixon said.

'We'll need someone to formally identify Ryan's body, but we'll be in touch when that can be arranged. Thank you, for your help. And, again, we're very sorry for your loss.'

Chapter 5

Whitney had called in as many members of the team as she could get hold of. Brian and Frank were already on duty, and Ellie and Doug were both available. Meena was away for the weekend and couldn't make it. When she arrived back with George, they were all seated at their desks, eyes focused on their computer screens. She wrote the victim's name on the whiteboard which took up a large portion of one of the walls.

'Thanks for coming in at short notice. As you know, Ryan Armstrong was found dead in a car park in the city, next to the snooker club he owned.'

'I can't believe it,' Doug said, shaking his head. 'What a loss.'

'You're a snooker fan?'

'You could say. I'm a member of the Palace Snooker Club, which Armstrong owned with Scott Marshall.'

'Marshall was one of the guests at the victim's house last night, the wife informed us when we broke the news to her. We'll be speaking to all of Armstrong's guests. Brian, who did you interview at the club?'

'Joe Dawson. He knew about Ryan as Molly had texted him. He'd tried to get hold of the manager, Glen Tibbs, but he was away for the weekend. He couldn't contact Scott Marshall as he didn't have his number so he closed the club for the rest of the day, and we left together. He'd caught the bus to work so hadn't seen Ryan's car in the car park, or he might have been the one to discover the body.'

'Thanks. We'll be visiting the club, but not yet. First, I want the CCTV footage surrounding the snooker club examined. The approximate time of death is between eleven and four, so until we have a more precise time, we'll check from nine p.m. until the time of the 999 call. Frank, I'll leave you to do this. Then, check out the cameras leading to and from the victim's house. See if you can pick up his car heading towards the snooker club, and also anything over the last few weeks that appears suspicious.'

'Bloody hell, guv. I'll be here all night, at this rate.'

'I'm sure the wife won't mind,' Doug quipped.

'I want you all to warn your families that you're going to be working late for the foreseeable future. Brian, the victim's wife mentioned a stalker who they took out an injunction against. Her name is Deborah. Track her down and get her in here for questioning. Ellie and Doug, I want a thorough background search on Armstrong and his friends. In particular, Scott Marshall, Tyrone Butler, Kurt Kastrati and Rory Clarke, who the wife believes were at the house last night. Get them in for an interview. We also need information on the victim's financial situation. His social media presence. His business. Also, find out if he has a manager.'

'Yes, guv,' they responded in unison.

'I'm going to see Dr Dexter at the morgue shortly and, hopefully, we'll find out the exact cause, and time of death. For now, work on the assumption he was shot between the hours of eleven and four and that's what killed him. I don't need to tell you this is going to be a high-profile case, and it's going to attract the attention of the media, not just locally, but nationally and probably internationally. We have to tread very carefully.'

'I have a contact, from when I was at the Met, who works for the snooker governing body,' Brian said. 'Shall I get in touch with him to see if I can find out anything about Armstrong, guv?'

'It's not hit the media yet, so we'll leave that one for now. Once the news has been released, and is public knowledge, then go for it. We don't want an accidental leak at this stage.'

Brian had only been with the team for three months and after a slightly tricky start, mainly because he knew Chief Superintendent Douglas, Whitney's arch-enemy, he appeared to be settling in well and was becoming an integral part of the team. Occasionally, his one-upmanship from being trained at the Met showed, but the other team members would soon put him in his place, in a roundabout way because he was their superior officer. She'd been feeling guilty recently because she hadn't taken the time to sit down with him and ask how it was going.

'I'm sure it will be out there soon enough,' Brian said. 'Before we even have a press conference, I expect. Did the wife know of any reason why her husband might've been shot?'

'We couldn't question her in any great depth because she was so distraught. But we'll follow up. She does have an alibi of sorts. She was staying with her parents and was up all night with her sick child while they were asleep in bed. I need to speak to the super regarding the best way to handle this. According to her voicemail, she's uncontactable today so I'll have to wait until tomorrow morning, unless she contacts me after hearing my message. She turned to George, who'd been standing next to her. 'Ready?'

'Yes.'

They drove to the morgue and once they arrived hurried into the lab. Claire was in the main area peering over the body.

'May we come through?' Whitney called.

'Yes,' Claire replied, without even turning around to greet them.

Armstrong was laid out on one of the stainless-steel tables in the centre of the room. He wasn't very tall, maybe about five foot eight with broad shoulders. He had an undercut hairstyle, and the top had blond highlights. He was clean-shaven and judging by the tautness of his abs, worked out.

'Was it the gunshot that killed him?' Whitney asked.

'Correct. There was only one shot and he would have died instantly. This is where the bullet entered the body.' Claire pointed to the hole in his chest, and Whitney and George both leant forward to take a look. 'Do you see the pattern of tiny abrasions around it?'

'Yes,' Whitney said, nodding.

'It's what we call stippling, and it tells me that the victim was shot at close range. Stippling is caused by the discharge of a gunshot or round. The gun would most likely have been less than two feet from the victim at the time of shooting. The bullet was lodged in the heart and remained intact. That's good news for you because it means you can match it to the murder weapon … when you find it.'

'*If* we find it. A high percentage of murder weapons are never found. Do you know what type of gun the bullet came from?'

'I'm not a firearms expert but will say that it most likely came from a .22 calibre handgun. We'll know more after it comes back from analysis by the lab.'

'Handguns are illegal,' Whitney said. 'Not that it would deter a would-be murderer. Can you confirm that he was shot in the car?'

'Yes, he was shot where he was found, as we could see by the blood pooled in the car seat.' Claire said. 'Wait until we hear back from forensics, and we'll know exactly what happened.'

'Can you tell if the victim tried to fight back?'

'There are no defensive wounds, which indicates that he was surprised and didn't have the chance to even raise his arms.'

'He'd had some friends around to his house on Saturday night. Do we know whether he was drunk or had been taking drugs?'

'I've sent his blood off to toxicology, so I'll let you know when the results are back.'

'While I remember, do you have his mobile?'

'His pockets were empty.'

'Not even his keys in there?'

'What is it about the word *empty* you don't understand?' Claire asked, staring at Whitney over the top of her glasses. 'They weren't anywhere in the car either, before you ask.'

'Okay, I get it,' Whitney said, giving a wry smile. 'Can you give me his exact time of death?'

'I've narrowed it down to between one and three in the morning.'

'So, he had an evening with his friends and could well have been over the limit. But someone, or something, persuaded him to get into his car and drive to the car park. What was it? And why was it important enough to risk the repercussions of being caught?'

Chapter 6

Whitney arrived at work early in the morning, having already heard on the radio about Ryan Armstrong's death. She was surprised it had remained a secret for twenty-four hours, considering who he was. They really needed to make an announcement to the media about the investigation. She pushed open the door to the station and saw Superintendent Clyde several yards in front of her, so she hurried over to catch up with her.

'Morning, ma'am. I take it you've heard about the murder of Ryan Armstrong. I tried calling you yesterday but couldn't get through. I left a message but didn't want to go into any detail in case someone else had access to your phone.'

The super stopped and turned to face Whitney. 'Yes, I heard it on my way in this morning. We were away yesterday and had no signal. It was unfortunate, as I would have liked to have known in advance, but we weren't home until gone midnight, which is why I didn't return your call.'

'No need to worry about that in the future, ma'am. I'm well used to having my sleep interrupted.'

'I also hadn't realised it was such a major incident.'

'Sorry, ma'am, I should have emphasised that in my message but, like I said, I didn't want to alert the wrong person.'

Jamieson, her previous boss, had never wanted disturbing when he was off duty, and she'd assumed that Clyde would be the same. When thinking about it rationally, it was hardly surprising her new boss didn't act in the same way as her old one as they were like chalk and cheese.

'No need to apologise. Does Chief Superintendent Douglas know?'

The hairs rose on the back of Whitney's neck at the mere mention of the man who had always had it in for her, and on several occasions had attempted to derail her career. He'd recently returned to the Lenchester force in a more senior position than he had been before. She'd tried to block all thoughts of him from her mind, but as he was Clyde's immediate superior, it wasn't always possible.

'I don't know, ma'am. He may have seen the dailies yesterday, if he was working. We do need to discuss strategy,' she added, wanting to deflect from a *Dickhead Douglas* discussion.

'We'll have to hold a press conference as soon as possible or the media will be hammering non-stop on PR's door.'

'We have nothing to tell them, other than to confirm the murder. So far, the pathologist has informed us that Armstrong was shot at point-blank range in the chest. We're waiting for the full report back from ballistics, although Dr Dexter believes it to be a .22 calibre handgun. Luckily, we have the bullet. We're gathering the CCTV footage from around the car park where his body was found. His wife stayed with her parents on Saturday night and we have no idea what Armstrong was doing out at that time of night, considering he'd hosted a small party at his house earlier.'

'I'll give a press conference later and explain the investigation is ongoing. You don't need to be a part of this one.'

Whitney was more than pleased about that as it wasn't often she was excused from dealing with the press.

'Fine, I'll leave that with you, ma'am.'

'Because of the nature of this case, I want you to update me each day on where we are with the investigation.'

'Yes, ma'am.'

They stepped in the lift together and the super got out at the fourth floor, leaving Whitney to continue to the fifth where she was based.

She still hadn't got used to the new station, even though they'd been there for three months. She missed their old Victorian building with its rattling pipes and out-of-date toilets. It also had character, whereas the new one, which was all-singing, all-dancing, had nothing appealing about it whatsoever. More importantly, it was out on the edge of the city and nowhere near her favourite coffee spots. And, as everyone would attest, without her coffee she could be as grumpy as hell. Having said that, she had to admit the coffee in the new canteen was good.

After stopping by her office and hanging up her jacket, she went through the second door leading into the incident room where the team were gathered, sitting at their desks.

'Good morning, everyone,' she said, calling them to attention. 'I want a rundown on where we are so far. Frank, the CCTV footage.'

'It was the weekend, so traffic was heavy in the vicinity because of the two nightclubs close by. Also, plenty of foot traffic. The victim drove along Fletcher Street and turned left into the car park at just after one in the morning. There are no cameras in the car park so that's all that was captured.'

'Did anyone else drive in there around that time?'

'None went in, although several cars drove out at midnight, but no more after that.'

'They could've been leaving the snooker club, as it closes then,' Brian said.

'Was it possible to tell if Armstrong was alone in his car?'

'From what I could see, yes he was, but the images weren't great so someone could've hidden from view.'

'Did you spot anyone walking into the car park?'

'No, but if they knew where the cameras were situated, kept close to the side of the building, and were wearing dark clothes, they could've avoided being seen.'

'That would've involved some surveillance. Check that out. What about cameras in the vicinity of the victim's house? Did you pick up anything?'

'Actually, yes. Although it's a residential area, there are several major roads leading to Pennington Grove all of which are covered by CCTV. I spotted Armstrong being followed over the last two weeks.'

A lead already?

'The stalker?' Whitney asked.

'The driver was male, in a Vauxhall Corsa. What alerted me was that when the car had parked up no one got in or out, so I don't think it's just a coincidence that it was around the same time as Armstrong.'

Whitney walked over and Brian followed. 'Show us.'

Using only two fingers and stabbing the keyboard, Frank called up the footage. 'This is from last Thursday. Here's Armstrong driving out of Pennington Grove and turning left. Look to the right and you'll see the other car pulling out of a parking space and starting to follow him. Now look at the next day, Friday, in the afternoon. Armstrong is out again, and he turns right into Mercia Road. See behind him? It's the same car. I found other sightings, too. Several near the snooker club.'

'Have you traced the car?'

'Not yet because the number plate was partially obstructed.'

'On every camera angle?' Brian asked.

'It could be dirt. Possibly done deliberately. I know the last two letters are WW. Also, there's a sticker in the left corner of the back window and I could make out the word 'rent'. The car could be a rental. I'll check it out.'

'Brian, did you locate the stalker?' She turned to her sergeant who was standing next to her.

'Yes, guv. Her name's Deborah Radley and she lives in Warwick.'

'Take Meena and bring her in for questioning.'

'Ellie, what were you looking into?'

'The victim's financial situation, guv. He's got plenty of money. Earnings from tournaments, advertising, endorsements and also the snooker club, which he owns in partnership with Scott Marshall.'

'Have you checked his social media presence?'

'Armstrong has a fan page, with over a hundred thousand followers, but he doesn't post much himself. I think maybe it's run by someone on his behalf. I'll find out who. He also has a manager, Dennis Blaine from DB Promotions, who's based in London.'

'Thanks. We need to interview him, although it's quite a distance and I can't afford the time at the moment.'

'We could use Zoom, guv,' Brian said. 'I can set it up for you.'

'Good idea. Where are we on tracking down Armstrong's friends who were at the house on Saturday night?'

'Tyrone Butler's in London at a funeral and will be back in Lenchester first thing tomorrow morning,' Ellie said. 'I've asked him to come into the station as soon as he returns. I know it's not ideal, but because it was a funeral I didn't insist on seeing him immediately. I did confirm that he was telling the truth about where he was. Kurt Kastrati and Rory Clarke are both coming in this afternoon. I haven't managed to get hold of Scott Marshall yet.'

'Okay. Someone contact forensics and see if there were any of the victim's possessions in the car. In particular, his phone and keys. Dr Dexter didn't see them but she didn't search everywhere. I'm going to interview the wife now she's had time to get over the initial shock.'

'It wasn't a shock if she was the one to have killed him,' Brian said.

'True. I'll try her parents' house first as she may still be there. I don't want to phone first. Forewarned is forearmed and all that.'

She went into her office and called George.

'I'm going to see Naomi Armstrong. Are you free?'

'Give me half an hour and I'll be with you.'

Chapter 7

George pulled into the station car park and spotted Whitney waiting by the side of the building, moving impatiently from foot to foot. She drew up beside her.

'Are you in a hurry?' she asked as the officer jumped into the car and fastened her seat belt.

'We've got a lot to do, so I thought I'd wait for you out here to save time.'

'How's Tiffany?' George asked as she pulled out into the traffic.

'Apart from the odd burst of hormones when she gets a bit snappy, she's doing really well. She's getting larger by the day. If I hadn't seen the scan myself, I'd swear she was having twins.'

'Do they run in your family?'

'Not that I know of. I've no idea about Lachlan's, though. Mind you, Tiffany weighed in at a little under nine pounds when she was born.'

'That's a lot for someone of your size,' George said, wincing.

'You're telling me, it's making my eyes water just

thinking about it. It was why I ran the gamut when it came to pain relief, finally ending up having an epidural. It was bliss, I couldn't feel a thing.'

'Has Tiffany decided on the type of birth she'd like?'

'Not yet. She's still got another twelve weeks to go, so there's plenty of time to work it out.'

When they arrived at the Dixons' house, Whitney knocked on the door. Mr Dixon answered.

'Is Naomi here?' Whitney said.

'You've just missed her. She's gone back home.'

'Is she alone?'

'She has her daughter with her. I offered to drive her back, but she said no. My wife's arranged to see her later. Naomi said she wanted to be on her own, despite us not wanting her to. But we learnt long ago that Naomi gets what she wants. She's very determined is our daughter.'

'How was she?' Whitney asked.

'She's coping, although I'm not sure it's hit her yet. She wants to stay strong for little Sienna.'

'Do you have CCTV here?'

'Unbelievable! You actually think she had something to do with this, don't you? Well, no, officer, we don't have CCTV but I'm sure the Crawleys' camera will have picked her up if she did leave, which I *know* she didn't. They live at 154.'

'I understand that this is difficult, Mr Dixon, but this is all part of our enquiries, and standard procedure. What car does your daughter drive, and also you and your wife?'

The tension eased a little from his face. 'Naomi has a Mazda CX-5. I have a Ford Mondeo and my wife a Ford Fiesta. The Crawleys are in their seventies and retired, so you should find them home as they don't go out often.'

'Thanks, we'll go there now.' They headed down the

path and turned left towards 154. 'Any observations?' Whitney asked.

'Before he got angry with you, I could see by the tightness of the lines around his eyes, and the way he was standing with his arms folded like he had a barrier across his chest, that he didn't agree with Naomi's decision to go home, but he couldn't do anything about it. There may be issues between her and her parents.'

'What sort of issues?'

'Difficult to pinpoint, but there was a certain unease about him. Obviously, in part, because of Ryan's death, but I sensed frustration because he couldn't look after her in the way he wanted to.'

'Typical response, though. It's hard to let go, however old a child is.'

'That's very astute of you,' George said.

'It's what being a parent does to you.'

They walked down the drive to the Crawleys' house. There was a camera above the front door. Just as Whitney raised her hand to press on the bell, the door opened by a tall thin woman, with grey hair piled up on her head into a bun.

'Yes?' she said, her eyes darting from Whitney to George.

'I'm Detective Chief Inspector Walker and this is Dr Cavendish. We'd like to speak to Mrs Crawley?' Whitney held out her warrant card.

Startled eyes stared back at them. 'That's me.'

'There's nothing to worry about. We have a few questions regarding your CCTV.'

The woman exhaled loudly and clamped a hand to her chest. 'Thank goodness. You had me worried for a moment. Come in.' She opened the door fully, and they walked past her into a square hall, with textured wallpaper which was tinged yellow with age.

'We'd like to see footage from late Saturday night into the early hours of Sunday morning from the camera that points towards the road. Are you able to show us?' Whitney asked.

'The computer is in the dining room. Our grand-daughter set it up and showed us how to use it. I think I remember what to do.'

They followed her into a room which had brown curtains with orange and yellow flowers of varying sizes on them. The carpet, worn in several places, was red with brown diamond shapes.

'Have you lived here long?' Whitney asked.

'Fifty-five years, since we got married.' She pulled out the chair at the head of the table, which was in front of the open laptop, and sat down. 'Now, let me think.' She stared at the screen and then hit some keys. 'Done it,' she said, looking at Whitney and George, a proud expression on her face. 'This is from eleven on Saturday.'

Whitney peered over her shoulder. 'Can you speed it up?'

'I don't know how.'

'Allow me,' George said, leaning across and pressing fast forward.

'Stop there,' Whitney said, as a car drove past at just after one. 'Do you recognise this car, Mrs Crawley?'

'Yes, it belongs to the young couple who live at 98.'

They continued looking through the footage, but there was no sign of any car belonging to Naomi or her parents.

'Thank you for your assistance,' Whitney said as they left the Crawley house.

'I'm glad to have helped. I didn't like to ask before, but

is this to do with Ryan Armstrong being killed? His in-laws live at 160.'

'I'm sorry, we're not allowed to discuss ongoing investigations.'

'I understand,' the elderly woman said, tapping the side of her nose.

They returned to George's car. 'That rules out his wife,' she said, pulling out into the road and heading in the direction of the Armstrong house.

'Maybe,' Whitney said. 'But she could've been involved, even if she didn't actually pull the trigger. I still have plenty of questions to ask her.'

When they arrived at Pennington Grove, there were three cars parked in the drive of Marsden House, including the CX-5. 'She must have visitors,' George said, pulling up behind the white Range Rover.

'Hello, Chelsea, we've come to see Mrs Armstrong.' Whitney said when the cleaner answered the door.

'I'll go get her.'

Chelsea ushered them into the hall where they waited until Naomi came out of the room on the right. She walked with purpose until getting closer to them and then slowed down, dragging her feet slightly. Was she putting on an act?

'We'd like to ask you a few more questions about yesterday if we may, Naomi?' Whitney said.

'I don't know whether I'm up to it.' She gave a sigh.

Again, forced?

'It won't take long. I noticed two other cars in the drive. Do you have someone with you?'

'Yes, Scott Marshall. He was my husband's partner at the snooker club and they were best friends. He came over to see how I was coping. Is it okay for him to be with me while we talk?'

'Yes, that will be fine,' Whitney said, nodding.

George frowned. Wouldn't it be best to keep them apart at this stage, considering they could both be suspects? Unless Whitney wanted to gauge their reactions to her questions and whether there were any undercurrents between them.

'Would you like me to make coffee, Mrs Armstrong?' Chelsea asked, as she hovered in the background.

'Would you like some?' Naomi asked.

'Yes, please.' Whitney and George both replied.

'Coffee for four, Chelsea.'

They followed Naomi into the lounge. The man sitting on the sofa jumped up. He looked to be in his thirties, and was tall with dark blonde hair that curled around his ears. His grey eyes were a little close together and darted from Whitney to George. What was he on edge about?

'It's the police, they want to talk to me about what happened.'

He walked over to them and held out a hand. 'I'm Scott Marshall. Ryan and I were friends and business partners. I was stunned by the shooting. If there's anything I can do to help, please let me know.'

Interesting. He managed to pull himself together quickly.

'Thank you,' Whitney said, after shaking his hand. 'Please, sit down.'

Naomi and Scott sat on the sofa and George and Whitney on the two easy chairs opposite.

'Had you noticed anything different about Ryan's behaviour recently?'

'He was the same as usual,' Naomi said.

'Do you know whether he was worried about anything? Finances, maybe.'

'Why would he worry about that?' Scott said. 'The

club's doing well. He was at the top of his game in snooker, and was inundated with sponsorship requests. Life couldn't have been better for him.'

There was an edge to the man's voice. Was his life different from his partner's?

'Naomi, do you agree?' Whitney asked.

'Yes, I do. We didn't have money troubles.'

'Did Ryan have any habits? Gambling. Drinking. Drugs.'

'Not that I know of.' She turned to Scott. 'He wouldn't have done any of that in front of me, what about you, Scott? Did you see anything like this when I wasn't around?'

'Absolutely not.' He shook his head. 'He never gambled or drank heavily and he definitely wouldn't have taken drugs. It would be too risky with random drug testing. Anyone found positive can virtually kiss their career goodbye.'

There was a knock at the door and Chelsea came in carrying a tray, which she put down on the coffee table and hurriedly left.

'Do help yourself,' Naomi said, to Whitney and George.

'How was your relationship with your husband, Naomi?' Whitney asked, as she passed a coffee to George and took one for herself.

'Good. Our fifth wedding anniversary is next month.'

'Did you argue much?'

'Ryan grew up in a household where his parents were at each other's throats most of the time. He refused to be like that, so no, we didn't argue.'

'That must have been frustrating for you.'

'Not at all. I avoid confrontation when I can.'

'Other than your husband's stalker, who you

mentioned yesterday, have you had further thoughts regarding anyone who might have held a grudge against Ryan?'

'I can't think of anyone. Everyone liked him. I mean, obviously, there must be people who were jealous of his success, but he was popular. I honestly don't know.' A single tear rolled down her cheek. She pulled out a tissue from her sleeve and dabbed it away.

'And what about you, Mr Marshall, you spent a lot of time together. Are you aware of anyone who held a grudge against him?'

'I'm not. As Naomi said, Ryan was very popular. People joined the snooker club in the hope of seeing him play.'

'And did they?'

'Yes, they did. We spent time practicing there, even though we both have tables at home. Members would watch and often ask us for selfies.'

'Didn't that interfere with his practice regime?'

'Not really. Ryan practicing at the club was part of our marketing plan, to bring in the punters, as he was more of a draw than me. He also practiced for hours at home, so he wasn't impacted.'

His body tensed slightly. Was he jealous of Armstrong's success? It wouldn't be unheard of in sporting circles.

'Was there anyone in particular who pestered him on a regular basis at the club?'

'Club members would come and chat for a few minutes and then leave him alone. He'd get messages on his social media page from fans all the time, but that goes with the territory. Nothing threatening, that I know of.'

'Mr Marshall, you were here on Saturday night?'

'Yes, at our regular monthly get-together.'

'What time did you leave?'

'I was the first to leave, I'm not one hundred per cent sure of the time. Before midnight I think.'

'How did you get home?'

'I called a taxi because I'd been drinking. And, before you ask, no one can vouch for me because my wife had gone to stay with her parents and taken our son Leo with her.' He stiffened.

'What's the name of the taxi firm?'

'I can't remember.'

'Show me your call log and we can find out.'

It was uncanny the way a person's movements could be so easily tracked. It made the police's job much easier.

He took out his phone and stared at it. 'I've just remembered. I didn't use my phone to call the taxi. I got one of the guys to do it for me.'

'Why?' Whitney asked, disbelief written on her face.

'Because they knew a firm.'

'Which one of the guys?' Whitney pushed.

'Um … sorry, can't remember that either. I must have had more to drink than I remember.'

'Was drinking to excess at these monthly get-togethers usual?'

'Sometimes. That's why we didn't drive.'

'Do you remember how much Ryan had to drink?'

'No idea. I didn't keep tabs on him. I'm pretty sure he wasn't out of it. He couldn't have been if he drove to the club.'

'How do you know he drove himself?'

'I-I just assumed he did as he was found in his car. That's what the media said.' He blinked several times in succession. Whitney's line of questioning was making him extremely uncomfortable.

'Where do you live?'

'Favell Drive. It's twenty minutes from here.'

'Do you have a security system, so we can check your arrival time?'

'We don't. My wife has been going on about getting one, but we haven't got around to it.'

'What happens now in regard to the club? Does Ryan's share go to you, Naomi?' Whitney asked.

'It's too early to be discussing this,' Marshall said, narrowing his eyes and giving a sharp nod in Naomi's direction.

'My solicitor will be dealing with it,' Naomi said.

'Do you have Ryan's phone? He didn't have it on him when he was found.'

'He never went anywhere without it. Even at home he always had it in his pocket. Apart from when we went to bed, and he left it beside him on top of the drawers beside our bed.'

'Please could you go and check if it's there, as he might have gone out without it. I'll come with you.'

George waited in the lounge with Scott until Whitney and Naomi returned a few minutes later. Whitney glanced at her and shook her head.

'Thank you for your help. Please don't leave the city without first letting us know, as we will need to speak to both of you again.'

'Am I a suspect?' Naomi asked, her hand in a tight ball and pushed against her chest. 'My parents will vouch for me, as I've already told you.'

'We're investigating all avenues. We'll see ourselves out.'

They left the house and headed back to the car.

'Was there anything of interest in the bedroom?' she asked.

'The bed hadn't been slept in and there was no phone.

So, we can assume he was still up when he was called out,' Whitney said.

'The fact that he'd only half cleared up also suggests the same.'

'True. And, what is it with these women that both of them had to stay overnight with *mummy and daddy* because their husbands were otherwise occupied? Can't they look after their children on their own?'

'Yes, I observed that myself. Very often pampered women crave attention and find being on their own for any length of time very difficult to deal with.'

'I'm not saying being with their parents is wrong. Just weird that both of them did it at the same time, that's all. But thinking about it in your terms, I can understand why they're doing it. Sort of.'

'I'll take your word for it. Where to next?'

'The station. I'm hoping the stalker has been brought in, and I'm expecting two of the friends who were at the party to come in, too. What did you make of Naomi and Scott?'

'If we hadn't known that she was married to Ryan, we'd be forgiven for assuming that Naomi and Scott were partners. The way she looked at him for support when you asked her a question. The way she leant in towards him and the mirroring of their body language. They both had their legs crossed, pointing at each other. Her left leg over her right, and his right over his left. In my professional opinion, they have a close relationship.'

'Close enough to kill Armstrong?'

'We have no evidence for that, but it shouldn't be discounted. I—'

Whitney's phone rang.

'Walker.' George glanced over at Whitney who was nodding her head. 'Okay, Brian. I still want to interview her, though. Arrange a time for her to come in. We won't be long.' She ended the call. 'Kurt Kastrati is already at the station. Deborah Radley, our stalker, has an ironclad alibi. She was in hospital. She went in on Friday with stomach pains and wasn't discharged until Sunday afternoon.'

'That rules her out. But she might have something useful for you if she's been following him recently.'

Chapter 8

The drive back to the station was delayed because of an accident on the main road into the city meaning that Whitney had no time to stop for a much-needed coffee in the canteen before heading to the incident room.

Brian was standing by the door, tapping his foot and checking his watch as they entered the incident room. 'What kept you?'

'Sorry, there was a hold-up,' she said, scanning the room, and noting the team were all working at their desks. She turned back to Brian. 'Come on, let's interview Kastrati. George will observe.'

She marched down the corridor to the lift, with the other two following.

'Finally,' Kastrati said, standing as Whitney and Brian entered. He was tall, towering over Whitney, with close-cropped blond hair and a pencil moustache, like the one Brad Pitt often grew.

'Sorry to keep you waiting, Mr Kastrati. Please, take a seat. I will be recording this interview.' She sat on the chair opposite, leant across Brian and pressed the *record* button. 'Interview on the eighth of March, those present: Detective Chief Inspector Walker, Detective Sergeant Chapman and ...' Whitney nodded at Kastrati.

'Kurt Kastrati.'

'Thank you for coming in to see us,' Whitney said.

'Well, anything I can do to help catch the monster who did this to Ryan.'

'I'd like to ask you about Saturday night. Please go through the events of the evening.'

'I went to Ryan's house for our monthly get-together. We've been doing the same thing for the last few years, unless Ryan's away at a tournament or some other engagement.'

'What do you do there?'

'We hang out together and have a laugh. Drink, eat, play a few games of snooker. A normal lads' night out.'

'How long have you known Ryan?'

'Over fifteen years, since we were kids. We met at a snooker club in Lenchester and hit it off straight away.'

'Do you play professionally?'

'I wish. I'm not a bad player, but not good enough to do it for a living.'

'What is your job?'

'I'm a builder. I have my own company.'

'On Saturday did anything strike you as different from usual?'

He shook his head. 'It was exactly the same as every other time. I arrived around seven and stayed until midnight.'

'Did you leave on your own?'

'I left with Rory. We got an Uber, and it dropped me off first and then took him.'

'And after that, where were you?'

'I was at home with my wife. She was up when I got back and can vouch for me if you need her to.'

'Please write down her details so we can contact her.' Whitney slid over her notebook and pen.

'Surely you're not accusing me. That's fucking ridiculous. I'd never have hurt him. We were friends. Good friends.' He glared at her.

'We're checking everybody's alibi so we can exclude them from our enquiries.'

'Okay, then,' he said, picking up the pen and writing in the notebook. He then pushed it back towards Whitney.

'We understand that Ryan had a stalker, and he had to take out an injunction against her.'

'You think it was her?' he asked, his eyes wide. 'I know she was a pain in the arse, but she'd never been violent in all the times she followed him. Which was often. We used to joke that if Ryan didn't watch out he'd find her hiding in the men's toilets watching him take a leak.'

'We don't believe it to be her. Do you know why he felt the need to take out an injunction against her?'

'Naomi discovered her in the garden taking photos of her and Sienna. Ryan didn't mind people being at the club, but he was angry about her snooping around at his house.'

'Were there other stalkers?'

'There were lots of people, both men and women, who wanted to hang around and be near him because he was famous.'

'Do you know of any issues between him and these people? Was he mean to any of them?'

'He was kind and took the time to talk to everyone He appreciated his fans, especially those who would spend money to watch him at tournaments.'

'Is there any person who you can think of who might have held a grudge against him?'

Kastrati gave a slow shake of his head. 'There's no one. I was gutted when I found out what had happened to him. He genuinely was one of the good guys.'

'What do you mean by that?'

'Let's put it this way. He was famous and could afford all the trappings that went along with it, but he didn't let it go to his head and didn't rub it in your face. If it had been …' He paused for a moment.

'What were you going to say?'

'Nothing. It's not relevant.'

'I think it could be,' George said in her ear.

Whitney gave a nod. 'Let me be the judge of that. Please continue.'

'Look, we're all friends, but Scott Marshall, who's also a professional snooker player on the circuit, does have a habit of making out he's better than the rest of us, even though he wasn't in the same league as Ryan.'

'How was he with members of the public?'

'It depended on his mood. Sometimes he treated them well, and other times he could be rude and arrogant. He wasn't as popular as Ryan, that's for sure.'

'Was there any animosity between Ryan and Scott?'

'They were business partners, and good friends. I never witnessed them falling out, but I often used to think that Scott took advantage of Ryan.' He paused for a moment. 'Maybe not advantage exactly, but he was the leader of the two of them. He decided what they did. It was his idea to buy the snooker club when it came up for sale.'

'Was Ryan reluctant about it?'

'No. But it wasn't his idea. I don't want you to think that I have an issue with Scott because I don't. We're all mates and we have a good time together when we hang out. But of the two of them, he's …' He shook his head. 'I've said enough.'

'He's what?' Whitney pushed.

Kurt paused and stared at his hands, the strain of betraying his friend clear on his face.

'He's the one who might have upset someone enough to get himself shot.' He held up both hands. 'But that's just my opinion. It doesn't mean anything. I don't know why anyone would want to kill Ryan.'

'Thank you for your time, Mr Kastrati. If you do think of anything else you believe might be useful in the investigation, please contact me.' Whitney handed him a card, which he took and placed into his jacket pocket. 'We'll be contacting your wife to confirm your alibi for Saturday night, and DS Chapman will escort you to the front entrance.' She paused. 'Actually, just one more question. Did you call a taxi for Scott Marshall on Saturday night?'

'No.' He shook his head.

'Do you know who did?'

'I don't. I remember Scott leaving first, but not long before I did.'

'Did you see the taxi pick him up?'

'We were all in the basement. The road can't be seen from there.'

'Okay. Thanks.'

Whitney waited until Brian and Kastrati had left and then went next door into the observation area.

'A useful interview,' George said.

'It certainly gave us an alternative view of Scott Marshall,' Whitney said. 'But so far nothing which indicates a motive for Armstrong's death. Let's go back to the incident room and find out when Rory Clarke is due to come in for his interview. If it's not for a while, we should have time to visit the snooker club.'

Chapter 9

The Palace Snooker Club was situated in an old, red-brick building. They parked in the street on the opposite side of the road and headed to the entrance. The door was propped open, and they stepped into a small foyer. On the wall was a sign indicating the snooker club was upstairs.

'This is a lovely building, it looks like it dates back to the late Victorian times,' George said. 'The ceilings are exquisite.'

'It was a theatre until the 1960s and then it was turned into a bingo hall. I remember my mum telling me about how she would come here with her parents on a Thursday to play bingo.' Whitney's voice faded as memories of the conversations she'd had with her mum came to mind. They weren't so frequent nowadays, as her mum's dementia had been getting steadily worse. Although when they'd visited the care home and told her about Tiffany being pregnant, she was very excited by the news.

'I imagine the acoustics would have been extraordinary,' George said.

The curved, dark wood staircase took them into a small

vestibule. Whitney tried the door, but it was locked. On the wall beside the door was a swipe pad and above it a bell which Whitney rang. A hatch, to the right of the door just above her eye level, was opened by a woman in her forties, her eyes were red, and tiny streaks of mascara were on her cheeks.

'Are you members?' the woman asked.

Whitney held up a warrant card. 'I'm Detective Chief Inspector Walker and this is Dr Cavendish. We're here to see Glen Tibbs.'

'Come in,' the woman said, as she pressed a buzzer releasing the catch on the door. The door opened into a large bar area and from a door to the right of them the woman walked out to meet them.

'Where is Mr Tibbs?' Whitney asked.

'He's in the office, I'll go and fetch him.'

She disappeared back through the door she'd just come out of, and Whitney scanned the large room. There was a man standing by the fruit machine feeding coins into the slot, and another sitting on a stool at the bar with a pint of beer in front of him. Further into the room were two men standing by the pool table. She walked over to the closest wall and stared at the photos lining it. Several of them featured the victim, holding up trophies.

'Where are the snooker tables?' she asked, turning to George.

'According to the signage, tables one to six are up the stairs over there,' George said pointing to an area off to the left where there was a small staircase. 'And tables seven to twelve are downstairs, over there.' She pointed beyond the pool table to the rear of the room. 'I'm assuming that must go down into what was the stage area of the theatre.'

'Hello, I'm Glen Tibbs.' Whitney turned at the sound of his voice.

'I'm DCI Walker and this is Dr Cavendish. Is there somewhere private we can talk?'

'Are you here about Ryan?'

'Yes.'

'We can go into the upstairs snooker room. It hasn't been opened up yet, so no one will be playing. My office is tiny and can house two people max, and that's only if they breathe in.'

'The snooker room is fine, as long as we won't be overheard,' Whitney said.

They followed him up the steps and into a large rectangular room housing six snooker tables, set in three blocks of two. On the wall beside each one was a mahogany scoreboard with gold lettering and a rack filled with cues. The tables had grey covers on them. Tibbs led them over to the snooker table in the far left corner, which had a bench seat against the wall and a circular table with four chairs around it.

'It still hasn't sunk in,' Tibbs said, as he sat on one of the chairs and gestured for Whitney and George to join him. 'Do you know any more about it? Like, why and who?'

'That's what we're investigating. We'd like to know more about Ryan's input into the club. Obviously, we know it's owned by him and Scott Marshall. What else can you tell us?'

'Ryan would be here several times a week, if he wasn't away at a tournament or doing media events. The members enjoyed seeing him. It's part of the appeal of the club and what makes it so successful.'

'Can anyone come in and play?'

'We're a members' only club, which is why the door is locked and people can't come in off the street. Members swipe their membership card to get in.'

'You still use actual cards?' George said, frowning.

'It's easier to control entry that way. Anyone could get in if we used a keypad entry system once they knew the number. It's not perfect and non-members occasionally do get in, but it's the best option.'

'How many members do you have?'

'Over a thousand on the books, but some of them might only come in once or twice a year. We have a hard-core of around two hundred, maybe a little less, who are regulars.'

'Do you allow non-members in?' Whitney asked, leaning in slightly.

'Only if they're invited. Members can bring in guests, but they have to sign them in. And, obviously, Ryan and Scott would meet people here. They'd let us know in advance if we were to expect anyone.'

'Did they often hold meetings at the club?'

'Sometimes, in the mornings during weekdays as that's when it's the quietest. We don't tend to get busy until after lunch.'

'Who did they meet with?'

'A variety of people. Salespeople from the brewery, or people who wanted to sponsor our tournaments. Business people from Lenchester. Charities wanting Ryan to promote them.'

'When was Ryan last here?'

'Friday. He'd been around quite a lot recently, as there wasn't a tournament on.'

'Were Ryan and Scott always here at the same time?'

'They were often together, but not all the time. Scott has always spent more time at the club because he doesn't have so many other commitments.'

'Do you have CCTV footage available for us to look at, so we can look at who Ryan met with recently?' Whitney asked, the camera on the wall facing them catching her eye.

'Yes, we do. I can email it to you if you'd like. It's all digital.'

'Please send me the last three weeks. Here's my card.' Whitney pulled out a card and handed it to him. 'Can you think of anyone who might have held a grudge against Ryan?'

He let out a long sigh. 'I can't. He got on well with everyone.'

The same story. A popular guy. So what was the motive?

'Is business going well?'

'Yes, exceptionally. The club's very popular with the snooker playing public.' His brow furrowed. 'What's going to happen to it now?'

'That's something you'll need to discuss with Scott Marshall. Can you tell me, what you were doing during the early hours of Sunday morning between one and three?'

'I was on duty Saturday night, and the last customer left around midnight. By the time we'd finished and locked up, it was twelve-thirty. I gave a lift to two members of staff, as usual, and then went straight home. I was there by one-fifteen.'

'Can anyone vouch for you?'

'My wife was in bed when I arrived back, but I accidentally woke her when tripping up the stairs, so she can. She moaned about the time, which is why I can be so exact.'

'We'd like to confirm that with her.'

'Yes, of course.'

Whitney took out her notebook and pen from her pocket and passed it over to him. 'Please write down her number.'

'That's her mobile, you can catch her anytime on there,' he said after giving it back to Whitney.

'Where do you park your car when you're here?'

'In the car park next door.'

'Were there any cars in on Saturday night when you left?'

He shook his head. 'Mine was the only one.'

'Thank you. I'd like you to email me the CCTV footage now before we leave to make sure it gets through.'

Chapter 10

Back in the incident room, Whitney called everyone to attention. 'I have some CCTV footage from the Palace Snooker Club, which the victim owned with Scott Marshall. Frank, I'm going to forward it to you. Ryan Armstrong was there on a regular basis so look for anything out of the ordinary, however small. Check to see who he was with, or if there was anyone at the club paying him particular attention. More than would be considered acceptable, bearing in mind he was famous and did attract attention.'

'Yes, guv.'

'Ellie, I want a thorough background check into Scott Marshall, including what car he drives and whether it can be seen on any CCTV footage close to the club at the time of the murder. Meena, you give her a hand. Brian, you said you could sort out a Zoom meeting with Dennis Blaine, the victim's manager. Arrange it for later this afternoon. I—'

'Guv, the front desk has just let me know that Rory

Clarke has arrived,' Doug interrupted, as he replaced the phone back on the desk.

'Thanks. I'll go down now.'

'Do you want me with you?' Brian asked.

She could manage without him, but she'd been making a concerted effort to include him, so he didn't feel marginalised. She occasionally called him Matt, after her previous DS, which didn't go down well, and she still had a tendency to compare the two of them.

'Yes. You can arrange the Zoom meeting after, this shouldn't take long.'

The three of them left and made their way to the interview room, with George, as usual, going to the observation area.

As they entered the interview room, they were faced with an attractive man who looked to be in his late thirties with thick grey hair pulled back into a ponytail 'Thank you for coming in to see us, Mr Clarke. We're going to record our conversation. Brian, could you do the honours?'

'Good work,' the psychologist said in her ear. 'It might appear a small gesture to you, but it will be extremely beneficial.'

She smiled to herself and gave a tiny nod of acknowledgement.

'Interview on Monday, the eighth of March. Those present: Detective Chief Inspector Walker, Detective Sergeant Chapman, and, please state your name for the recording,' Brian said.

'Rory Wayne Clarke,' he said, in an unmistakeable Scouse accent.

'I understand that you were at the Armstrong house on Saturday night. Please can you give us a rundown on how the evening went,' Whitney said.

'Sure. I got there late because I'd been detained. If you

know what I mean.' He winked at Whitney, his blue eyes twinkling.

'I have no idea, Rory. You'll have to enlighten me.'

She had *every* idea but she wasn't going to let on.

'I was with a woman I met at the football match. We went back to her place. Do you want more?' he asked, grinning.

'What time did you arrive at Ryan's?' she asked, ignoring the question.

'Just after half-eight. I got a taxi.'

'What was happening when you arrived?'

'They were in the middle of a game of doubles. Ryan and Kurt were thrashing Scott and Tyrone. Scott was losing his rag.'

'Why?'

'There was two grand riding on the game, and he was fucking up the easiest of shots.'

Why hadn't Kastrati or Marshall told them about this? They'd implied it was a regular evening, with nothing out of the ordinary going on.

'Was this usual?'

'Oh yeah. No point in playing without betting on the game. It's what we always did. Scott's a sore loser. Always has been.'

That explained it.

'You've known him a long time?'

'He's my cousin. When I moved down here, he introduced me to Ryan and the others. It helped that I'm a good snooker player. Obviously not in Ryan and Scott's league, but good enough to make a game of it.'

'Was there anything unusual about Saturday night?'

'Nothing. We played snooker. We drank. We ate. Exactly the same as it always is.'

'Except that Scott Marshall lost his temper.'

'That's not unusual. It depends on how well he plays. He's not consistent, and that's why he's never been as successful as Ryan.'

'What time did you leave?'

'I cadged a lift with Kurt in his Uber. It dropped him off first and then took me. Around midnight, maybe?'

'Can anyone confirm the time you arrived home?'

'I'm living with my aunt and uncle, as a temporary measure, so they can.' Some of his bravado dropped away. Did he have problems?

'Why temporary?'

'I got into a bit of financial difficulty and lost my house. They didn't want to see me on the streets, which I'm grateful for.'

'Are they Scott's parents?'

'The other side of the family.'

'Are you working?'

'Yes, I'm a football agent. I run an agency in partnership with another guy.'

'What does that involve?'

It was a new one on her.

'I scout talent here and overseas for the bigger clubs.'

'Have you signed anyone I've heard of?' Brian asked, leaning forward slightly.

'I may have in the past, although recently it's not been easy. I do have a player from Ukraine who's currently at Aston Villa in their youth squad and have high hopes for a young lad from Poland.'

'Did either your aunt or uncle see you when you arrived home?' Whitney asked.

'Yes, my aunt was up. I can give you her number if you'd like to check.'

'Yes, please.' Whitney passed over her notebook. 'Jot it down here. Do you know of anyone who might have held a grudge against Ryan? Or anyone he'd upset in the past.'

He paused for a moment. 'Ryan wasn't that type of guy. He didn't fall out with people. He was easy-going and laid-back.'

'Ask what he's like as a player.' George said.

'Did he have a killer instinct when playing snooker?'

'Oh, yes. On the table he wasn't Mr Nice Guy. But he didn't play dirty. He was focused and wouldn't allow anything to distract him. He was mesmerising to watch when he was on a roll.'

'Did he have any issues with other players?'

'Not that I know of. Whether he won or lost, once matches were over, he was back to his usual self.'

'Did you call a taxi for Scott Marshall on Saturday night?'

'I don't think so. But couldn't say one hundred per cent. Why?'

'Someone did, and we don't know who. Can you check your call log?'

He pulled out his phone, unlocked it, pressed some keys and peered at the screen. 'According to this I made a call at eleven thirty-five to a number I don't recognise. Shall I call it so we can see who answers?'

'Yes, please. Put it on speaker.'

He pressed the number. 'Westfield Taxis,' a woman's voice said after several rings. He ended the call without speaking. 'It must have been me, after all.'

'Thank you. If you do think of anything that might help, please contact me.' She handed him her card. 'DS Chapman will see you out.'

He'd given as much as she needed. Especially his take on Scott Marshall, which was interesting as it added to what they'd already been told.

She opened the door for them to leave and once they had, she went into the observation room to see George.

'Thoughts?'

'As yet, no motive. There's agreement among the friendship group about the nature of the relationship between Armstrong and Marshall, which isn't out of the ordinary.'

'Really? What makes you say that?'

'Very often in a friendship one person is more dominant than the other. This is the case between Armstrong and Marshall. I also suspect that Marshall, despite his outward appearance lacks confidence in his ability, hence his inconsistency and the need to prove himself. Armstrong, from what little we know, had a far more relaxed demeanour and was confident in respect of his talent.'

'Do you suspect Marshall of being involved in the murder?'

'It's a hypothesis worth considering, until you ask yourself why? Without Armstrong, the club won't be so successful, and he wouldn't be so high profile among the snooker loving public. In conclusion, without evidence to the contrary, no, I don't believe so.'

Chapter 11

'Where are we on the victim's phone?' Whitney asked when she returned to the incident room, having said goodbye to George who'd gone to the university. She scanned the room, but there was no reply. 'Anyone? Who contacted forensics?' Again there was silence. 'Ellie?'

'Not me. I thought someone else was going to.'

'Come on, you lot. Don't drop the ball now, this case is too important. Meena, find out about the mobile. Doug, contact Westfield Taxis and find out where they took Scott Marshall after picking him up from the victim's house on Saturday night. Brian is our Zoom conversation set up?'

'Yes, guv. It's in fifteen minutes, in your office.'

'Okay. Has anyone got anything else to report before we go?'

'I've been looking at car hire companies and think I've tracked down the place that hired out the car which had been following Armstrong. They were closed when I called. There was an after-hours number which went through to a voicemail, so I didn't leave a message,' Brian said.

'Why were they closed so early?'

'No idea, guv.' Brian said.

'We'll visit tomorrow and find out.'

They went into her office, and she sat at her desk staring at the screen.

'I've already been in and downloaded Zoom onto your computer. I hope you don't mind.'

'Not at all, I couldn't have done it. Bring a chair around and sit next to me.' She waited until he was seated, before turning to him. 'While we've got a few minutes, tell me how it's going now you're more settled into the team.'

His eyes narrowed slightly. 'Good thanks, guv.'

Had he been hanging out with George? That told her nothing.

'And what about Meena?' she asked, remembering he was less than complimentary about the DC when he'd first arrived.

'I'll admit, I misjudged her. She's doing really well. When she was at Willesden, she wasn't given enough opportunity to shine. I retract what I said about her, she's fitting in well and making a good contribution.'

That was good to hear as Whitney, too, thought Meena made a good addition to the squad.

'And what about the rest of them?' she asked, curious to hear his opinion as they could take a while to get used to.

'They're a great bunch. Occasionally a little disrespectful, but it's done in fun and is because they're used to working with you. Nothing I can't handle.'

'Good. Now we've settled into a routine, I'm very happy with the way the team is gelling. In no small part due to the way you've integrated into it.'

He gave a nonchalant shrug, but Whitney could see through it. Her view mattered to him.

'Let's sign in,' he said glancing at his watch. 'I take it this is still the same. You speak, I listen.'

'We'll see how it goes,' she said.

Brian was very different from Matt and in the interests of good relations between them she was considering letting him take more of a lead in interviews. Only *considering*, she hadn't yet made a final decision. It was a big step to take and nothing to do with his skills, but more because of the way she liked to work.

They logged in and were joined by a silver-haired man sitting behind his desk. He had a deep tan, as if he'd been overseas recently. And as for his suit, it looked as if it cost more than Whitney would spend on clothes in a whole year. But that's what she'd expect from a manager to the stars. He had an image to maintain.

'Thank you for speaking to us, Mr Blaine. I'm Detective Chief Inspector Walker and this is Detective Sergeant Chapman. We'd like to speak to you about Ryan Armstrong.'

'Please, call me Dennis. We were all devastated when the news of Ryan's shooting was announced. Where are you on the investigation? Do you know who did it and why?'

'At the moment, we're in the early stages of our enquiry. We can only tell you what you've been told already, that he was shot and his body found in the car park beside the snooker club he owned. What we'd like to know is whether you know of anyone who held a grudge against Ryan?'

He leant forward slightly, resting his arms on his desk. 'Celebrities attract the attention of people who might wish to harm them. Often the celeb in question doesn't even know they're being targeted.'

'But do you know of anyone in particular who might

have had it in for him? Were there incidents in the past which might be relevant?'

'Several years ago, there was a woman who was obsessed with Ryan and turned up at all of his tournaments. But after a couple of years she disappeared, and we didn't see her again.'

'So this wasn't the stalker that he had to take out the injunction against?' she checked, although it couldn't be if she'd disappeared over two years ago.

'This was someone else.'

'How long ago did this obsession start and do you know the woman's name?'

He frowned. 'It must be at least five years because I remember she was at the NEC in Birmingham when they held the Davenport Tournament, and that's been held at the Crucible in Sheffield for the last four years. I don't know anything about her as she didn't ever cause a disturbance. She was just always there, staring at Ryan wherever he went. We didn't report her to the police as we didn't believe it to be necessary.'

She doubted this woman had anything to do with the murder.

'Have there been any incidents recently you can think of that might help us? We've checked with his stalker and she has an alibi.'

'None.' He shook his head. 'Everything had been going well. Ryan was the golden boy of sport and every major company had approached us with a view to using him for endorsing their products. He was making a killing.'

As was he, no doubt. No wonder he could afford such expensive clothes.

'Did he make more money from endorsing than from playing snooker?' Brian asked.

He glanced at Whitney and she gave a nod, indicating that she didn't mind him asking the question.

'Absolutely. The prize money is good for the top players, but not enough to live the lifestyle Ryan did. As with most sports stars, he earnt more away from the game.'

'Do you represent Scott Marshall, Armstrong's partner?' Brian asked.

'I did, but we had to drop him as a client. He wasn't doing very well on the circuit, and requests for endorsements had dried up because of it. He was qualifying for competitions, but rarely got further than the last sixteen. It was at a time when I'd lost one of my senior staff members and we were stretched.'

'How did he take it?' Whitney asked.

'Not well. He tried to persuade me to give him another chance. I told him if his performance improved, we'd consider it.'

'Did you mean it?'

He shrugged. 'This is business. I'm not in it for the good of my health.'

'It's a good job he's a partner of the Palace Snooker Club, if he doesn't earn much at snooker. By all accounts it's doing well,' Whitney said.

'So I'm given to believe. I haven't been there. I don't tend to travel much out of London unless it's overseas.'

'Is there anything you can think of that might help us with the investigation?' Whitney asked. It was like banging her head against a brick wall. No one had anything useful to assist them.

'Not really. He was one of the better sportspeople that we handled. He didn't go crazy and, as far as I'm aware, his marriage was strong. Obviously, you don't know what goes on behind closed doors, but we often hear rumours and I hadn't heard anything regarding him. He was squeaky clean. This is why it was such a shock. I'm sorry, I can't help you further.'

'Can you tell me what you were doing between one and three on Sunday morning? We're asking everybody we speak to so we can eliminate them from our enquiries.'

'I was at the airport in Hawaii, my flight had been delayed. I'd been on holiday.'

That explained the tan.

'Can anyone vouch for you?'

'Everybody at the airport. But if you need to see my tickets, I'll ask my secretary to send them over. Or you can get in touch with customs, they'll confirm it. I have another meeting in five minutes. Are we done here?'

Whitney bristled. Who did he think was in charge?

'We are for now. We may need to speak to you again.'

'Sure. Get in touch with my secretary and she'll schedule you in.'

He left the meeting, and Whitney turned to Brian. 'Everyone we speak to is in agreement. Ryan Armstrong was a likeable, good family man. A squeaky clean sportsman. So why was he killed? There's got to be something we're missing.'

'Finding the man who was following him should help. Tomorrow our luck might change.'

Whitney laughed. 'Don't talk about luck in front of George or she'll give you short shrift. According to her, *luck* doesn't come into it.'

'Do you agree?'

'Actually, no. Investigations do require an element of luck. As for coincidences …'

'Don't tell me, Dr Cavendish doesn't believe in those either.'

'Mention it in front of her and see the response. I dare you.'

'Are you setting me up?' Brian arched an eyebrow.

'My lips are sealed.' She drew a pretend zip over her mouth. 'Right, tell the rest of the guys we'll meet back here early tomorrow morning for a briefing, after which you and I will go to the car hire place.'

She watched as Brian left her office for the incident room and smiled to herself.

He was okay.

Chapter 12

'Watch out, guv,' Brian shouted, grabbing hold of her arm so she narrowly missed an oncoming car.

Her heart was in her mouth. 'Where the hell did that come from?' She watched the dirty white Corsa nip into a parking space reserved for staff and marched over. She stood by the driver's door, tapping her foot on the ground. 'Didn't you see me?' she snapped as the young man who'd been driving got out. He was wearing a royal blue polo shirt with *Rent Me Car Hire* on it.

'Keep your hair on, missus. I didn't hit you, did I? I'm late for work. Can't stop.'

'Actually, you can,' Whitney said, holding out her warrant card, and stepping in front of him to prevent him from leaving.

'Shit,' he said through clenched teeth.

'Indeed. I could charge you with dangerous driving.' She locked eyes with him.

'I'm sorry,' he said, bowing his head. 'Please don't do anything or I could lose my job. I work in valeting. My wife's having a baby soon and we need the money.'

Whitney gave a sigh, allowing her more benevolent side to take over. 'Well, don't do it again. We're here about one of your cars, so if you take us to the office, you'll have an excuse for being late as we stopped you.'

'Thanks.' He gave a grateful smile.

They followed him to the small wooden structure that resembled a garden shed.

'The cops are here to see you, Mary.' He turned to Whitney. 'She can sort you out. See ya. And thanks.'

After he left, Whitney went up to the desk and showed her warrant card. 'I'm Detective Chief Inspector Walker and this is Detective Sergeant Chapman. We'd like some information about a car that we believe was hired from you. It's a blue Vauxhall Corsa and the last two letters on the registration are WW.'

'I'm not sure we're allowed to give out that sort of information as it's confidential,' Mary said, leaning forward and covering whatever was in front of her on the desk with her arms, as if she thought Whitney was trying to read it upside-down.

'Well, it's either that or I get a search warrant and we then tear the place apart. We need this information urgently as it's in connection with a recent murder.' She always played the search warrant card in times like these as it usually did the trick and saved them time.

Mary bit down on her bottom lip. 'I'm new here, so let me check with the manager what she wants to do.'

She turned over the document on her desk, and hurried away, going through a door at the rear of the office. Whitney was tempted to turn it over and see what was so secret that it had to be hidden, but thought better of it.

After a minute or two, an older woman came out, followed by the receptionist.

'I'm Kate Harris, the manager of this branch. I understand you want to know about one of our cars.'

'We're trying to trace a man who we believe rented a blue Vauxhall Corsa from you. We have the last two letters of the registration, which are WW.'

'Let me check. It's been fairly quiet these last couple of months so it should be easy to find.' Kate sat at the desk, looked at the computer screen as she tapped at the keyboard and nodded. 'We did hire out a car for two weeks with those details. It was brought back yesterday afternoon. It was rented by a man called Colin Jenkins.'

'What particulars of his do you have?'

'A photocopy of his driver's licence, and his address and phone number.'

'How did he pay?'

'By cash and we also put a hold on his credit card as security in case of damage but …' Kate paused and turned to the receptionist who was standing behind her. 'Mary, your name is attached to this booking, and there was no hold put on the customer's card. Why not?' She pointed at the screen.

'Umm … I'm not sure.' Mary peered over Kate's shoulder and stared at the screen. 'Oh, I remember, now. The man was in a hurry and he said it was fine because he'd used us before and there wouldn't be a problem because you knew him. He was very insistent. I thought it would be okay. It happened in my first week and I was on my own because you'd gone out. I forgot to mention it. I'm sorry.'

'We'll speak about this later.' Kate printed off the customer details and handed the copy to Whitney.

'Thank you. We tried to contact you yesterday, but you were closed before five. Is that usual?'

'Our hours are eight until six, but yesterday we were

short-staffed as Mary had gone home sick with a migraine and, as it was quiet, I made the decision to close early. I'm sorry you couldn't reach us, but we do have an after-hours number. Did you call it?'

'Yes, but we weren't prepared to leave a message. Has the vehicle been cleaned yet?'

'It's due to be done today.'

'You'll have to cancel the clean as I don't want it touched. It was potentially used in a murder.'

'A murder?' Kate's eyes widened.

'Where is the car, we'd like to take a look?'

'I'll take you over there,' Kate said, standing up and hurrying around to where Whitney and Brian were standing.

They followed her into the car park and over to where the blue car was parked beside several other vehicles. Whitney pulled out some disposable gloves from her pocket and handed them to Brian.

'I've got some,' guv,' he said.

'I'm so used to being with George, I forgot you have your own.' She opened the driver's door and looked in. It was empty and relatively clean. 'If he was the shooter, there could be some gunshot residue on the steering wheel. Forensics will find it.' She shut the door and then walked around to the rear and opened the boot. Again, there was nothing left in there. 'Thanks,' she said to the manager, as she pulled down the boot and closed it. 'Our vehicle recovery operator will arrange for it to be removed and taken to our premises for further exam-ination.'

'When can we use it again?' Kate said.

'We can't release it back to you until all examinations have taken place, and I can't say how long that will be, I'm afraid. We're going to put up a cordon around the car until it's taken away. Please arrange for the cars either side of it to be moved elsewhere.'.

'I'll get the cordon,' Brian said, heading back to his car and pulling out some tape and bollards, which he placed around the suspect's car.

Whitney moved out of the manager's earshot and pulled out her phone. She called the station and arranged for the car to be removed. Then she rang Ellie.

'Yes, guv,' the officer said.

'We're on our way back. The man who rented the car is Colin Jenkins. I'll text his driving licence number over. Find his details as I want him brought in for questioning as soon as possible.'

'Yes, guv.'

After waiting until the area surrounding the Corsa was clear, Brian drove them back to the station.

Whitney went straight over to Ellie's desk.

'Have you found the guy who hired the car?'

'No, guv. There's no record of that license number or person. His documents must have been fake.'

'Here's a photocopy of the licence. Check it out.' She pulled out the piece of paper and handed it over.

'I can run the photo on the licence through the facial recognition database to see if it throws up anything. Obviously, I won't get a hit unless he's got a record.'

Whitney called everyone else to attention. 'We've just been to *Rent Me Car Hire* company and they've given us the details of the person who'd been following Ryan Armstrong. Unfortunately, it turns out he gave them false information. Ellie's investigating it now. Forensics will be going over the car, and once we've identified the suspect, we'll bring him in for questioning.'

'Guv, Tyrone Butler's here,' Doug called out.

'Thanks. Come on, Brian, let's speak to him. Although

if it's anything like the other interviews, we're not going to get much, other than Armstrong was perfect and Marshall's dodgy.'

'We should speak to Marshall again, as the only time he's been interviewed was with Mrs Armstrong,' Brian said as they headed out of the incident room and went to the lift to take them to the ground floor.

'All in good time. We're already learning plenty about him, which will assist us when we do question him. We know that he was the more dominant of the pair, which isn't out of the ordinary, and that he's a poor loser. Although, that doesn't make him a killer.'

When they entered the interview room the man sitting at the table stood and stepped towards them.

'I'm Tyrone Butler,' he said, holding out his hand for Brian to shake. He was around five feet eight inches tall and had a shaved head and a smattering of freckles over his face. He smiled, lighting up his green eyes. He wasn't attractive in the traditional sense, but Whitney warmed to him. He had a sincere quality about him. Not that she'd let her guard down. Experience had shown her that even the most *genuine* of people could do despicable things.

'DS Chapman, and this is my guv, DCI Walker.'

'Please sit down, Mr Butler,' Whitney said. 'I understand you've been to a funeral. I'm sorry to hear that. Was it someone close?'

'It was my father-in-law, which is why I couldn't get back before now to help you.'

'I totally understand. As you know, you're here because of what happened to Ryan Armstrong. I'll be recording this interview.' She went through the usual interview protocol and then looked at him. 'You were at the Armstrong house on Saturday night with the other guys. Could you give a rundown of how the evening went?'

He nodded. 'It was our usual session. Nothing out of the ordinary. We had a few drinks, something to eat and played a few games of snooker.'

'Including doubles where you and Scott Marshall got beaten by Ryan and Kurt.'

He frowned. 'You know about that?'

'Yes. Scott Marshall was very angry about it, I understand.'

'I wouldn't say *very* angry. He acted as he always did when things don't go his way. We've known him for years and are well used to his behaviour.'

'There was a lot of money riding on the game. Was that usual?'

'To be honest, when Scott wanted to make it two grand, I was shocked. Usually, we play for no more than five hundred. But he was insistent, so we all went along with it.'

'Were you angry with Mr Marshall when he messed up? Were you in for fifty per cent of the bet?'

'The bet was between Ryan and Scott. Kurt and I weren't a part of it, other than playing. No way would you see me betting that much.'

'Did they often bet between themselves?'

'No. I admit that was a bit odd.'

'Did you question why?'

'No point. If that's what Scott wanted to do, then that's what happened.'

'Were any of you really drunk?' Whitney asked.

'We all had a few. Too many to drive, but no one was really out of it.'

'Apart from the doubles match, did you notice any tension between Scott and Ryan during the night?'

'Nothing out of the ordinary. I'm assuming you know that there were often niggles between the two of them.'

Whitney shook her head. That was the first they'd heard of it.

'Can you be more specific?'

'It was usually to do with the snooker club. On Saturday, Scott was going on about the club staffing and how it should be reduced to improve profits. Ryan didn't want to, saying that trimming the staff was a short-sighted option as they had a big tournament coming up that would put the club on the map. It was going to be on the telly and that would bring in loads more members.'

'How did Scott react to that?'

'Swore and muttered a bit. Told Ryan he should leave the business side of things to him and then didn't mention it again. Really, it was nothing out of the ordinary. Surely, you don't imagine Scott had anything to do with the shooting?'

'Do you?' Whitney asked, putting the question back to him.

'No I don't. They've been friends for too long. Scott's all mouth. Why cut off the hand that feeds you? He needed Ryan more than the other way around, everyone knew that.'

'Why?'

'The snooker club does well *because of Ryan*. They got this prestigious tournament *because of Ryan*. Scott gets to hang out with the big guns of snooker *because of Ryan*. Now Ryan's gone, Scott's life is going to change big time. He'll find himself excluded from all the places he'd previously enjoyed being a part of. There's no way Scott would want Ryan dead. No way at all.'

They seemed strong enough reasons for Marshall not to dispose of his friend. But it was only hearsay. What if Ryan had threatened to exclude him? Scott could have killed him in temper.

'Can you think of anyone who might have held a grudge against Ryan?'

'I take it you know about his stalker? Then again, she'd never threatened him in the past. So why start now? In that case, no. I can't think of anyone.'

'What were you doing between the hours of one and three on Sunday morning?'

'I was at home. My wife picked me up around midnight, maybe a little earlier, and we went home. We stayed up for a while talking and then went to bed.'

'Didn't your wife mind you going out as her father had only just died?'

'It was her suggestion that I should go. My father-in-law actually died a few weeks ago, but he died unexpectedly, so we had to wait until after the post-mortem before holding the funeral.'

'I think that's all for now. Thank you for your time,' Whitney said, leaning in front of Brian and stopping the recording. 'If you do think of anything, please get in touch. DS Chapman will escort you out of the station.'

After Brian and Butler had left, Whitney headed back to the incident room.

'Guv,' Ellie called out as soon as she'd entered the room. 'I've found the man who hired the car. His name is William Palmer, and he's got a record.'

'Is this William Palmer from Lenchester, aka *Bill the Blagger*?' Frank called out, looking up from his screen.

'Do you know him?' Ellie asked.

'Too right I do. He's been around for years. He's a PI and a right dodgy one at that. I'm sure you'll find his record is for breaking and entering, and other iffy stuff. He was a wannabe police officer but got turned down and decided to become a private investigator.'

'What you're saying is we're not going to find that he

belongs to the Association of Private Investigators,' Whitney said.

'You've got it in one, guv.'

'I want him here for questioning pronto. Ellie text me his address and I'll arrange for uniform to bring him in.'

She went into her office and phoned George.

'Can you get in today? A potential suspect is being brought in.'

'I have a tutorial shortly, but that will only take thirty minutes. Other than that, it's fairly quiet. This is the last week of term, and lectures have finished. It's just a question of students handing in their assignments. I'll be with you in an hour.'

Chapter 13

'Read the research paper by Madison et al. and that will give you an alternative viewpoint,' George said to the student sitting opposite her at the table in her office. He was a high-flyer, and she wanted to push him. She hoped that after finishing his undergraduate studies, he'd apply to do postgrad. He was insightful, hard-working, and showed exceptional promise.

'Thank you, Dr Cavendish.'

There was a knock at the door and, before she had time to call out, Robin, her head of department, stuck his head in.

'Sorry to interrupt, do you have a minute?'

She glanced at her watch. 'I have another appointment. Can it wait until tomorrow?'

'It's about the next research committee meeting, I'm not going to be there and I wanted you to chair it. I was going to run through the agenda with you.'

'Then it can wait, as it's not until next week. I'll speak to you tomorrow.'

'Well …'

'I'm in the middle of a tutorial,' she said, nodding at her student.

'Okay. Come and see me first thing.'

She had little time for him, as he allowed himself to be swayed by others, as she'd found to her cost when her ex-boyfriend, who also worked at the university, had tried to ruin her working relationship with the police. He hadn't succeeded. But that was down to her and not her head of department acting appropriately.

'Are you happy with what I've asked you to do?' she asked, returning her attention to the student.

'Yes, thank you. Apart from … I did want to ask you something.'

'What is it?'

'You work with Lenchester Police on their cases, and I wondered if you'd ever considered having someone accompany you, to gain some work experience. Me.'

She hadn't been expecting that.

'It's not my decision to make. I can ask Detective Chief Inspector Walker whether she'd accept someone being with me but, to be frank, I'm not sure it would be possible because of the sensitive nature of the work.'

'If you could ask, that would be awesome. I'm planning my next steps and would like to experience working with the police. They have a fast track scheme for entrants with degrees.'

'After our conversations regarding being accepted for postgraduate study, I'd assumed you were going to continue here. With your ability, you should give it serious consideration.'

'It's an option, and I haven't totally discounted it, but I've been in education for eighteen years and maybe it's time for me to step into the real world. Working for the police would be cool.'

Students were so idealistic at that age. But she wouldn't disillusion him. He had to make his own decisions.

'Don't do anything before thinking everything through carefully. I'll let you know what the DCI says.'

'Thank you,' he said, grinning, as he picked up his bag and left her office.

She took her coat from the back of the door, left the campus and drove to the station.

On arrival, she headed straight for Whitney's office and knocked on the door.

'Come in.'

She opened the door and walked in. 'Hello.'

'I'm glad you're here,' Whitney said, as she stood and came over to where George was standing. 'William Palmer has just arrived. To get you up to speed, he's the person who'd been following Ryan Armstrong. He hired a car, using a fake driving licence. He paid by cash, and because the woman he dealt with was new she didn't run his credit card through the system to put a hold on it. It turns out he's a private eye and, according to Frank, he's dodgy. He has a record. Let's go and grab Brian and we'll interview him.'

'Do we have time for a quick word before we go?' she asked.

'Sure. What is it?'

'One of my students has asked to do some work experience here with me. He's thinking of joining the force through the fast-track scheme. Is it possible?'

'We don't offer work placements, because of the sensitive and dangerous nature of the work. But we do have Force Insight Days, which give anyone interested in joining the chance to find out more about us and what goes on in the different departments. I don't mind chatting to him, too, if you'd like me to.'

'Thank you. I'd hoped he'd stay on and do his masters and PhD. Students like him don't come along very often. He has an exceptional, analytical mind and could make a huge contribution to the discipline, internationally.'

'Do you want me to try to put him off? I could introduce him to *Dickhead*. That ought to scare anyone away.' She laughed.

'It's kind of you to offer, but that wouldn't be fair. It's his decision to make. I'll just have to hope he decides to stay with me. Not that there's anything wrong with him becoming a police officer, I have the utmost respect for what you do here.'

'You don't have to explain. I totally understand. Right now, though, we don't have time to discuss this further.'

They collected Brian from the incident room and headed to the ground floor and the interview room where Palmer was being held.

George slipped into the observation room and sat on one of the stools. She scrutinised the overweight, balding man who was obviously uncomfortable as he fidgeted in his seat. He was in his fifties and wore a casual brown leather bomber jacket with a dark-green T-shirt underneath. His fingers drummed erratically on the table. Definitely nervous.

'Why am I here?' he asked as soon as Whitney and Brian entered the room.

'Because we wish to talk to you,' Whitney answered as she started the recording equipment.

'Ask some non-contentious questions to give me a baseline from which to assess his body language,' George said into the mic, conscious that, as a PI, he might be familiar with interrogation techniques and body language, using them to his advantage.

'What's your occupation?' Whitney asked.

'Perfect,' she said.

'You know what I am.'

'I'd like you to tell me for the recording.'

'I'm a private investigator.'

'How long have you been doing that job?'

'Twenty-five years.'

'What is your marital status?'

'Divorced and much happier because of it. Now can we get to the point?' He scowled at Whitney.

'Thanks,' George said. 'Ask what you like, now.'

'Do you use your own car for work?'

'Yes.'

'Then why did you hire a car from *Rent Me Car Hire* for two weeks, dropping it off last night.'

His eyes widened. 'I … I …' He faltered. 'How do you know?'

'Because we went through their records.'

'B-but …' His fists clenched into balls on the table.

'Were you going to add that we couldn't know because you'd falsified your documents?' Whitney asked, interrupting him. 'That doesn't mean we can't track you down. We used the photo on your fake licence and found you that way. I'm surprised you hadn't thought of that. A rookie mistake, if you ask me. Now perhaps you could give us an explanation regarding what you were doing and why?'

'It's confidential.'

'Notice how every time you ask a question he looks at Brian to give his answer? He doesn't like being questioned by a woman,' George said. 'You can use it to unnerve him further. He's already struggling.'

'No, it's not, if you know what's good for you,' Whitney said, her tone even more aggressive than before. George approved.

'It's still confidential.'

'We're investigating the murder of Ryan Armstrong and we know you've been following him because you were picked up on the CCTV footage on several occasions. We want to know why.' Whitney said.

'I was working for a client.'

'Who is this client?'

'I don't know as I didn't deal directly with them.'

'And you expect us to believe you? This isn't a B-movie.'

'It's the truth. I was contacted by a go-between. And before you ask I don't know their name, either. I was paid to follow Armstrong and report his movements back to my contact.'

'How did they pay you?'

'They left cash in an envelope at my office.'

'Where? Under the mat? Or did you give them a key, and they left it on your desk?'

'It was posted through the letter box in a brown envelope.'

'Of course, it was.' Whitney arched her eyebrow. 'Surely you can see this doesn't add up.'

'I'm telling the truth.'

'Let's suppose I believe you. Why did you hire a car and fake your documents? What was the point in that?'

'Because they told me to.'

George shook her head at the childish response.

'Who's *they*?'

'My contact. Part of the contract was for me not to be traced.' He let out a sigh.

'And yet you failed. You do know it's illegal to falsify official documents. Did you ask why it was to be kept off the radar?'

'Of course I didn't. They were paying me good money to follow Armstrong, that's all I cared about.'

'Did they specify how long you were to watch him?'

'No, but after Armstrong was killed I stopped. I haven't heard from them since then. They still owe me for last week, so they'd better get in touch.'

'What were you doing between the hours of one and three early Sunday morning?'

He looked daggers at Whitney. 'You're not pinning his murder on me. I went out to the pub on Saturday night, had a skinful, came home and fell asleep on the sofa.'

'Weren't you meant to be following Armstrong then?'

'I knew he was at home as I saw him greet all his friends when they arrived. I assumed he wouldn't be going out again.'

'How were you able to see that?'

'I was positioned across the street from his house using high-powered binoculars.'

'Can anyone vouch for you during the times in question?'

'No, I live on my own.'

'Where were you drinking?'

'I went to The Crown on Lawrence Street. They called a taxi for me around midnight, maybe a bit later. Ask them, they'll be my alibi. I could hardly stand, so certainly couldn't drive to the snooker club, murder the bloke and then scarper.'

'I'm inclined to believe him,' George said. 'None of his body language indicates he's lying.'

'We'll be getting in touch with the pub to confirm your story. Let's go back to this mysterious client. How did they contact you in the first place to offer you the job?'

'They found me online.'

'And why did they choose you? Was it because they knew you skirt on the wrong side of the law most of the time and would do things other PIs wouldn't consider?'

'I resent those assumptions. Okay, so I have a record. That doesn't mean I break the law all the time.'

'Doesn't it? What about the fake documents you used?'

'That's different. I don't know why they chose me. You'll have to ask them.'

'How do you suggest we do that, seeing as we don't know who they are? Are you sure the go-between didn't tell you their name?'

'The first time he called he said he had a client from overseas who wanted me to follow Ryan Armstrong and report back daily on what he did.'

'Ah … so we've gone from *they* to *he*. That's progress. Do you have a phone number for this *go-between* so you could give your report?'

'I don't. He phoned me each evening at nine o'clock.'

Whitney gave an exasperated sigh. 'You're really not helping yourself. Let's try something else. During the time you followed Armstrong, where did he go?'

'My notes are on my phone. May I?'

'Be my guest,' Whitney said.

He pulled out his phone from his pocket and stared at the screen for a few seconds. 'He went to his snooker club regularly. He met his friends at various pubs. He also went to the gym. Twice he drove to Watford Gap service station and met an officer from the Metropolitan Police Force. A DI Clifford.'

Whitney sat upright in her chair. 'How do you know that's who he was?'

'I took a note of his car registration and used my contacts to find out who it was registered to. I also took photos of the DI and checked him out online. I'm a private investigator. Finding out who people are is like bread and butter to me.'

'Apart from discovering who the people are who hired you,' Whitney retorted.

'I didn't even try.' He shrugged and sat back in his chair.

'He's getting complacent, Whitney. He thinks he's getting the better of you,' she said.

'When you informed the *go-between* who Armstrong had been meeting, what was his reaction?'

'There was none.'

'Have you had any contact with him since Armstrong's death?'

'I've already told you I haven't and that I'm still owed money.'

'Returning to when you hired the car with fake credentials. What would you have done if they had insisted on putting a hold on the credit card?'

'I would have gone elsewhere to rent the car. There's always somewhere you can do a deal.'

'We are going to be further investigating your use of false documentation and will be looking to press charges. DS Chapman will escort you out of the station and we will be in touch. Interview suspended.'

George left the observation room after Brian had walked past with Palmer, then she went into the corridor and waited for Whitney, who came out holding a folder.

'He possibly knew more than he told you,' she said to Whitney.

'Regarding what?'

'Who the go-between was. He said he didn't try to find out but, by the very nature of his work, I believe he tried. It was the way he dismissed it so quickly. Either he found out and was scared off, or he tried and wasn't able to discover his name, which would also have rung warning bells with him.'

'We'll question him again, but more important for now is that we know Armstrong had been meeting with this detective from the Met. I'm going to contact him and see what he knows.'

'I'm going back to work to finish off some admin, do you need me tomorrow?'

'Yes, please. First thing in the morning, if you can make it.'

'I've arranged to see my head of department, but he can wait.'

'Thanks. It's such a high-profile case, we really need all hands on deck to get it solved before the likes of Douglas interfere and want to take the investigation away from me.'

Chapter 14

Whitney opened the police database and found the contact details for DI Sebastian Clifford from the Met. She called the number listed.

'Clifford,' he answered, after it had been ringing for a while and she was just about to hang up.

'This is DCI Whitney Walker from the Lenchester force.'

'How may I help you?' His voice was deep, yet had a warmth about it. But that aside, he sounded as posh as George, if not more so. Is that even possible?

'I'd like to speak to you about Ryan Armstrong, the snooker player who was shot and killed in the early hours of Sunday morning.'

'I am aware of his death.'

'We've been informed that the victim met with you on two occasions recently.'

There was silence for a few seconds, during which time she heard him suck in a breath. 'Who made this claim?'

'A private investigator from Lenchester who'd been employed, by sources as yet unknown to us, to follow

Armstrong. He'd been working for them for the last two weeks. He's not in the frame for the shooting as he's got an alibi. He was paid in cash and claims not to know who his employers were. He only had conversations on the phone with a go-between and his payment was left at his office. He maintains that you met Armstrong twice at Watford Gap service station. Firstly, do you confirm that these meetings took place? And, secondly, what were they about?'

'I'm unable to comment.'

For goodness' sake. Suspects played the *no comment* card she didn't expect it from a fellow officer.

'You have got to be kidding me. Your answer is not acceptable. I'm the senior investigating officer on this case, as well as your superior officer.'

'Are you pulling rank?' he asked.

He didn't sound angry. If anything, there was a dry, almost humorous, edge to his voice.

'Rank has nothing to do with it. I would like to find out about your meeting with Armstrong. It could be an important factor in apprehending his killer, as I'm sure you can appreciate.'

'I am unable to discuss this with you. It's confidential.'

'Guv.'

'Pardon?'

'It's confidential, *guv.*'

Okay, she was being petty, but she didn't like being given the runaround, especially by an officer of a lower rank. Though, one thing she could imply from their conversation was that he did actually meet with the victim, or he would have denied it. It would have been pointless not to.

'My mistake. It's confidential, *guv.*' Again with the dry tone.

'Well, it can't remain so if it's integral to my investigation. I'll have to take this further if you're not prepared to answer my questions.'

'That's your prerogative, but for now I can't comment without first consulting with my superior officer.'

'I *am* your superior officer.' She forced herself to remain calm, despite wanting to take the phone and bash him over the head with it.

'In the special squad of which I'm a member we follow a specific chain of command.'

She was getting absolutely nowhere with this infuriating man. Her fists were clenched and her body tense. But he hardly seemed ruffled.

'So, just to be crystal clear, are you refusing to assist me?'

'If you wish to put it in those words—'

'Yes, I do, and rest assured I will be taking this further.' She ended the call without giving him a chance to reply.

Fuming, she left her office and went straight to see the super. She knocked on the door which was slightly ajar.

'Enter,' Clyde called out.

'Do you have a moment, ma'am?'

'Yes, come and sit down.' Clyde placed the pen she was holding on her desk and gave Whitney her full attention.

'We've got a lead regarding the killing of Ryan Armstrong. It involves a private investigator who was being paid to follow him. He informed us that the victim had twice met with a DI Clifford from the Met. I've contacted Clifford who's part of some *special squad* and he point blank refused to give me any information whatsoever regarding his liaison with Armstrong, despite me being his superior officer.'

She was about to mention that he sounded really posh, then thought better of it as it had no bearing on the case.

'I see. We don't wish to tread on their toes if they're in the middle of an investigation, but—'

'But this is a murder enquiry and should take precedence over anything they're doing,' Whitney said, interrupting.

'Not necessarily. Leave it with me and I will contact the Met and let you know how we're going to proceed.'

'Thank you, ma'am. I hope you have better luck than I did.'

She returned to the incident room and stood in front of the board. 'Listen up, everyone. I want to give you an update on where we are. William Palmer, the PI, was paid to follow Armstrong. He has an alibi for the shooting but, more importantly, he informed us that the victim had twice met up with a DI from the Met at Watford Gap service station. I got in touch with this DI and got zip. It's unacceptable, and I've now passed it on to the super to sort out.' She picked up the board pen and wrote up Palmer's name.

'Who was the officer you spoke to?' Brian asked, as she was about to add Clifford's name. She'd forgotten Brian had trained there. Maybe he would have a way in, if the super failed. Though that was hardly likely. If anyone could get Clifford to comply, it was Clyde.

'DI Clifford,' she said, turning to face him. 'Do you know him by any chance?'

'You mean, the viscount?'

'The what?'

'He's a real viscount, as in an aristocrat.' He smirked as Whitney looked in his direction, open-mouthed.

'Come on, Sarge. We're not that gullible,' Frank said. 'Since when do any of that lot work for the police. Can you imagine it? We'd be spending our entire life bowing and curtseying every time we saw them.'

'I'd love to see you curtsey with your bad knees. You'd fall arse over tit,' Doug said, laughing.

'I can curtsey, just watch.' Frank stood, put one foot behind the other and dipped down about six inches.

'You call that a curtsey, you barely moved.'

'Doug. Frank. Stop it,' Whitney shouted. She was in no mood for their antics. 'Brian, tell me the truth about Clifford.'

'It's true. Google Sebastian Clifford and you'll see all about him and his family.'

'He's right, guv,' Meena called out. 'I've got him up here on the screen. He's the second son of Viscount Worthington. The title was created in 1754 and it passes to the eldest son, who is Clifford's brother Hubert.'

'Can you imagine being called Hubert at school? You'd get the piss taken out of you big time,' Frank said.

'So, DI Clifford himself isn't actually a viscount,' Whitney said.

'Semantics, he's still from the aristocracy and different from the rest of us,' Brian said.

'What's he doing on the force then?' Whitney shook her head. It was weird enough getting to know George and her background, which was totally alien to her. But this took it to a whole new level. Not that she was going to have anything to do with the man. It wasn't like they worked together.

'No idea. It's not something I remember having been talked about. Or, if it was, nothing was mentioned to me.'

'Do you know him personally?'

'I never worked with him. I only know of him because having an aristocrat working at the Met went around like wildfire.'

'Well, I don't care who he is. The fact is, he fobbed me off and wouldn't give me any information. Just let him try it on with the super and see how far he gets. Aristocrat or not.'

'He's a good guy,' Brian said. 'There must have been a genuine reason for him not helping us.'

'Wait a minute. You just said that you hadn't worked together, but now you're defending him. What am I missing?'

'Nothing. I'm just repeating what I heard from people who knew him well. I'll be honest, there was never a bad word said against him.'

'Does he know of you?'

'I doubt it. We never came in contact with each other.'

The door to the incident room opened and Whitney's attention was diverted as she saw the super heading towards her. It was still weird to have her boss regularly coming to see her, rather than the other way around. When Jamieson was in charge, he rarely set foot in the incident room and if he did, she always went on full alert as it invariably meant she was in for a bollocking.

'Whitney, can I have a quick word in private?' Clyde asked, as she walked over to the board.

'Of course, ma'am.'

They went through to her office and Whitney closed the door behind them. They both remained standing.

'I've spoken to my counterpart at the Met and then to DI Clifford. He confirmed that he does know Ryan Armstrong and that he did meet with him, as you discovered.'

'That's fantastic. Thanks, ma'am. Is he going to cooperate with us?'

She knew her boss would deliver the goods. Nice guy, or not, DI Clifford wasn't going to get in the way of her operation.

'It's a little more complicated than that. It's linked to a

long-standing investigation, and Clifford wasn't prepared to jeopardise the progress they'd made so far. He—'

'That's ridiculous. This is a murder enquiry and has to be more important. Surely—'

'Whitney, stop.' The super held up her hand. 'I'm fully cognisant of the priorities necessary for solving this case, and so is DI Clifford. He acknowledges our need to have as much information as possible, and with this in mind I have arranged for him to come to Lenchester to assist you with the case.'

Assist. What the hell did that mean?

'In what way will he be helping us, ma'am?'

'An assessment of how it's going to work will be undertaken when he arrives. It's hoped that working together will be mutually beneficial.'

Whitney sucked in a long breath. The one thing she didn't want was some jumped-up officer from the Met trying to muscle in on her case.

'Who's going to be in charge?'

'Obviously, you are, Whitney. You're the SIO and senior officer,' Clyde said, an incredulous expression on her face. 'I'm relying on you to make this collaboration work, as it will be in both of our interests. I also don't wish it to get back to the Met that we were being deliberately officious in any way.'

'No, ma'am. You can rely on me. When's Clifford going to be here?' She hoped it wouldn't be for a few days so they could get stuck into more investigating without him there.

'First thing tomorrow morning.'

Damn.

'I'll look forward to it.'

The super opened the door leading into the corridor. 'I expect to hear from you regarding progress.'

Whitney marched back into the incident room.

'Everything okay, guv?' Frank asked. 'You've a face like thunder.'

'I'm fine. Wanted to let you all know that we're being joined tomorrow by DI Clifford from the Met. We're going to work *together* on the case.'

She glanced around as all eyes were on her. They had to be professional about this.

'An extra pair of hands will be useful. He'll have a different perspective,' Brian said.

'Yes, I'm sure it will be most *useful*.'

Out of the corner of her eye, Whitney noticed a look pass between Frank and Doug. They most likely knew her exact thoughts on it.

'Guv, Deborah Radley's here,' Meena said.

'Who?' She frowned.

'Armstrong's stalker. You wanted to interview her.'

'Oh yes. Brian, you can come with me.'

They walked in silence to the lift and then to the interview room, Whitney engrossed in her thoughts and Brian texting. When they entered the interview room, Deborah Radley looked up at them, her body tense and her eyes rimmed red. Her hands were clenched on the table.

'Thank you for coming in to see us,' Whitney said, as she pulled out a seat opposite and sat down. 'I hope you're feeling better after being in hospital.'

'It was a false alarm. I was rushed in with severe abdominal pains, but it turned out to be irritable bowel syndrome and they let me go home.'

'We'd like to talk to you about Ryan Armstrong and the restraining order against you.'

'It's not as bad as you think. I love Ryan. *Loved*. It's like a bad dream, knowing he's dead. I didn't do anything wrong. I didn't threaten him or his family. They told the police I was a stalker, but that's not true.'

'Weren't you found in his garden taking photos of his wife and child?'

She blushed. 'Yes, but not for the reasons you're thinking. I'm writing a biography of him and thought I'd get some photos for the book.'

'Did Ryan authorise this book?' Whitney asked.

'No, he didn't. It was going to be a surprise.'

'Are you still writing it?'

'I've completed the first draft. But now he's dead … I …' A sob escaped her lips. 'I'm never going to see him again. My life's over.'

Whitney reached over for the box of tissues and slid it in front of the woman. She took one out and wiped her eyes.

'Why didn't you explain about the book when the injunction was taken out?'

'It was a waste of time. Ryan wouldn't have listened. His partner, Scott Marshall, had it in for me. I wouldn't be surprised if he was the one to suggest it to Ryan, just to get his own back on me.'

'For what?'

'One time when I was at the snooker club watching Ryan play, I went to the Ladies' and when I came out Scott Marshall was waiting for me. He trapped me in the corner and …'

'Did he assault you?'

'Not exactly. He said that if I was good to him, he'd get me some time alone with Ryan.'

'Did you take him up on the offer?' Brian asked.

'No, I did not. Do you think I'm a slut? It's only Ryan I want.'

'How does this relate to the injunction?' Whitney asked.

'I think Scott sowed the seed in Ryan's mind to get back at me for turning him down.'

The evidence against Marshall's character was adding up. But did that make him a killer?

'According to our records, you were following him all the time and the fact you went to his house was bound to be worrying.'

'With hindsight, I shouldn't have gone there. But you know the reason why.'

'Since the injunction, did you continue to follow Ryan, keeping your distance?'

'Not all the time.'

'Did you notice anyone else following him, or acting suspicious around him?'

'No.' She shook her head.

'Presumably you have photos and notes that you used when writing your manuscript.'

'Yes.'

'I'd like copies of everything you have. You may have recorded something of use.'

'I'm sure there's nothing, or I'd have spotted it.'

'Not necessarily. Email everything you have to this address.' Whitney handed over a business card. 'You may go now.'

After seeing Radley out of the station, they returned to the incident room.

'Ellie, what have you turned up on Scott Marshall?'

'He's married with one child, in a house worth over a million which is owned outright by his wife. She's the only daughter of Gordon Elliot.'

'*The* Gordon Elliott, millionaire businessman who

somehow manages to avoid paying any taxes, if the media is to be believed,' Doug said.

'That's the one. Marshall is active on social media, usually posting photos of himself with the victim playing snooker. I've done some research into the family finances, and his wife is the one with the money. Shall I go deeper?'

'Keep it on the back-burner. Brian, I want Marshall in here tomorrow. Arrange it, please.'

Chapter 15

Detective Inspector Sebastian Clifford drummed his fingers on the steering wheel. He'd left London at six, hoping to avoid the traffic, especially as he was heading away from the city, but it had been nose to tail the whole way and he was now stuck on the M1. It was gone eight and he hadn't even reached Milton Keynes, where he'd intended stopping for breakfast. His stomach grumbled in response to the thought.

Although he'd been in contact with Ryan Armstrong over recent months, he'd never been to Lenchester, keeping their meetings away from there to prevent being spotted. It appeared that he'd failed and that was unacceptable.

Was it his fault Armstrong had been shot?

The thought had been plaguing him ever since he'd heard the news of Ryan's death on the TV. Their next meeting had been planned for the day after the shooting, prior to the tournament due to be held at the Palace Snooker Club that week. Would it still go ahead? It was prestigious and had players from all over the country attending. He'd hoped it would provide them with some good leads. He was banking on it, as his investigation had stalled recently.

Had Armstrong confided in anyone about his arrangement with the special squad? Was that why he'd been shot? At their last meeting he'd assured Clifford he hadn't and that not even his wife knew about their meetings. Clifford had no reason to doubt him. He'd been cultivating Armstrong for some time before getting him to come on board to help with the case. In particular, before they could move forward he needed to be confident that Armstrong was clean and not involved in any illegal activity.

So much money was lost nationally and internationally from match-fixing. Not just in snooker, the area Clifford was currently focusing on, but in all other sports, which other members of the special squad he belonged to were concentrating on.

He wasn't naive enough to believe he could clean up the whole snooker industry, but he could do something about it. Make it much fairer for the public who paid to watch, and also for the players who were often in vulnerable situations. It wasn't unusual for players to have death threats made against their family if they didn't comply with throwing games, or making certain errors at a particular time. And they weren't idle threats. The mother of a player from Thailand was threatened with having both legs broken if he refused to comply with a request made of him. He wouldn't agree, and she ended up in a wheelchair for the rest of her life. He never played snooker again.

It wasn't acceptable.

Clifford could do without having to involve members of another force, though. The more people who knew about his work, the less likely it was to succeed.

He worked best solo, but from his brief discussion with DCI Walker, he suspected there was little chance of that happening. As to how much he would share with the officer and her team … after discussing it with his boss, he would play it by ear. Give away as little as possible, without being seen to jeopardise their investigation.

But if there were any indications at all that the shooting was linked to his operation, he'd be taking the case back to London quicker than the DCI could say *I'm in charge.* Words he expected to be levelled at him on a regular basis if his conversation with Walker yesterday was anything to go by.

Finally, he made it to Lenchester, a location he knew little of, having never visited, and he drove through the city until reaching the outskirts and the new purpose-built station, which he'd researched online before leaving. He parked in the visitors' car park and stared at the modern building. It looked impressive, with the sun bouncing off the thousands of large windowpanes. It wasn't his cup of tea. He much preferred buildings with some history. But this was a workplace and with that in mind, he could acknowledge that it was impressive.

He strode in through the main entrance door and went up to the reception.

'DI Clifford to see DCI Walker,' he said, staring down at the civilian on the desk and holding out his warrant card.

'Just one moment,' the woman replied.

How was Walker, and her team, going to react to him? In his experience, the Met had an unjustified reputation for believing they were better than officers from other forces.

He'd have to take it steady and bring them on board, otherwise this would be a collaboration in name only.

Chapter 16

'They're sending a DI Sebastian Clifford from the Met to work with us on the case. He's part of some *special squad* which I know nothing about,' Whitney said to George, making quote marks with her fingers. 'If he tries to take over, sparks will fly, I can one hundred per cent assure you of that. And you'll never guess what. He's one of yours.'

The psychologist had no sooner arrived in the incident room, a short while ago, when Whitney had whisked her away to the office so she could let off steam about their soon to arrive *guest*. It had been preying on her mind ever since she'd learnt about his visit. The more she thought about it, the more annoyed she got. He should have handed over the information they needed and not been so precious about it. She bet he thought it was beneath him to work at Lenchester, instead of his precious Met. Well, she'd show him. Just one step out of line … one step … and he'll be sorry.

'What do you mean, *he's one of mine*? One of my what?' George asked, frowning.

'According to Brian, he's the son of Viscount

Worthington. You do know him, don't you? Is he a friend of yours?'

A scowling face stared back at her. 'Whitney, contrary to what you believe, there isn't a club to which all *posh people*, as you refer to us, belong. How many times do I have to explain this to you?' She released an exasperated sigh.

'You are posh, though, aren't you?' Whitney pressed, ignoring the niggle at the back of her mind that she might be pushing George a little too far.

'That's the label you've given me. And in answer to your question, no, I don't know him personally, although I have heard of Viscount Worthington and the Clifford family.'

'Ha. I knew it. Did you go to school with this chap? Or did your brother?'

'Firstly, I went to an all-girl's school, as I believe you already know. Secondly, I have no idea which school Clifford went to, so I cannot comment on whether my brother, James, is acquainted with him. If it was Eton, then James may know the man. Thirdly, I'd rather you ceased jumping to conclusions based on illogical assumptions.' George folded her arms, her lips together in a flat line.

That told her.

'Point taken. Anyway, whether or not you know him, he's arriving today to help us on the case, so I'm glad you're here.' She was about to say, *to explain his aristocratic behaviour,* then thought better of it. She'd already overstepped the mark, and George might leave if she continued. She glanced at her watch. 'It's already nine-thirty, and he was meant to be here first thing. Where is he? Is Met time different from ours?' The phone on her desk rang, and she picked it up. 'Walker.'

'There's a DI Clifford here to see you.'

She'd spoken too soon.

'Give him a visitor's pass and I'll send someone down to collect him. Also, arrange for a permanent pass, as we've no idea how long he'll be here.'

'Will do.'

'Clifford's arrived,' she said, replacing the phone. 'I'll be back in a sec.' She went into the incident room. Meena was closest, so she headed in her direction. 'DI Clifford is here. Could you go downstairs and collect him? Please bring him straight to me.'

'Yes, guv.'

She returned to her office and sat down at the coffee table opposite George. 'Should I have gone downstairs to meet him myself?'

'Is that appropriate behaviour?'

'Not really, as I'm his superior officer, but it would have been more welcoming. Except, welcoming is not how I'm feeling at this precise moment.' She wouldn't have admitted her feelings to anyone other than George as she knew the psychologist would keep it to herself.

'You're not going to help the relationship with that attitude.'

'He doesn't know. I promise to play nice.' Who was she trying to convince? 'We'll have a meeting in here first and then I'll introduce him to the rest of the team.'

'Are you sure you want me here with you?'

'Quite sure. You're the go-between. You can interpret what he says.' George glared at her. 'Joking,' she said, holding her hands up in mock surrender. 'It's just, you know what it's like being around people like him.'

'You have an extremely unfounded and biased view of people who've had a different upbringing from you.'

'Leave me with my own little prejudices, I haven't held it against you, have I?'

'Not now, but when we first met you were decidedly judgemental and—'

A knock at the door interrupted her.

'He's here,' Whitney said lowering her voice, and standing. She smoothed down her trousers, which had wrinkled at the knee. Next to her, George also stood. 'Come in.'

The door opened, and Whitney clamped her mouth together. Whoa. He was one of the tallest men she'd ever seen, and very solid in stature. He filled the doorway. Not only that, his angular jaw and dark hair and eyes made him most striking.

'DI Clifford, guv,' Meena said, appearing positively tiny standing next to him.

'Thank you, Meena. You can go now.' She glanced up at Clifford. 'I'm DCI Walker and this is Dr Cavendish. George. She's a forensic psychologist who works with us on our more serious cases, of which this is one. Come on in.'

'It's a pleasure to meet you both,' he said, stepping inside the office, and flashing a disarming smile which caught her unawares. 'Is there anywhere around here that I can get a good cup of coffee and a Danish pastry? I missed breakfast.'

Whitney glimpsed at George. He'd passed the first test.

'There's the canteen downstairs and the coffee isn't too bad. Well, not for me. George, what's your opinion as you're far more discerning than me in that respect?'

'It's passable.'

'High praise indeed. Let's all go, and we can discuss the case,' Whitney suggested, as she could do with a coffee, even though it had been less than an hour since her last one.

'That sounds like an excellent idea,' Clifford said.

As they left Whitney's office and were heading down

the corridor towards the lift, she found herself sandwiched between them. It was like being in *Land of the Giants*. Clifford even towered over George. He had to be at least six feet six or maybe more.

'How was the journey up here?' she asked, making small talk, knowing that George wouldn't.

'There was an accident on the M1 which is why I'm late. I'd intended arriving between eight to eight-thirty, but there was almost an hour's hold-up because the motorway was down to a single lane. A lorry had shed its load.'

'That's a pain,' she said. 'But at least you finally made it.'

They went into the canteen and Clifford paid for coffees and a Danish for each of them. He was certainly getting off to a good start. But she wasn't going to be complacent, as he could be using it to put her off guard, and then he'd jump in and try to take over.

She was being paranoid. Which was ridiculous. She was the senior officer, and should know better.

They sat at a round table in the corner far away from the other people in there, so they had some privacy.

'Let's talk about the case,' he said, demolishing half of his pastry in a single bite. 'Mmm. This is good.'

'When I spoke to you yesterday, you refused to disclose anything related to your meetings with Ryan Armstrong. Can I take it that, as you're here working with us, we are now going to be informed of the relationship between the two of you?'

Clifford leant back in his chair and studied her, not in a threatening way, but more like he was deliberating before answering. Was it that confidential?

'What I'm about to tell you goes no further.' He looked from Whitney to George, as if wanting confirmation.

'That's not possible. My team needs to be kept in the

picture or they won't be able to work on the case. Keeping them in the dark isn't an option.'

'How many are there?' The expression on his face was unreadable. Was he about to relent?

'There's Brian Chapman, my sergeant and—'

'Chapman? I know that name.'

Brian said they weren't acquainted. Had he been lying about that?

'He trained at the Met and spent several years there. He mentioned that he knew of you but said you wouldn't know him.'

'I didn't ever meet him, personally, but I remember coming across his name on several reports. There was one relating to a drug bust in Enfield on July the eighteenth, 2015. I was collecting information on one of the charged. He also filed a report on March the fourth 2018 following a police chase which he was part of. And—'

'You remember *every* report you've read?' George asked.

'Yes.'

'Do you have a photographic memory?' Whitney asked. She'd love to have that ability. She could put it to so many good uses.

'There's no proof that it exists,' George said. 'I suspect what DI Clifford has is HSAM. Highly superior autobiographical memory. It's exceptionally rare.'

'You're right. Well done. That's exactly what I have. Most people have never heard of it.'

'This is George we're talking about,' Whitney said. 'What she doesn't know isn't worth knowing. How does HSAM work exactly?'

'I'm able to recall events from the past in great detail, and can tell you when and where they occurred. Do you want to know what I had for lunch this day a year ago?' He gave a wry smile.

'Wow. It would be so cool to have that talent,' Whitney said.

'Be careful what you wish for. Some things a person has no desire to remember. Although, I admit it can be useful, if channelled correctly.'

'Like when studying for exams?'

'It does help with recall, but exams are far more than a regurgitation of facts. Applying and evaluating the knowledge is paramount, and that's a completely different skill set. But we digress. Who else is on your team?'

'I have four detective constables, Frank Taylor, Ellie Naylor, Doug Baines, and Meena Singh. They're a loyal and conscientious bunch, and I trust them implicitly to keep confidential what we discuss with them. Ellie's a brilliant researcher and a great asset. You won't find better.'

'I'll second that,' George said. 'Her skills are extraordinary.'

'Good, she'll be useful. What you're asking is that including the two of you we allow seven people in our investigatory bubble. That's a lot to manage. One small slip and the whole operation could go tits up.'

She didn't mention that it was eight if you counted the super.

'Think of us as one,' she reassured him. 'You have my word there'll be no leaks from any officers in the squad.'

'It appears I don't have an option but to go along with it.' He sniffed his coffee and took a sip. 'Not bad. I can certainly live with it while I'm here.'

Which hopefully wouldn't be too long, even if she was warming to him. A little.

'See, George. What did I say?'

'I haven't disputed that it's drinkable, but it's not the best you can get.'

'George seems to forget that this is a police station and we don't have the budget for the *best you can get.*' Whitney laughed, and Clifford cracked a smile as well. 'Back to our discussion, why were you meeting with the victim?'

He put his mug on the table and leant back in the chair, keeping his eyes fixed on her. 'We're investigating a syndicate in southeast Asia who are involved in match-fixing in snooker. Betting is huge in sport and having advance notice of an outcome is extremely lucrative. Sportspeople are regularly approached to fix matches. They're offered money to do so, but if they refuse, it can be very dangerous. There have been family members killed when a sportsperson has refused to comply with what's requested.'

'In our country?'

'Death threats and killings have taken place in parts of Asia, but it's only a matter of time before it happens here.'

'So this group from overseas will ask someone to throw a match and then put large amounts of money on the person or team they know will win?' Whitney asked.

'It's not just the outcome of a match. People will bet on anything, even two drops of rain running down a window-pane. Take football, where manipulating play is common. It's not unusual for people to bet on players getting sent off. The bet would specify a time frame and the name of the player. So, for example, a player could be told to get them-selves sent off within the first fifteen minutes of a match. There are all manner of things to bet on.'

'And it's the same in snooker?'

'It's extremely prevalent in snooker. Most professional players will be approached at sometime in their careers to throw a match. Armstrong was clean, but there are some players who will take bribes to fix matches. It's easier if both players have agreed, but even if only one does, it's still possible to engineer outcomes. During my meetings with Armstrong, we'd agreed he would give us inside information about what was going on.'

'Had he provided you with any before he died?' George asked.

'A little, but it was early stages as I hadn't been working with him for long. It took a while to get it off the ground because I had to convince him to help. He knew the potential risks.'

'Yet, despite having a wife and young child, he agreed. And you were okay with that?' Whitney asked.

She'd only just met the man, but he didn't come across as the sort to put an informant in danger.

'I'll be honest, the risks we'd envisaged weren't life-threatening. More the affect it might have had on his career.'

'But you said that family members had been killed in Asia. Surely you must have thought of that?' Whitney said.

'It didn't seem pertinent. Our meetings were very low-key and I had no idea we were being watched.' A pained expression crossed his face.

Guilt?

'Had Armstrong been approached to throw any matches in the past?'

'Several times, the most recent being last year and he'd turned them down. He couldn't give us any information about the people who approached him because it was all done very clandestinely.'

'Were there any repercussions after he refused to take the bribe?'

'None that we know of. I don't want to give the impression that there are repercussions for everyone who refuses to take a bribe and fix a match, because there aren't. It's rare, but that doesn't mean it won't become more common.'

'Does match-fixing take place during major sporting events?'

'Not usually. If anything, it's the less popular events which syndicates focus on. In football, preseason matches are often targeted, as they don't attract media attention. It's much easier to fix something then. It's been known for whole teams to be in on it, and they'll use a friend or family member to bet on the outcome for them. Like I said, it's rife.'

'Do you feel responsible for Ryan Armstrong's death?' Whitney asked.

Judging by his double take he was surprised that she'd asked but he'd get used to her forthrightness.

'We're not yet in the position of being able to apportion blame. That's why I'm here so we can investigate what has happened. But what we don't want is for other members of the snooker community to know that he was working with us.'

'Could he have told anyone what he was doing, like his wife or business partner, and it got back to the syndicate?'

'There's always that risk, but he was instructed not to mention it to anyone, and he agreed. He knew there were risks, so why take any unnecessary ones. He didn't strike me as that type of man.'

'It might have been discovered by accident. William Palmer, the PI who'd been paid to follow him, reported your meetings to the people who had engaged his services. If these people belong to the same organisation you're targeting, they may very well be responsible for the shooting.'

'That's my thinking, especially if they know who I am.'

'They do because Palmer told us, and he would have told them.'

A shadow crossed Clifford's face. 'We want to clean up the sport but not at the expense of Armstrong's life.'

He showed compassion. Whitney approved.

'Once we've finished here, I'll introduce you to the team, and then we'll bring Palmer back in. You and I will interview him, and George will observe, feeding back to us throughout, which will assist in the questioning. Is that okay with you?'

Why did she ask? Was she seeking his approval?

'You're in charge.'

'Yes, I am,' she said, allowing herself a tiny smile.

She pulled out her phone and called the desk sergeant, asking him to instruct uniform to pick up Palmer and bring him in.

'In the interest of openness, I need to let you know that my boss wants me to bring the case back to the squad,' Clifford said, once she'd ended her call.

He wormed his way into her good books, and then he dropped that on her. Did he think she was that gullible?

'Why?'

'If there's proof that Armstrong's death was a direct consequence of working with me, then my department should take over the case as we have all the information relating to the organisation who could be responsible.'

'This is my case, and you should be passing that information to me.'

'For now, we'll work on it together. The higher-ups will decide what happens based on what we discover over the next few days.'

'We'll see about that,' Whitney muttered under her breath.

Chapter 17

After their chat in the station canteen the three of them headed back to the incident room. George had been surprised at how well Whitney was dealing with having Clifford join them on the case. From his actions, it had seemed that he'd already got the measure of Whitney, until he mentioned taking the case back to the Met. That wasn't a good move on his part. He'd learn very quickly that Whitney would not give up without a fight. But, watching them together was interesting from a psychological perspective.

They walked into the room, where the team were busy at their desks and Whitney called them to attention. 'This is DI Clifford from the Met. He's here to help us with the case. Before his death, the victim had just begun working as an informant for his squad and—'

'That fact is to be kept within these four walls,' Clifford interrupted.

'Everyone here is fully aware of the need for discretion,' Whitney said, her voice flat. 'The squad is investigating an international syndicate who they believe may have infiltrated the country in various sports with a view to influencing outcomes of matches so large bets can be placed. Armstrong was going to help on the snooker side.'

'You mean players throwing matches?' Frank said.

'Match throwing is the main area we're investigating, although bets are made on more than just the outcomes,' Clifford said.

'That was Frank, over there is Brian, Meena and Doug,' Whitney said, pointing to each one in turn. We're bringing Palmer in again and DI Clifford will be interviewing him with me while Dr Cavendish observes. While we're gone, Ellie, look at the interaction between Palmer and this go-between he mentioned. He might have been paid cash, but there has to be some way of pinpointing this man. Doug, I'll forward you the email that's just come through from Armstrong's stalker. She was writing a biography about him and has sent me the manuscript and her notes. Take a look for anything which might help.'

'Yes, guv. By the way, I got in touch with Westfield Taxis and the driver who took the booking made from Rory Clarke's phone is away in Spain until next week.'

'Couldn't the office tell you anything about the job? Aren't the journeys all monitored nowadays?'

'It seems his app wasn't working, so he was going old-school on the radio. As far as the records show, he was dropped at home, but we won't know for certain until the driver returns.'

'Okay. Meena, the victim's phone?'

'It wasn't in the car.'

'That means it's missing. Find out the last time it was used, and where. Brian, where are we with the alibis for the other men at the party?'

'All corroborated, guv. An email has also come in from the pathologist. No drugs in Armstrong's system, but the amount of alcohol in his blood would have put him over the limit.'

'Thanks, Brian. So, whatever it was that took him away from his house, must have been important.' Her phone rang. 'Walker.' She nodded. 'We'll be there shortly.' She ended the call. 'Palmer's here.'

Whitney forwarded the email to Doug, and they left to go downstairs.

'Please, call me Seb. There's no need for DI Clifford,' he said as they were on their way.

'Noted,' Whitney said. 'For the record, I'm guv, not ma'am.'

'Yes, I realised that from our conversation yesterday.'

George headed into the observation room. Palmer was fidgeting in exactly the same way he had in the previous interview. Clifford walked in first and pulled out the chair on the left.

'I sit there,' Whitney said.

He nodded and sat in the chair beside her. Whitney leant across him and started the recording.

'Interview on Wednesday, March the tenth. Those present: Detective Chief Inspector Walker, Detective Inspector Clifford. Please state your name.'

'William Lewis Palmer. You know that from before.'

'And this is another interview and procedures have to be followed.'

'Why have you brought me back in? I told you everything I know.'

'DI Clifford has joined to help with the investigation. You know him, of course, because you were following Armstrong when they met.'

'Yes, that's right, I did.' Palmer nodded at him.

'Where were you situated at the time I was meeting with Armstrong?' Clifford asked.

Whitney didn't bristle in the slightest at Clifford asking questions. She must have been expecting it.

What George hadn't admitted to Whitney, and wasn't going to because it would only add fuel to her fire, was that she believed she'd been to at least one event in the past that Clifford, or members of his family, had attended. Viscount Worthington was one of the patrons of a private hospital where her father was senior consultant and on the board. They held regular fundraising events. Having HSAM, Clifford would have remembered if they'd actually met, although presumably not if they hadn't been introduced and there were lots of people there.

'I sat in my car and parked close so I could observe you together.'

'Did you take photos?'

'Yes.'

'I wish to see them, forward them to us.'

'Why?'

'Because DI Clifford told you to,' Whitney snapped. She pulled out her card from her pocket and slid it over to him. 'Here's my card. Send them to the email address on there. Are the photos on your phone?'

'Yes.'

'Do it now. We'll wait.'

Palmer took out his phone from his pocket and spent the next few minutes forwarding the photos. 'Done. You have all the pictures I took from both of your meetings. Okay?' He glared at Whitney.

'I'll check.' She picked her phone up from the table. 'They're here.'

'Did you overhear our conversation?' Clifford asked, leaning forward slightly.

Palmer jerked backwards and flinched. Was this a tactic Clifford adopted to intimidate? If so, it worked well and appeared cleverly practiced. His body size and presence was a useful asset.

'No, I wasn't told to report on conversations. My contact wanted to know where Armstrong went and who he met.' Palmer's eyes darted between Clifford and Whitney.

'Let's return to this *contact* of yours. In your previous interview you informed us that you didn't try to find out who he was.'

'Yeah. So what? It's true.'

'He's lying. Look at his pursed lips,' George said.

'I don't believe you. I suggest you think again and tell us the truth.'

'It's more than my life's worth to tell you any more than I already have. You don't mess with these people.' He threw his hands up in despair.

'How do you know, if you've no idea who they are?' Whitney challenged.

'Armstrong's dead, isn't he? Do you think it's a coincidence? Because I don't.'

'We can protect you,' Clifford said, his voice softer than before.

'What? Like you did Armstrong? No thanks.' He folded his arms tightly across his chest and sat back in the chair.

'Some protection is better than none at all,' Clifford said.

'Yeah, right.'

'This is heading nowhere, Whitney. He'll back himself into a corner and won't answer any question. Move on,' George said.

'You said that you were left cash for your services. Your contact must've told you when he was going to leave it, as you wouldn't want it to be on the floor with the rest of the post, in case someone else picked it up,' Whitney said.

'He left it inside the office on my desk.'

'Who let him in?'

'Um …'

'Did you give him a key? This is making no sense.'

'Look … okay. I'll tell you. But if anything happens to me it's on your head. I was there when he came with the money.'

'So you have actually met this person?' Whitney said, sighing.

'Yes,' he muttered.

'How many times?'

'Once when he asked me to do the job and twice more when he paid me.'

'How much were you paid?' Clifford asked.

'I don't remember.'

'Try again,' Clifford said, his voice low but no-nonsense.

'I got ten grand a week.'

'Which means you've earnt twenty thousand so far?' Whitney said.

'Yes.'

'How long did they employ you for?'

'They didn't give a time frame, just that I was to be paid ten thousand a week. Armstrong being shot ended my income.'

'Did this person give you a name?'

'Jad.'

'Describe him?' Whitney said.

'Medium height. Medium build. Dark hair. That's it.'

'Not helpful. What was he wearing?'

'Jeans, T-shirt and navy blazer.'

'Age? Ethnicity? Come on, you're a PI, give us a proper description.'

'He's East Asian. I'd say mid to late thirties.'

'Did he say how long the job would last?'

'I've already told you, he said they'd pay me ten grand a week until they said to stop.'

'When you reported that Armstrong had met with DI Clifford, did you give them his name?'

'No.' He averted his eyes.

'Yes, he did,' George said.

'Don't lie to us or you'll have perverting the course of justice added to your list of charges.'

'Does that mean I'm being charged for the false documents?'

'We're looking into it. So, to recap. You met with *Jad* who paid you cash and didn't give you an end date for this job. Does he live locally?'

'I've no idea. He drives a car with a UK plate.'

'What sort of car is it?'

'I honestly don't remember.' He shook his head vigorously.

'Don't give me that crap. I'm betting you got the number plate and checked him out,' Whitney said.

'This could get me in so much trouble. All I can tell you is he drives a red BMW. I have a photo on my phone. I didn't check him out in case he discovered what I'd done. He might not have been big, like you,' he nodded at Clifford. 'But the chilling tone in his voice was enough for me to realise I'd be stupid to cross him.' He picked up his phone and called up the photo. Whitney wrote down the details.

'Show me your call log. I want Jad's number.'

'He probably used a burner.'

'We'll check.'

After writing down the number, Whitney turned off the recording equipment. 'We may wish to speak to you again, so don't go anywhere without checking with us first. I want to know immediately if this Jad person contacts you again.'

Chapter 18

After returning to the incident room, Whitney headed straight for Ellie's desk. 'We're looking for a man called Jad who drives a red BMW, and this is the registration number.' She held out her notebook for Ellie to copy it down. 'He's the one who met with Palmer and paid him. See what you can find out about him.'

'Yes, guv,' Ellie said, turning her head back to the screen, her fingers speeding over the keyboard.

Whitney returned to where George and Clifford were waiting. 'Let's go to my office and we'll discuss the case further.'

For the moment, she was prepared not to talk in front of the others until she had Clifford's assurance that it was okay. She knew he'd want to keep some things close to his chest, and if she was to be privy to what they were, then she'd play his game. She'd already got the measure of him. He seemed a genuine guy, but she didn't trust him not to attempt to take over if he was unhappy with the way things were progressing.

Once they were seated around the coffee table, she looked at Clifford.

'Tell me more about this syndicate you're investigating.'

'There's not a lot I can share with you other a substantial number of hours have been spent investigating them. I understand how frustrating it is for you, but you have to accept that I'm not at liberty to disclose everything we have on our files. It really is on a need-to-know basis. I don't make the rules.'

He was right, and she accepted that he had no choice, but that didn't make it any less annoying.

'Have you come across a person called Jad before?'

'Jad is a very common name in eastern Asia, in particular Singapore.'

Was he giving her a clue?

'This syndicate you're centring on, are they based in Singapore?'

He leant back in his chair and stretched out his legs.

'You didn't hear it from me,' Clifford said.

'Thank you. Now we've established that Singapore is where your squad is focusing their efforts, should we assume this Jad is part of their organisation?'

'That much, I'll tell you.'

'Is there anything else you can tell me?'

'There's—'

A knock at the door interrupted him and Ellie walked in. 'I've found your man, guv. His name's Jad Tan and the car's registered in his name. He rents a flat in Clapham, London, and he comes from Singapore.'

'Excellent work.' Whitney said, not even bothering to suppress her grin. Maybe they wouldn't need Clifford's input, after all.

'I've also got other things to share with you regarding Armstrong.'

'We'll be out in a minute so everyone can hear.'

'Thanks, guv,' Ellie said, turning and leaving the office.

'Now we know our go-between is Jad Tan from Singapore, can you confirm whether he's on your radar or not?'

'His name has come up, but he hasn't been at the forefront of the investigation. We believed him to be on the periphery. With him in the frame, it's definitely pointing to this shooting being directly linked to the Singaporean syndicate.'

'Not so fast. I accept that Armstrong was being targeted by them, but we don't know yet whether they were the ones who authorised the shooting. It could be a coincidence.' She glanced at George, fully expecting to be blasted for using the word, but the psychologist remained silent. 'Until such time as we can be sure of a link, the case remains with us.'

He leant back in his chair and hooked his hands behind his head, keeping his eyes fixed on Whitney. 'I do have to report in, but I'll wait a while longer and see what we turn up.'

She nodded her assent. 'We should bring Jad Tan in for questioning.'

'No, that's not possible. We can't alert him or we run the risk of him fleeing the country. If he's more involved than we'd first assumed it could jeopardise our whole operation.'

She gave an exasperated sigh. Talk about one step forward and two steps back. 'We'll try to manage without him for the moment but, for the record, I'm not happy about it.'

'That much is obvious,' Clifford said in a dry tone.

George laughed and Whitney turned, surprised. 'What?'

'I was amused by the altercation between the two of you.'

'I'm glad someone finds it funny.'

George looked at Clifford. 'Whitney won't stand for people blocking her.'

'I consider myself warned.' He grinned.

'If you two have quite finished, let's see what Ellie has for us,' Whitney snapped, which she followed with a grin as she didn't want Clifford to think she took George's comments seriously. In fact, she enjoyed it when the psychologist cracked the occasional joke. 'Hopefully we'll find something *else* we can use to progress the investigation.'

Clifford's phone rang and he looked at the screen. 'Sorry, I've got to answer this. Hello, Jill. Is everything okay?' He nodded. 'Keep an eye on her and if she's still lethargic tomorrow let me know and we'll take it from there. You know what she's like, she could've eaten something dodgy in the park.'

Might he have to return to London?

'Is everything okay?' Whitney asked, once he'd ended the call.

'It's my dog Elsa, she's not well. My neighbour looks after her when I'm away. Hopefully she'll be fine by the morning.'

'Sorry to hear that. What sort of dog is she?'

'A yellow Labrador. I'm sure she'll be fine, this isn't the first time it's happened. Labs are dustbins and will eat anything.'

'Are you okay to go into the incident room, now?'

'Of course.'

They headed out of the office and she called the team to attention. 'Ellie's going to share what she's managed to discover about our victim.'

'Thanks, guv. I've been looking into Armstrong's finances and his money came from a variety of sources. He had tournament winnings, and he gave exhibition matches. Also, he endorsed products and was used in advertisements. The snooker club was profitable, too. Not hugely but enough for him not to have to invest further money into it.'

'So, nothing to ring any alarm bells, then?' Whitney said. 'Do you have anything to add?' she asked, nodding at Clifford.

'We did a thorough investigation into Armstrong before we got him on board. We discovered no financial irregularities.'

'Guv,' Brian called out. 'Scott Marshall's arrived, and he's waiting in one of the interview rooms. How do you want to play this?'

She glanced from Clifford to Brian, debating which one to take. Probably best if it was the former.

'Thanks, Brian. I'll go with DI Clifford and take Dr Cavendish to observe.'

A shadow crossed Brian's face. He'd understand it was nothing personal. And she didn't have time to dwell on it. Her time was better spent focusing on the case and dealing with Armstrong's partner.

Scott Marshall smiled as they walked into the interview room, a relaxed expression on his face. Had he got over the death of his best friend so soon?

'How may I help?' Marshall said, as they sat opposite him.

'We'd like to talk to you about your relationship with Ryan Armstrong,' Whitney said, after she'd set the recording equipment and gone through the usual protocol.

'He was my best friend and business partner. I'm

devastated that he's dead.' The smile on his face vanished and hurt shone from his eyes.

Was it an act?

'Was the snooker club your first business together?'

'Yes, it was. We'd been talking about finding a joint venture for a while, preferably snooker related, and when this club came up for sale we snapped it up.'

'How is the business structured?'

'We formed a limited company. Fifty per cent of the shares each. We employ a manager to run the club and have joint overall responsibility.'

'Meaning Ryan's shares go to his estate,' Clifford said.

'That's correct. It's the same as for me.'

'With a joint share, how did you deal with any business disagreements? Did one of you have a deciding vote?' Clifford asked.

'We trusted each other's judgement and rarely had business disputes. But if the occasion arose when we did, we each had a deciding vote on certain aspects of the business. My areas were suppliers and staff, and Ryan's were members and marketing. It worked well. We also agreed, before taking on the business, that we wouldn't allow our partnership to impact our personal lives.'

'Regarding your personal relationship, would you say that you and Ryan argued much?' Whitney asked, following up on what he'd said.

'No more than any friends do. We'd been friends for years, so of course we disagreed sometimes.'

'On the night he was shot, is it true you lost two thousand pounds in a bet over a game of snooker you were playing?'

He rubbed his temple. 'Yes.'

'That's a lot of money?' Whitney asked.

'I know people who bet ten times that without batting an eyelid. I wouldn't call it a lot.'

'It is to me. I understand the bet was larger than usual. Why?'

'No reason in particular. I just felt like it.'

'Did you lose your temper when Ryan and his partner beat you?'

Was he going to admit what she'd already been told?

He paled. 'I was cross with myself for playing badly and missing easy shots. I've beaten Ryan hundreds of times in the past. He wasn't invincible, even if he was one of the world's top players.'

'There's more to this than he's letting on. I believe there's a deep-seated feeling of inadequacy when he compares himself with the victim,' George said.

She'd been sensing that, too.

'Is it right that you lose your temper when things don't go your way?'

He couldn't meet her eyes. 'Sometimes.'

'We've heard that it's more than *sometimes*. That your temper is well known.'

He balled his fist and cupped it in his other hand. 'Look, I'm not like Ryan. I won't put up with shit. If that means speaking my mind, then I will. Where's the harm in that?'

'Do you ever get violent when losing your temper?'

'No.'

She arched her eyebrows. 'So, you don't lash out in a fit of rage when, for example, Ryan beats you?'

'What are you accusing me of? I'd never have harmed Ryan. I wasn't anywhere near the club when he was shot.'

'Yes, you've already told us you were at home, yet there's no one who can vouch for you.'

'It's not my fault I was alone.'

'You live in a lovely house … it must have cost a fortune. More than you'd earn from the snooker circuit, or from the snooker club.'

'If you've been checking me out, then you know our money comes from my wife's trust fund. That's not a crime.'

'No one said it was. How does it feel, being a kept man?' Whitney taunted.

'I'm *not* a kept man,' he snarled. 'How dare you suggest it? Do you think being a professional snooker player happens without putting in hours and hours of practice? And then there's my snooker club. Do you think the manager does everything? He operates under my guidance. So, you can stop with your snide comments or …' His fists clenched on the table and he leant forward, fury in his eyes.

'Enough,' Clifford said, his voice cold and flat. 'Keep your temper in check.'

'Good job,' George said in her ear. 'A clear indication of how he struggles to control himself.'

'Sorry,' Marshall said, sucking in a breath and bowing his head.

'I want to go back to Saturday night. In our previous interview you mentioned getting a taxi and leaving before twelve, but you don't remember which taxi firm you used because someone else called them for you.'

'That's correct.'

'Does the firm Westfield Taxis ring a bell?'

'Um …'

'Were you picked up by one of their taxis?'

He frowned. 'I don't know.'

'He's hiding something,' George said. 'It could be that he drove and doesn't want to admit it because he was over the limit.'

'How much did you have to drink?'

'The same as everyone else. Some beer. A couple of whiskies. We usually have a skinful, which is why none of us drive.' He leant on his elbow, partially shielding his mouth with his hand.

'And you definitely got a taxi and didn't drive.'

'How many times do I have to tell you? One of the guys phoned for me.'

'Was it Rory Clarke?'

'It could have been. Yes.'

'When you returned home, was your car there?'

'Yes. Of course it was.'

'Did you take it out for a drive?'

'No. No. No.' He thumped the table. 'I've had enough of this. I'm saying nothing more without my solicitor present.' He folded his arms across his chest and scowled in her direction.

'Do you think you need one?' Whitney gave her stock answer.

Marshall turned his head and stared at the window.

'We will end this interview now and you're free to go. But know that we'll be speaking to you again.'

Chapter 19

Whitney opened the door of the incident room, and the sound of laughter echoed in the hallway. Seated on a table between Frank and Doug, with her legs swinging, was Tiffany. Her hand covering her mouth as she was laughing.

'What are you doing here?' she asked, walking over.

A raft of guilty expressions stared back at her.

Tiffany grinned. 'I was bored at home and decided to come and see you as it was getting late. I caught the bus in and thought maybe we could go out for dinner, if you're not finishing late. What do you think?'

'I don't see why not. I have to eat sometime.'

'Awesome. It was a right mission getting here, it's quite a walk from the bus stop. When the woman on reception phoned upstairs to speak to you, Frank took the call and came to fetch me.'

'It was my pleasure. I've been telling Tiffany what it's like to be a good parent,' Frank said.

'And I've been warning Tiffany not to listen to him,' Doug added. 'We all know the hassle he's been through with his kids.'

'That doesn't mean I can't offer some good advice,' Frank said, feigning a hurt expression. 'I want Tiffany to make the most of the time before her children have minds of their own and stop being affectionate and compliant.'

They all knew how difficult it had been for Frank and his wife with their daughter, who wouldn't leave home for years and then ended up moving back complete with husband and children in tow. She'd moved out again, but for how long remained to be seen. Whitney suspected he exaggerated how bad it was for effect, though.

'Thank you, Frank, for your input,' she said.

'Do you know whether you're having a boy or a girl?' Frank asked.

'Yes, but we're keeping it a secret.' Tiffany looked over at Whitney conspiratorially.

Whitney turned to Clifford, who was standing beside George a few feet away. 'This is my daughter. Tiffany, this is DI Clifford, from the Met. He's come to help us with a case.'

'Call me Seb,' Clifford said, striding over and holding out his hand for her to shake.

'Go and sit in my office, I'll be in shortly,' Whitney said.

Tiffany hoisted herself down from the table. 'No one warned me I'd be getting this big.' She laughed, and walked towards Whitney's office, with one hand massaging her back.

Whitney waited until her office door was closed. She trusted her daughter, but it wouldn't look good for her to be discussing the case with her there, especially with Clifford around.

'We've questioned Scott Marshall, who certainly has a temper, which he showed when provoked. He claims he was at home at the time of the murder, but there's no one to corroborate that. He maintains he was drinking on Saturday night and wasn't capable of driving. George believes he's hiding something, but we're unsure whether it's anything to do with Armstrong's murder. He remains a person of interest, but as we don't have sufficient evidence to hold him, we need to keep on digging. Tomorrow morning we'll visit the snooker club again with a view to asking more pointed questions.'

'I won't be with you,' Clifford said.

She turned to him. 'Why? I'd have thought visiting the club would have been a useful exercise for you?'

She was more than happy for it to be just her and George, but was surprised that Clifford didn't wish to be with them. What was he planning? Going back to the Met and leaving them to get on with solving the case themselves? Wishful thinking.

'I'll be visiting, but not with you. I'll pretend to be a customer.'

'You won't get in, it's a members' only club?'

'Trust me, it won't be a problem. If you see me, don't speak. Act like you don't know me.'

Whitney flashed him one of her looks. 'I'll pretend you didn't say that as I'm fully aware of the need for your identity to be kept secret.'

He bowed his head. 'Understood.'

'I want everyone in early tomorrow morning.' She turned to George. 'Do you fancy grabbing a bite to eat with me and Tiffany, if you're not seeing Ross?'

'I'd love to.'

As they headed towards her office, Whitney glanced over her shoulder. Should she have invited Clifford to join them, as he'd probably be spending the evening on his own. They couldn't talk freely when he was there, so he could entertain himself. He wasn't her responsibility.

'Are you ready to go,' she said to Tiffany, who was sitting behind the desk, playing on her phone. 'Do you have any preferences on where we should eat?'

Tiffany looked up and smiled. 'I've had a craving for fish and chips *all* day. Soaked in vinegar.'

'Shall we eat in or grab a takeaway and go home?'

Whitney would prefer the latter, as all she wanted to do was put her feet up with a glass or three of wine.

'I want to talk to you anyway, so let's get a takeaway.'

'Do you mind George coming?' Whitney assumed not, but thought she should check.

'Of course not. George is one of the family.'

'My sentiments exactly.'

'I'll go in George's car if that's okay? It's a lot more comfortable than yours.'

'It's fine with me,' George said.

'It looks like that's sorted then. I'll get the fish and chips and you two go back home and warm the plates. I'll see you back there.'

It took Whitney longer than expected as there had been a queue at the takeaway. As she walked in the house she could hear George and Tiffany talking. It was funny how George was more relaxed with Tiffany than anybody else. Whitney wasn't jealous. She loved the bond between the two of them.

'I'm back,' she called as she headed into the kitchen.

The table was set, and the plates were warming in the oven. Whitney dished out their dinner, opened some wine for her and George, and gave Tiffany an apple juice.

Halfway through the meal, when there was a lull in the conversation, Tiffany rested her cutlery on her plate. 'I've made a decision,' she announced, her eyes on Whitney.

'What about, the colour of the nursery?' she asked, as

they'd been discussing it in depth recently and couldn't decide.

'Don't be daft. This is something serious. I've decided that I do want to meet my father.'

Whitney coughed violently, almost choking on the chip in her mouth. She grabbed her glass of wine and took a large gulp.

'What the … Don't do that to me.'

'Sorry. But I thought you'd want to know.'

'Of course, I do, but not when I've got a mouthful of chips.'

After their most recent conversation about Martin, she wasn't convinced that Tiffany would agree to seeing him. Martin would be delighted. But was she?

Yes, in principle, but once it happened it could change everything.

She'd spent all these years as the only parent Tiffany had. Now her daughter had two. Would that make a difference?

'What made you finally decide?' she asked.

'I've been thinking of the baby and how Lachlan is the father. I'm not going to hold it against him that what we had wasn't the real thing and that he wanted to go back to Australia. Once the baby is born, they should know each other, if it's what Lachlan wants. It would be unfair of me to exclude him.'

'Like I did, you mean,' Whitney said, picking up her fork and moving the food around her plate.

'That's not what I meant, Mum. Your situation was different. You mustn't feel guilty for what happened all those years ago. Lachlan and I have been texting, and he's going to come over for a visit once the baby's been born.'

Whitney swallowed hard. Please don't let Tiffany decide to return to Australia with him.

'Do you think you might get back together as a couple?'

'No way. He's going to visit, that's all. Just because we're not together doesn't mean he's not a nice guy. I want to do what's best for the baby.'

'When you were growing up, how did you feel about not having your father around?' Whitney asked, holding her breath as she waited for her daughter's reply.

'It didn't bother me. And I'm not just saying that. I had you, Granny, Gramps and Rob, we were a family. But being pregnant has changed my perspective on things, and I do want to meet Martin and get to know him.'

'You'll really like him. All my preconceptions about him couldn't be further from the truth. He's a nice man, and he's not going to push you into any relationship if you don't want one. He thought he couldn't have children, as he wasn't able to with his wife. He feels so lucky knowing about you. But I'll leave him to talk to you about that. What's your view, George?'

'From a psychological point of view, in most instances it's good for a child to have a good relationship with both parents.'

'Even yours?' Whitney quipped.

'Mum,' Tiffany said, frowning in her direction. 'Leave George's parents out of this.'

'Sorry, I didn't mean to upset you. It was a stupid quip.'

'You didn't upset me. Tiffany, your mother's correct, my parents are very different from most and had a strained relationship with their children, unlike the one you have had with your mother. I believe meeting your father will be a positive experience for you.'

'So that's sorted,' Whitney said. 'I'll let him know and see when he's free to meet. Possibly Saturday or Sunday.'

'So soon?' Tiffany said, a look of panic marching across her face.

'Not if you'd rather wait. I thought you'd want to get it over with.'

'I'm being silly. Let's blame it on the hormones. Whenever he wants to visit is fine with me.'

'We'll make it very informal, no pressure. I'll cook something.'

'Are you sure about that?' Tiffany said, pulling a face.

'I could always ask George to cook for us,' she suggested, smiling in her friend's direction.

'I'm happy to oblige.'

'I don't think the three of us facing him is a good idea,' Tiffany said.

'I could make something for you and drop it over. I don't need to be with you while he's here. Or I could take your mother out for a drink and leave the two of you alone to get to know each other,' George said.

'I'm not sure about that, either,' Tiffany said, biting down on her bottom lip.

'Let's wait and see what he says. Then we'll make a decision. We don't need to decide right now.'

Whitney didn't want to put Tiffany off meeting Martin. Although she did agree with George that leaving them alone might be the best thing to do. Even though she'd worry like crazy about what was going on if she wasn't there to supervise. But Martin wouldn't push it. He'd be sensitive to Tiffany's needs and wouldn't make it difficult for her.

And just think, if they hit it off and Whitney and he carried on their relationship they could be a real family.

She shuddered. Why did that scare her?

It didn't. It just made her nervous.

Chapter 20

George followed Whitney up the stairs to the snooker club entrance. In stark contrast to their last visit, when they reached the top the door was propped open, and they were able to walk in without having to obtain permission. There were people milling around everywhere.

'What are all these people doing here? It wasn't like this the last time,' Whitney said.

They stood beside the bar, both of them scanning the area, when Glen Tibbs walked out through the door leading to the bar. He glanced at them and frowned as it registered who they were.

'I can't talk to you today,' he said, hurrying over to them. 'At least not for a while.'

'What's going on here?' Whitney asked.

'It's the start of the East Midlands tournament. The finalists will qualify for the world championships. It's the last chance for those who haven't already qualified. It's on for seven days.'

'Tournament aside, we're investigating a murder, and

have further questions to put to you. It can't wait,' Whitney said.

He gave an exasperated sigh. 'Give me ten minutes and then I'll be with you, but not for long. I've already got problems. The first two matches start in thirty minutes and one of the referees hasn't turned up. And on top of that I've got a player claiming that table one hasn't been ironed properly. It has, as I supervised it myself. There's no time to do it again.'

'Ironed?' Whitney asked.

'After a table is brushed it's ironed to make sure the nap of the cloth is flat.'

'What difference does that make?'

'Tables have to be perfect to ensure positional ball control and speed.'

Although she knew nothing about snooker, George found all these details fascinating.

'And do you iron every day?' she asked.

'Daily during a tournament. Normally we only iron three times a week and on the other days we block the table. That's where we take a specially made block of wood, cover it with some cloth and run it along the table.'

'I had no idea it was so involved,' she said.

'Our tables are the best on the market and covered with Strachan cloth. The man we employ to look after them has worked on the tables used at the Crucible in Sheffield during the world championships. I'm putting this player's complaint down to nerves. Anyway, as you can see, I've got my hands full.' He gestured at the people milling around. 'And you're not here to learn about how we care for our tables.'

'We'll wait for you here,' Whitney said. 'Are you open to the public or are all these people part of the tournament?'

'At the moment it's mainly players and the media who are here. The public will be arriving any time from now. We have a seating area and matches are televised so people can watch in the lounge area.' He pointed to the wall where there was a large screen.

'Does anyone monitor who comes in? Surely—'

'I'm sorry to be rude, but I've got to go.' He pointed at his watch. 'I'll catch up with you shortly.' He rushed away before Whitney had time to respond.

'Perhaps we should come back when he's not so busy,' George suggested.

'The tournament's on all week and we don't have time to wait until it's over. I'm going to have a word with the man behind the bar. He wasn't here the last time we visited.'

George glanced at the young man. He had a tea towel slung over his shoulder and a cloth in his hand which he was using to wipe down the bar.

'Good morning, ladies. What can I get you?' he asked as they approached.

Whitney showed her warrant card. 'DCI Walker and Dr Cavendish, we'd like to talk to you about Ryan Armstrong.'

He tossed the cloth he was holding into the sink at the back of the bar and moved closer to them.

'I'm not allowed to leave in case someone needs serving, but I can answer some questions here if you like. Can I get you anything? Tea. Coffee. Something stronger.'

'Coffee would be good, thanks.'

He poured them two coffees from the jug on the rear counter and passed them over, with some long-life milk capsules and sugar on the side.

George grimaced. 'Do you have real milk?'

'No, sorry, this is it.'

'Hey, Joe,' a voice called out from beyond the end of the bar. 'Can you put the lights on above the pool table?'

'Sorry, mate.' He headed over to a bank of switches and turned one on. 'This is going to be a crazy week.'

'But that's good for business. Do you often have tournaments here?' Whitney asked.

'Fairly regularly, but this is the first time we've held the East Midlands qualifier. It was because of Ryan that we got it. It's bloody tragic that he's not going to be here to see it. Bloody tragic.'

'Were you surprised they decided to go ahead with it after what happened to him?'

'This tournament is a big deal. I don't see how it could be cancelled because the winner qualifies for the worlds.'

'Could it have been held at another club?'

'Not at such short notice. We've been planning this for months.'

'The time leading up to Ryan's death, did you notice anyone suspicious hanging around especially when he was here?'

'Not that I remember.'

'Do you know all the people who visit the club?'

'I've been here for years, since before Ryan and Scott bought the place, and know most of our members. I work three days a week and a couple of evenings. This week it will be different as we've got the players and their friends and families here. I don't know all of them.'

George glanced over to see the manager in the far corner of the lounge talking intently with someone.

'Who's Glen Tibbs talking to?' she asked.

He squinted and peered over to where they were standing. 'I'm not sure who he is. I don't think he's a member. But I could be wrong.'

The way their bodies were hunched over was suspicious. She'd follow up with Whitney once they'd finished with Joe.

'How well did you know Ryan?' Whitney asked.

'He was here a lot and wasn't stuck up even though he was famous. He was a good guy and spoke to everybody. Always had time for a chat. Everyone liked him.'

'Can you think of any reason why someone would want to harm him?'

'No. I never heard a bad word against him. That was why it was such a shock.' He glanced from side to side, before moving in a little closer. 'You know, if it was going to be either one of the two owners who was shot, my money would have been on it being Scott.'

'What makes you say that?'

'He's not as well liked as Ryan and always seems to be doing deals on the side. Take the beer. We have an exclusive contract with the brewery, but he'll often bring in drink he's *picked up* for us to sell. That sort of thing. But you didn't hear that from me. I can't risk losing my job. I—'

'Excuse me?' called a voice from the end of the bar.

George glanced over and saw it was Clifford. She gave a tiny nod in Whitney's direction as she had her back to him.

'I've got to go,' Joe said.

'It's Clifford,' she said quietly. 'He's speaking to Joe, but I can't work out what about. Now he's walked away and is heading towards Tibbs.'

They stepped away from the bar and stood so they could both see Clifford. They watched as he interrupted the manager and took him to one side. After a few moments, Clifford reached into his pocket and passed something over to him. He then left and went downstairs towards the snooker room.

'Was Clifford giving Tibbs money?' Whitney asked.

'It looked like it. Was he placing a bet? We'll find out when we see him. Tibbs has been acting in a suspicious manner. I observed him with the man he was talking to before Clifford interrupted and whatever it was they were discussing, they didn't want to be overheard.'

Whitney looked at her watch. 'I'll give Tibbs five more minutes and, if he's not here, we'll go and find him.'

'No need,' George said, spotting him heading in their direction. 'He's coming over now.'

'I'm free for a quick chat, but not for too long,' Tibbs said as he reached them. 'We'll have to do it in here so I can keep an eye on everything. We can sit over there.' He nodded to an empty table close to the door.

'Not ideal, but it will have to do. We saw you engrossed in a conversation at the end of the lounge area. What was that about?' Whitney asked once they were all seated.

'A media person, wanting to know about the tournament and trying to get information about Ryan. Bloody bottom feeders.' He rubbed his nose and averted his eyes.

George didn't believe him for one moment, but now wasn't the time to challenge him.

Whitney cast a glance in her direction and arched an eyebrow.

'And then you were talking to that big man. What did he want?'

'He wanted to know more about the tournament and when the matches were on. He's come from out of town to watch.'

'Does he have to join the club to come in every day?'

'It's different during the tournament. We allow people who aren't members to watch, but we do keep an eye on them and we've got our security cameras.'

'Can these people play snooker if they want?'

'No. Six of our tables are being used for the tournament and the other six are for members use only.'

'Tell us more about the tournament,' Whitney said.

'The first matches won't be televised, but the ones later in the week will, and that's when the whole place will be buzzing. You think it's busy now, but this is nothing when compared with how it will get later in the week. It's when the top players will be playing each other.'

'Is Scott Marshall in the tournament?'

'He withdrew once he'd qualified for the worlds.'

Whitney frowned. 'But I keep hearing he's not that good.'

'You've got that wrong. He's a very good player, just not in Ryan's league. Thirty-two players take part in the world championships chosen from qualifying events around the country and world ranking. Over the last ten years, Scott has qualified five times. Ryan was automatically allowed to participate because of his ranking.'

'Are you expecting Scott here today?'

'He said he'd be here later. He should be around all week as it's our tournament.'

'How does he get on with members and staff? Is he as popular as Ryan was?'

'He's more difficult to deal with,' Tibbs admitted.

'Did you ever notice any animosity between him and Ryan?'

'Not really. They were partners and best friends. Scott took the lead in their friendship, but that didn't seem to bother Ryan.'

'Was Scott jealous of Ryan's popularity?'

'Well …' He paused and drew in a breath. 'He envied Ryan's talent and made no bones about it. If you speak to him, though, he'll tell you how many times he's beaten Ryan in the past. But never when it counts. I wouldn't have put it past Ryan to let him win sometimes. Whether Ryan's popularity with others was an issue for Scott, I can't say.'

'Has Scott discussed your position here and what's going to happen to the club now Ryan's no longer here?'

'Why? Has he said something to you? Am I going to lose my job?'

'We can't answer that. I suggest you take it up with him.'

'Glen?' Joe called out from behind the bar.

'Sorry, I've got to go,' he said, standing and acknowledging his staff member with a wave of his hand.

'Okay. But we'll be back.'

Chapter 21

Whitney was standing by the board with George when Clifford marched in. She sucked in a breath, still in awe of his sheer size and commanding presence. They'd been back at the station for two hours, so what had he been doing at the snooker club for all that time?

'What can you tell us?' she asked when he reached them.

'Glen Tibbs is engaged in illegal betting. I stayed for a while, watched some of the matches, and kept an eye out. I was able to place a bet with him, without any questions being asked, and witnessed several others doing the same.'

'Yes, we saw that, too. If it was that easy for you to do, does that mean it's out in the open for anyone at the club to take part?'

'Yes and no. It's all done on the QT. If people approach Tibbs, then he'll oblige. I only placed a small bet, not wanting to stand out.'

'I'll ask Frank to check the CCTV footage from the club and see whether it's a regular occurrence. If there's nothing on the tapes, we can assume he's just doing it for this tournament.' She went over to the officer's desk. 'Frank, go through the snooker club footage concentrating on the manager, Glen Tibbs. He's taking illegal bets for this tournament and we want to know if this is something he does on a regular basis.'

'Yes, guv,' Frank said.

'Make it top priority.'

She headed back to Clifford and George.

'Do you believe Tibbs is linked to the syndicate you're investigating?' George asked.

'It's unclear at the moment, until we look at footage from this tournament, analyse games and look for indicators as to when a game is being thrown.'

'You can tell?'

'There are nuances in people's behaviour, their facial expressions and body language, which give an indication of the exact time there's an intentional mistake.'

'Fascinating,' George said. 'I'd be interested in learning more. It's not an area I've researched before.'

'When I'm back at the Met, I'll send over some training videos for you to look at.'

'I'd appreciate that very much. Thank you.'

'My pleasure. If Tibbs knows that some people have been paid to throw a match, he could be cashing in on the side. It's not likely a lot of money will change hands as I imagine he only takes small bets. The big money will be placed at the bookies. There could be one of two things going on at the club. Either Tibbs is in cahoots with the syndicate, maybe keeping an eye out and making sure players do what they're supposed to, and also doubledipping by taking money on the side. Or, it's simply him taking bets with no link to the syndicate at all. We'll need to bring him in for questioning.'

'What are your plans for finding out whether he's

connected to the syndicate and how this links back to Armstrong's shooting?' Whitney asked.

This would be make or break. If a connection was established, they would lose the case. No question. She might not have a say in that happening, but she'd need cast-iron assurances and proof of the link if there was one, before she'd give up.

'I'll contact my officers at the Met and ask them to check for any connections between Tibbs and the syndicate. Questioning him will also assist.'

'You think he'll tell you?'

Surely, he couldn't be so naïve.

'That's what we'll find out.'

'By the way, how's your dog?' Whitney said.

'She's a lot better today, thanks for asking.'

'So you—' The door to the incident room opened and Whitney tensed. 'What the …' she muttered through gritted teeth, as Douglas walked in and made a beeline for them.

'Sir,' she said.

'Clifford, how are you?' Douglas's voice boomed out as he slapped the officer on the back. 'I heard you were here and came to say hello. I'm sure your expertise will expedite the solving of this case. We can't drag our feet. Not with the media breathing down our necks at all hours of the day.'

'I'm well, thank you, sir. We're making good progress.'

'Excellent, that's what I wanted to hear. Pop into my office before you return to London and we'll go out for a drink to catch up. I'd like to hear how the old gang are doing.'

Old gang? The man was a superintendent, not some DC.

'Yes, sir.'

'Right. I'll leave you to it.' Douglas turned and marched out, his arms swinging by his side.

'Wanker,' Whitney muttered louder than she'd intended.

'I take it you're not a fan,' Clifford said, arching an eyebrow.

Should she tell him the truth? If they were such good mates would he blab to Douglas? Did she care? It wasn't like he didn't already know her views on him.

'Is anyone?'

'The promotion boards, judging by his progress in the force.' He grinned, accentuating the laughter lines around his eyes.

'I've known him for over twenty years, since he was a sergeant here at Lenchester.' She shook her head. 'Enough said. Anyway, this isn't the time or place to swap stories about him. After the case is solved and over a few drinks, maybe I'll open up a bit more.'

'That works for me,' Clifford said. 'Back to Tibbs, we need to know more about his financial situation.'

'Ellie,' Whitney called out. 'Stop what you're doing and look into the finances of Glen Tibbs, the manager of the snooker club. In particular, check if there have been large amounts of money going into his bank account on a regular basis.'

'Yes, guv.'

'I'll ask uniform to bring him in, so we can question him properly.'

'I don't wish to usurp your authority, but that's not a good idea with the tournament on. It would be better if we didn't create a fuss.'

'*Usurp my authority?* Seriously, who speaks like that?' she said before she could stop herself. She glanced at George who was frowning in her direction. 'No offence meant.'

'None taken,' Clifford said.

'Although you did make a good point. We need to get him out of there without creating a fuss.'

'The afternoon matches don't begin until two, so it might be easier if we do it now while they're having lunch. We have no idea whether there are members of the syndicate there, so we need to be discreet. Although they'd expect him to be questioned regarding Armstrong's murder. In fact, it would look odd if he wasn't. But it's best to be as unobtrusive as possible.'

'George and I are known there, so you go and take DS Chapman. No one will suspect you're police, and that will make it easier.' Whitney faced her sergeant. 'Brian, go with DI Clifford to pick up Glen Tibbs.'

'Yes, guv.' He went to the coat stand and grabbed his jacket off the hanger.

'Forget the jacket, it's too smart for the snooker club,' Clifford said. 'Also, dispense with the tie and we'll go in casually, as if we're customers wanting to watch the matches.'

Whitney smiled to herself. Brian's work clothes were a throwback from his time at the Met. Interesting that Clifford didn't look so expensively dressed, doubly so because of who he was. Unless he'd deliberately dressed down and kept his good stuff for his aristocratic friends.

'Doug, have you gone through the stalker's notes and manuscript yet?' she asked after Clifford and Brian had left.

'Yes, guv. Nothing there for us to use. It was literally hundreds of pages of idolising nonsense. I never knew there were so many ways to declare your undying love for someone.'

'It was worth a shot.'

'Guv,' Frank called out. 'Take a look at this. Tibbs takes

bets on a regular basis by the looks of things. There are many instances when money changes hands.' She strode over and stared at the footage on the screen.

'Keep it for DI Clifford to have a look at when he gets back. Can you work out whether there's any pattern to his behaviour? Does he just take bets during matches? Is it possible to tell?'

'It happens all the time, even when there's no one playing. There's one incident here when a crowd of people are watching a horse race on the telly and he's openly taking money from them.'

'Okay, it's clear there's illegal gambling going on, but what we don't know is if it's connected to Clifford's investigation. I'm no expert, but it doesn't look like it is. And you know what that means. That the case will remain ours, and he will return to the Met. Any joy on Tibbs's finances yet, Ellie?'

'I'm in his bank account now. There are regular amounts of money going in and out, as you'd expect, but nothing out of the ordinary.'

'Any payments from overseas?'

'No.'

'Further evidence that the betting is done independently but, again, it's not our area of expertise, so we'll have to wait for Clifford to come back.' She turned to George. 'Let's grab a coffee while we're waiting.'

As they left the incident room, her phone rang. She glanced at the screen. It was Martin.

'Are you going to answer?' George asked.

'What? Um … yes.' She nodded. 'Hello. I'm at work.'

'I won't keep you long. What are you doing tonight? Can I come over to meet Tiffany?'

She swallowed hard. 'That's short notice.'

'You did say in your text that Tiffany was free most evenings.'

True. But she hadn't expected him to want to come over quite so soon. She'd only texted him last night after George had left. Was it going to be possible to get home in time, as she couldn't leave Tiffany to meet him on her own?

'Okay. Is eight o'clock okay? I'll make us something to eat?' Crap. Why did she offer to do that? She wasn't thinking straight.

'Excellent. I'll see you later.'

She ended the call and glanced at George. 'The meeting with Tiffany is happening tonight. And I've only gone and offered to cook. What the hell? I need my head tested. I'll have to tell Tiffany.' She called her daughter's number.

'Hey, Mum. Are you checking up on me?'

'I've just got off the phone with Martin. He wants to come over tonight and I've invited him for dinner if you're okay with it?'

'Um … Yeah. Sure. Dinner? We haven't much in.'

'I'll stop at the supermarket on the way home. I can make us a chilli, at least we know that will turn out okay. I've asked him around for eight. I'll try to be back by six to cook and tidy up. Are you sure it's okay? I can cancel if it isn't.' Her breath caught in the back of her throat as she waited for her daughter's reply, half hoping she'd suggest they rearranged the meeting.

'It's fine. Let's get it over with.'

'Try not to worry. I'll be with you and if it gets too awkward, I'll ask him to leave.'

'Thanks, Mum. Love you.'

'How was she?' George asked, as she ended the call.

'A lot calmer than me. Let's get to the canteen quick, I need a triple shot of caffeine.'

~

Twenty minutes later, Whitney and George returned to the incident room.

'Guv,' Brian said. 'I was about to call you. We have Tibbs in the interview room.'

'Where's DI Clifford?' she asked after scanning the room and not seeing him.

'He's gone to get a drink.'

'Did you have any issues bringing him in?'

'He wanted to know why he was being questioned again as you'd already spoken to him twice, and he was moaning about it being a really inconvenient time, but he did have another person there who he left in charge.'

'Was Scott Marshall at the club?'

'We didn't see him.'

The door opened, and Clifford walked in, holding a can of drink.

'Are you ready?' she asked him.

'Yes.'

'You and I will interview, and George can observe.'

'I thought I might be able to interview,' Brian said, his mouth turned down.

'Sorry, not this time. We can't have three of us in there, it would be overkill. If you'd like to observe with Dr Cavendish, you can.'

'Okay, guv. Thanks.'

The four of them went downstairs, and George and Brian stepped into the observation area while Whitney and Clifford continued to the interview room. Whitney pressed the button on the recording equipment. 'Interview on

March the eleventh. Those present: Detective Chief Inspector Walker, Detective Inspector Clifford and … please state your name for the recording.'

'Glen Robert Tibbs. Now, perhaps you can tell me why I'm here, and why you came into my club pretending to be a punter when in fact you are a copper?' He scowled in Clifford's direction.

'You're here because we want to talk to you about Ryan Armstrong and other activities that are going on at the snooker club,' Whitney said.

'What do you mean *other activities*?' He shifted awkwardly in his seat and clenched and unclenched his fists as he rested his hands on the table.

'We understand that you've been engaged in illegal betting at the snooker club,' Whitney said.

Tibbs stared down at the table, not answering.

'You took a bet from me,' Clifford said.

'That was a one-off,' Tibbs said, as he glanced up at them.

'That's not the truth,' Whitney said. 'We've gone through some of the CCTV footage from the club and there were several instances of you taking bets. Not just on snooker matches, but on horse racing, too.'

Clifford frowned in her direction. Damn. She hadn't mentioned it to him before they'd come down for the interview.

'So what? It's not hurting anyone, and it's not like I make loads of cash. It's a little thing on the side that I do for the members. It adds a bit of fun, that's all.'

'What's the highest stake you would take?' Clifford asked.

'Ten pounds max. Very occasionally I've gone up to twenty, but it depends on the odds. I'm not going to be out of pocket.'

'Did Ryan Armstrong know about this?'

He avoided eye contact and ran his fingers through his hair.

'He's about to tell you a lie,' George said.

'Yes, he knew.'

'Are you're sure about that, because from your behaviour, I don't think he did.' Whitney said, a flat tone to her voice.

'Okay. Ryan saw me taking a bet once and said it wasn't to happen again because it could damage the club's reputation as it wasn't legal.'

'But you still continued doing it. Why?'

'Scott knew, and he said as long as it didn't get in the way of me doing my job he'd turn a blind eye.'

'So, what you're saying is that Ryan and Scott, despite being partners, differed in what they allowed you to do?'

'Yes, but it wasn't anything major.'

'It's illegal,' Clifford said. 'That does make it major. Now, what about in terms of players throwing matches? Were you aware of when this was going to happen, and did you take bets on these matches, or place them yourself at a local bookies?'

He looked askance at them. 'What the hell are you talking about? I have nothing to do with any match-fixing, nor does it happen at our club. All I do is take a few bets on the side for matches or other sporting events that are going on. You can't start blaming something like that on me. My job is to keep the customers happy, and that's what I do.'

'They'd do better online,' Clifford said.

'Except those bets can be traced. My way, anyone who bets and wants to make a few quid can keep it a secret.'

'If we ask Scott Marshall will he confirm that he permitted you to engage in this activity?' Whitney asked.

'Not if it gets him in trouble. He's more concerned with not rocking the boat for himself.'

'Meaning?'

'Out of the two partners, he's the one you have to be careful of. He always has deals going on, and not all of them are above board.'

'And Ryan wasn't like that?'

'He was straight and trusting. Probably too trusting. He couldn't even see what was going on under his nose. He …' His words fell away.

'He's wishing he hadn't said that,' George said.

'Carry on,' Whitney pushed.

'It's nothing to do with any illegal betting. It doesn't matter.'

'We'll decide what matters, and if you want to get back to the tournament, you'll answer our questions.'

He laid his hands flat on the table and looked over at her, a nervous expression cloaking his eyes. 'Look, you didn't hear this from me, right? Naomi, Ryan's wife, and Scott Marshall are having an affair.'

'How do you know?'

'I spotted them in a pub car park *together* a few months ago. They didn't know I was there. It wasn't a pub I usually frequent. They're still seeing each other, I'm sure.'

'Have you seen them together since?'

'Naomi occasionally came to the club when Ryan wasn't there, but Scott was, pretending she was looking for her husband. Then she'd spend some time with Scott out in the open, so it looked as if they were friends, but I knew what was going on. You could see the looks that were going on between them.'

'Does anyone else at the club know?'

'Not from me. I know when to keep my mouth shut. What I don't get is why she'd want to be with Scott. Ryan could give her a great time. The travel. The holidays. The lifestyle. Scott's nothing without his wife's money and, knowing him, he'd never leave her.'

'That's all conjecture,' Whitney said.

'Can I go now? I need to get back. I've told you everything I know.'

'Returning to your illegal betting operation, it has to stop now, or we'll take it further and arrest you,' Clifford said. 'Consider this to be a warning.'

'What about the bets I've taken for the tournament?'

'Return the money.'

'Great,' Tibbs muttered. 'What I've told you about the affair. I don't want to lose my job. Don't tell Scott you heard it from me.'

'We'll do what we can to keep you out of it but can't promise. One of my officers will take you back to the club. Wait here.' Whitney ended the recording and left the room, with Clifford behind her. She went next door to the observation area.

'Brian, take Tibbs back to the club. Tomorrow we'll visit Naomi Armstrong and find out more about this affair. You needn't come with us for this one, Sebastian.'

'Because?' he said looking at her.

'I can't see this affair being anything to do with your enquiry.'

'We don't know that for sure.'

'In view of the fact that she's just lost her husband, it would be unfair for us to go in mob-handed. I think it's best if George and I go and we'll report back to you and the rest of the team. If the affair was the motive, it means your syndicate has nothing to do with it and the case remains ours.' She forced back a smile. As much as she thought he was an okay bloke, she'd be far happier when he'd left Lenchester and returned to the Met.

'If that's how you want to play it. You're SIO.'

Was he annoyed? If he was, he'd get over it.

'What are you going to do now?'

'I'm going to prepare a report for my superior officers. That will take the rest of the afternoon and into tomorrow.'

'Good. I assume you'll be sending me a copy.'

'This is for my boss's eyes only.'

Chapter 22

Whitney's eyes were glued to the large retro-style metal clock on the kitchen wall. The hands seemed to have stuck. Had it stopped working? Should she change the batteries?

'Mum, give it a rest,' Tiffany said. 'You're not going to make him arrive any quicker. You're making me nervous. Have a drink or something. Anything, just stop staring at the clock. You're not going to make the time go any faster.'

'I don't need one. I'm sorry. I'll be glad when he's here, and I can settle.'

Since arriving home and the reality of what was about to happen had hit her, she'd been going back and forth in her mind, wondering whether it was the right thing to do. It was such a massive decision that Tiffany had made, and Whitney didn't want to have forced her into it.

'Look, it's going to be fine. We're just going to meet and get to know each other.'

Since when did Tiffany get to be so adult. Surely, Whitney should be the one reassuring her. She walked over to the cooker and gave the chilli a stir. Should she put the rice on now or wait until he arrived? She'd do it now. It would give her something to do. She reboiled the kettle, went to the cupboard and took out the rice, measuring it into the saucepan.

'Aren't you nervous, even a little bit? I'm impressed with how laid-back you're being.'

'Of course, I am, but I'm going to take it as it comes.'

Maybe there was more of Martin in Tiffany than she'd realised. In fact, the more she got to know and like him, the more she could see him in her daughter. But she wasn't going to share that with Tiffany. Not now. It wasn't the right time. They had to take it one step at a time. She wished she'd asked George to come round and they could have chatted while Tiffany and Martin were together.

'Good idea,' Whitney said, nodding.

'Don't worry, we have another five minutes before—'

The doorbell rang, interrupting them.

'He's here. He's early. I'm going to let him in. Are you sure you're okay? I can tell him to go, I—'

'Mum, go.'

'Should we sit in the kitchen or go into the lounge?'

'We'll stay in the kitchen, as we've got to eat and it's almost ready.'

'Good idea. Maybe you should go to the door and let him in, while I stay here getting it ready,' Whitney suggested.

'No, I'm like a beached whale and I'm not budging,' Tiffany said, patting her stomach.

'Right. Okay. Stupid suggestion.' She hurried out of the kitchen and to the front door. When she opened it, Martin leant in and kissed her on the cheek.

'How are you?' he asked.

'I'm fine. Fine. Yep. Fine.' She nodded her head so vigorously it was in danger of falling off.

It was ridiculous that she held down a high-powered

job, managed a team of officers, and was responsible for taking criminals off the street, yet here she was acting like a child.

'You're all over the place,' he said, resting his hand on her arm. 'You know, it's going to be okay?'

'Yes, I do. Tiffany's said the same. It's just me. Come on in.' She opened the door further so he could step inside.

'Something smells nice.' He sniffed.

'Chilli. The only dish I can make which doesn't get spoilt, unless I forget it's on and burn it. That's happened on more than one occasion, but I'll save those stories for another time.'

He held out a bottle of white wine. 'Is this okay?'

She glanced at the label. 'Lovely. It will need chilling for a while before we open it.'

'I took it from the fridge at the supermarket, it's still cold,' he said, his brow furrowed.

She laughed. 'I've been hanging around with George for long enough to know that between buying it and arriving here, its temperature will have increased.'

They headed through to the kitchen, and she took a deep breath. Tiffany stood when Martin walked in and smiled.

'Hello, Martin, I'm Tiffany.' She held out her hand.

'Hello, Tiffany.' He stepped towards her and shook it.

It all sounded very stilted. Whitney opened the fridge and placed the wine on one of the shelves.

'Can I get you a beer or something?' she asked, enjoying the coolness from the open fridge on her face. She hoped she wasn't blushing. That would be embarrassing.

'I'll wait for the wine.'

'It won't be too long.' She closed the fridge door.

'Mum, open it now.'

'It has to be at a certain temperature so we experience it as it should be.'

'So George says. But seeing as she isn't here and you know nothing about wine and can't tell one spice from the next, why don't you open it and live dangerously.'

Martin laughed, and the tension eased from her body.

'You're right. But don't tell George.' She opened the bottle and poured a glass for Martin and herself, and gave Tiffany an apple juice. Whitney turned her back on them and focused on stirring the chilli.

'Tell me a little about yourself,' Martin said.

'As I'm sure Mum told you, I was at university studying engineering and then decided to take some time off and go overseas to Australia because I felt a bit stuck. Now I've had some time out I've decided that once I've had the baby, I may go back and finish my degree.'

Whitney stirred furiously. She hadn't known Tiffany was planning to return to study. That pleased her an awful lot. She'd deliberately not approached it with Tiffany because she didn't want to be one of those mums who put unnecessary pressure on their kids.

'So, engineering. What got you into that?'

It would be the bridges. It had always been bridges from when she was as young as three and had her first Lego set. No dolls for her. It was bricks and cars all the way.

'I've always been fascinated by buildings and bridges. I especially love bridges.'

Whitney smiled to herself.

'You do? Me too,' Martin said. 'If you could name a bridge anywhere in the world to visit, which one would it be?'

What the … He loved bridges. What a coincidence. *Sorry, George.*

'I've always wanted to see the Golden Gate Bridge in San Francisco,' Tiffany said, a wistful tone to her voice.

'You'd love it. It's an amazing feat of engineering. When I was there, I spent hours simply staring at it. I took hundreds of photos. I'll show them to you, sometime.'

'Thanks. I'd love to see them. Have you seen the Harbour Bridge in Sydney? It was awesome. I went with my friend, but she didn't appreciate it. It didn't stop me enjoying it though.'

'Yes, I've seen it. There aren't many famous bridges I haven't visited. And I agree with you, it's incredible. Did you see it at New Year when they have the fireworks display?'

'Not in real life as I was back here. I've seen videos of it though. Millions of dollars of fireworks. Did you do the bridge walk when you were there?'

'I did. Not for the faint-hearted. Some people struggled, but it was amazing to see the construction so close.'

'I know. I did it twice and thought about applying for a job as one of the guides, but my friend didn't want to move to Sydney and by that time I'd met Lachlan.'

Whitney tried to concentrate on serving up dinner, but it was hard listening to them talk. It was like they'd known each other forever.

'Dinner's ready,' she said, bringing the plates to the table, trying to act all nonchalant, while inside she was a mess. A good mess, though.

She sat at the head of the table, opposite Tiffany, and Martin sat between them.

The conversation between the two of them flowed, and Whitney hardly spoke. She was surplus to requirements.

'Anyone for coffee?' she said once they'd finished eating.

'I'll have a decaf please,' Tiffany said.

'Same for me,' Martin said.

'You two go into the lounge and I'll bring it in.'

She waited until they'd left the room, filled the kettle and grabbed the phone, hitting speed dial for George.

'Whitney?'

'I've got to tell you,' she whispered, not wanting Tiffany and Martin to hear. 'This is going amazingly well. Better than I could have ever imagined. It's like they've known each other for ages. Who'd have thought it? Don't answer that because you'll come out with something logical. And you'll never guess what, they've both got this mad passion for bridges. Coincidence or what?' She giggled, not sure whether it was because of her joke or from the relief of everything going so well. She suspected it was a bit of both.

'I'm exceptionally pleased for you. I know how worried you were.'

'Thank you. I feel fit to burst I'm so happy and I wanted to share it with you. I'd better go as they're expecting coffee. Can you come in tomorrow morning so we can visit Naomi Armstrong?'

'We've already arranged this.'

'Have we? Oh yes. Sorry. My head's all over the place. I'll see you tomorrow and fill you in on how the rest of the evening goes.'

Chapter 23

'Did you see Clifford's face as we left?' Whitney asked George as she drove into the heavy morning traffic towards Pennington Grove where Naomi Armstrong lived. 'I don't think he was too happy about being left behind, even though we'd discussed it all yesterday.'

'You could have gone with him instead of me, although it wouldn't have been a good use of his time, considering the affair is a different issue to his.'

'Exactly. I didn't want him with me, anyway. He might be good at investigating syndicates, but this is murder. You have much more to offer. Although I will admit that from what I've seen so far, I'm quite impressed, considering he comes from the Met and you know what officers from there can be like.'

'I have no idea, but I'm sure you can enlighten me.'

'Full of their own self-importance. Look at Brian. Okay, he's all right now. But, you know, they think if they say they trained and worked at the Met it makes them somehow better than the rest of us. And let's not forget Dickhead. His few years there made him even more obnoxious than he was before, if that's possible. And as for his *let's go for a drink* comment to Clifford, what was all that about? Knowing Douglas, probably because of Clifford being a viscount.'

'*Son* of a viscount. There's a difference.'

'Whatever. He's still an aristocrat, and that impresses some people. Not me, though.'

Whitney's inverted snobbery amused George, but she knew better than to express her opinion, as her friend would be most affronted.

'Is Naomi expecting us?' she asked, changing the subject.

'No because I didn't want to warn her.'

George turned into Pennington Grove and slowed down outside Marsden House. The gates were open, so she drove up the drive and parked in front of the house next to a green Ford Mondeo.

'She has a visitor. Not Scott Marshall, by the looks of things as it's not his car.'

'Good. We don't want him here for this conversation. The car probably belongs to Naomi's dad as he drives a Mondeo'

Whitney rang the bell and after a few moments, Naomi opened the door. She was fully made-up, although it didn't hide the red rings around her eyes, and was wearing a pair of beige trousers, with a dark brown silk blouse. Was she going somewhere?

'Mrs Armstrong, we'd like to come in and ask you some more questions,' Whitney said.

'I'm going out with my parents. We're going to see the undertaker in preparation for when Ryan is given back to us. They've just arrived.'

'We won't keep you too long,' Whitney said. 'We'd like

to speak to you alone as issues have arisen which are best discussed in private.'

Panic shot across her face. 'They're in the kitchen with my daughter. We'll go into the media room.'

They followed her down the corridor and into a large square room with a giant screen on one of the walls and ten La-Z-Boy recliners in a semicircle. Naomi gestured for them to sit in the front row. It was a strange room for her to have chosen, unless it was because it had been sound-proofed.

'What is it? Do you know who shot Ryan?'

'Not yet, but during our enquiries we've discovered that you and Scott Marshall have been in a relationship. Is that correct?'

She flushed a bright shade of red, her hand clutching at her chest. No answer was required. She was clearly guilty.

'Who told you that?' Her voice was barely above a whisper.

'We're not at liberty to discuss our sources but can you confirm it's the case?'

She bit down on her bottom lip. 'I suppose it was going to come out sooner or later, but before we've even buried Ryan couldn't be worse timing. Have you spoken to Scott about it?' She paused. 'I suppose not, or he would have told me,' she added before Whitney had time to answer.

'Did your husband know anything about you and Scott?'

'I don't think so. We were very discreet and met at out of the way places. But not discreet enough, if somebody knew about it.'

'How long have you been seeing each other?'

'It started last March, so almost a year. We didn't mean

for it to happen. We've been discussing moving in together. I was going to leave Ryan, and Scott was going to leave Jess. We hadn't decided on a date, though. The guilt has plagued me for months. It's not something I'd ever done before.'

'Does Scott's wife know about the two of you?'

'Not as far as I know. Like I said, we kept it all very quiet because we knew that once it was out in the open everything would change. In particular, the club.'

'Why? What exactly would happen to it?'

'I imagine it would have to be sold as Ryan and Scott couldn't have continued working together under those circumstances.'

'So, the fact Ryan is now dead means a lot of the issues you and Scott faced have been removed.'

Her eyes widened. 'Surely you can't think that *I* killed Ryan to save awkwardness with him and Scott. That's ridiculous. I loved my husband.'

'I thought you said you loved Scott,' Whitney said.

'It's complicated. I loved Ryan, but I'm *in love* with Scott. Ryan was a good man and a great father. I've been eaten up with guilt, but the heart does its own thing. We don't have control over it.'

George cringed. Talking about the heart as if it was some animate object that made decisions was totally beyond her. As far as she was concerned, the woman was using it as an excuse for her behaviour. 'That's debatable,' she said.

'Scott and I want to spend the rest of our lives together. We know we'll have to wait for an acceptable amount of time to pass now, but it will happen. Is there anything else you want? I don't want to be late for my appointment.'

'We're investigating the death of your husband and from what we've ascertained, you and Scott Marshall are the two people who stand to gain the most. So, yes, we do have other things to discuss. Namely, your affair,' Whitney said.

Tears filled Naomi's eyes, and she pulled a tissue out from her sleeve and dabbed them away. 'You make it sound so dirty. But it wasn't like that at all. We both fought against it happening. You have to believe me.'

'Did Ryan have any life insurance?' Whitney asked.

She nodded. 'Yes.'

'When was the policy taken out?'

'When he turned professional. Before I knew him.'

'Are you the beneficiary?'

'I don't know. Probably. Or Sienna. I don't know where the documents are so can't check for you.'

'How would you get away to see Mr Marshall without your husband suspecting?'

'When Ryan was away, it was no problem. Scott would sometimes come here. When he was home, we'd find a way.' She glanced at her watch.

'We will be speaking to you again. But for now, you may go to your appointment.'

'Thanks. I'll see you out.'

'A motive?' Whitney asked George once they were back in the car.

'There was nothing in her behaviour to indicate she was lying. But it could be a motive for Marshall, of which she was unaware. It would save the club from being sold, assuming Armstrong has left everything to Naomi, and that would leave Marshall in total control. Has the will been read yet?'

'I've no idea. I'll give Brian a call.' Whitney pulled her phone from her pocket and hit one of the keys. 'It's me. Find out if Armstrong's will has been read yet. Also, ask Ellie how she's getting on with her analysis of Marshall's finances.' She paused. 'Yes. It's fine to approach them. I thought you already had. We'll be back in half an hour.'

'Are you going to bring in Marshall?' George asked, once Whitney had ended the call.

'Not until we've collated all of our research. Brian's getting in touch with his contact at the snooker governing body, in case there's anything about Marshall or Armstrong that relates to our enquiries. I could've sworn I told him to wait until after news of the death had hit the media and then do it. He didn't need to ask for permission.'

'He didn't want to cross you.'

'Hmm. If you say so. A less kind person might suggest that he'd forgotten to do it and was doing this to save getting in trouble.'

Chapter 24

'Claire,' Whitney called out, spotting the pathologist in front of them as they walked into the station. They quickly caught up with her. 'What are you doing here? You haven't come to see me, have you?'

'I've been delegated to attend a meeting with your top brass. Aren't I the lucky one? I was instructed that it was formal and I should dress accordingly.'

Yikes. Who would have the nerve to say that to Claire?

'And you listened to them? You must be going soft in your old age.' She couldn't resist a dig and was happy to take the pointed comment should it come her way.

'It was Ralph.'

Claire's new husband. Whitney had yet to meet him, but he must be something special if he could get away with those comments. Although Claire's outfit was still outlandish, the only difference being that she'd added a formal black jacket to her pink and white striped dress, orange tights and royal blue lace-up shoes. She'd love to be a fly on the wall when the others at the meeting were introduced to her.

'Do you know who else is going to be there?'

'Haven't a clue. All I know is it's being chaired by Sandra Littleton, the chief constable. We're looking at improving the partnership between pathology and the police.'

'What's wrong with our relationship?' She glanced at George. 'Have you noticed any issues, as an outsider?'

'None.'

'We have an acceptable partnership with you and your team, but that can't be said for others in the police force. Some officers we deal with have no respect for our role, demanding we do things their way and not valuing the process. Others are just plain thick, and as far as I'm concerned, should be kept well away from the morgue. There are also budgetary constraints that need discussing. A lovely way to spend an afternoon, I don't think, especially when I've got two bodies demanding my attention.'

'The chief constable is pretty good at not wasting time, so I'm sure you won't be there longer than necessary.'

'I hope you're right. How's the Armstrong investigation going? Are you any nearer to finding his killer? The world championships won't be the same without him there.'

'We're making slow progress. Do you know yet the type of gun used in the shooting?'

'I had confirmation this morning that it was a .22 calibre handgun, as I suggested. You'll have the report later.'

'So where did the murderer get the weapon?'

'That's up to you to discover. All I'm doing is letting you know what type of weapon was used. Having said that, out of the kindness of my heart I will tell you that I've come across these in the past, so I expect that they are readily accessible.'

'And you couldn't have said that straight away?' Whitney shook her head.

'Where's the fun in that? Now point me in the direction of the conference room.'

'You'll need to report in at reception first, and they'll give you a visitor's pass. They'll direct you to the room the meeting will be in.'

George and Whitney left Claire and took the lift to the fifth floor.

'Attention, everybody,' Whitney said, when they walked in. Clifford was seated at one of the spare desks at the far end of the room, away from the rest of the team. He looked up, too, when she spoke. 'We've been to see Naomi Armstrong, and she confirmed that she's been having an affair with Marshall and informed us that they'd planned to move in together.'

'That's a good enough reason to shoot him then, isn't it?' Frank said.

'A bit too obvious,' Doug said. 'It's like something from those TV crime dramas.'

'We do have to consider the advantages for Scott and Naomi of Ryan being dead. Brian, what's the situation with the will?'

'Everything is left to Naomi, including all of his business interests. She would have known the contents as they both updated their wills at the same time after they bought the snooker club, and their daughter was born, two years ago.'

'So, with Ryan out of the way she'll inherit half of the snooker club and there'll be no messy divorce. That's a huge advantage. Ellie, Naomi told us about a life insurance policy, did you find that when you researched Ryan's finances?'

'Yes, there is a personal policy on Armstrong, but not a business one.'

'You'd have thought the bank would've insisted on them having one,' Whitney said.

'The club was paid for outright and there isn't a mortgage, so I doubt the bank would've required them to have one,' Ellie said.

'Brian, did you get anything from the snooker governing body?'

'I spoke to the chap I know, and he told me that Marshall had been the one to push for this tournament to be held at the Palace. Originally, they'd said no, but reconsidered after being let down by another venue.'

Clifford got up from his seat and walked over to join the rest of them.

'Is Marshall's wife aware of the affair?' he asked.

'According to Naomi, no. She said that although they'd been planning to leave Ryan and Jessica, they hadn't done anything about it and wouldn't do anything for a while now, out of respect for Ryan. We'll see what Marshall says when we interview him. Ellie, any more on his finances?'

'Yes, guv. While digging, I found an account in his name only. All the others were joint. Large amounts of money were paid into it on a regular basis.'

'Did you track where this money came from?' Whitney asked, her skin prickling as it always did when an investigation turned something up.

'Yes, guv. This is where it overlaps with my research into William Palmer. Marshall's money also came from Singapore. It's cleverly done, going via three different accounts in Singapore and then through a fourth in Malaysia.'

Whitney exchanged a glance with Clifford. 'Did Marshall come up at all during your operation, Sebastian?'

'Seb,' he muttered.

Had he mentioned that before?

'Sorry, *Seb.*'

'No, he didn't. But if he is attached to the syndicate, it would make sense for him to push for having the tournament at his venue. It would be much easier to ensure players did what they were meant to. Assuming they wanted matches fixed, which I'm not convinced about as it's a high-profile tournament.'

'Guv,' Meena called out. 'I've just taken a call from Rory Clarke about the taxi. He remembered that he'd called it for himself but then went with Kurt instead in his Uber. He doesn't remember cancelling it.'

'Why did it take him this long to get back to us?'

'I didn't ask. Sorry,' Meena said.

'So Scott Marshall didn't take the taxi after all, in which case how did he get home, and when? I want him in now for questioning. The last time he was here at the station he ended up refusing to speak without his solicitor present. Brian, take Meena and go to see him. Make it casual and say we'd like further help with the investigation. He may agree to being interviewed alone. Let me know when he's here.'

'I want to be part of this interview to speak to him about the betting going on at the club and his links with Singapore,' Clifford said. 'If he murdered Ryan because of his involvement with me, the syndicate could've provided him with the gun and Naomi could've been part of it.'

'If she was, then she must be a bloody good actress because George couldn't detect from her body language that she was lying, and in the ten plus investigations she's helped me with, she's got a one hundred per cent success rate with her witness assessments. We need to question

Marshall about the affair before we discuss the syndicate with him.'

'We can cover both. If the money in his account is from the syndicate, then this is an important breakthrough. Ellie, can I take a look at the account showing the payments?' He walked over to her desk and stood behind her.

'Here.' Ellie slid her chair to the side, giving him space to look.

'This can't wait,' he said, turning back to face Whitney. 'Let me interview with you.'

If he was right, then she'd be stupid not to let him take part. Their priority was to find the killer, and she shouldn't let her prejudices get in the way.

'Okay. We'll talk to him first about the affair, and I'll lead the questioning. Then we'll introduce the syndicate, and you can lead. By that time, he may be demanding his solicitor, so it may be delayed.'

'That's fine.'

'I recommend that, like me, you have George in your ear.'

'Excuse me?'

'George will observe, and you can have an earpiece. She'll advise on the direction you should take the interview based on the body language and responses from Marshall.'

'Do you think that will help?' he asked, turning to George.

'It's my area of expertise, if you want it. No one is twisting your arm to accept.'

'How could I refuse? Thank you.' He gave a tiny bow of his head.

Whitney stifled a grin. It was like being in the middle of a scene from *Downton Abbey*. 'That's sorted, then. Brian, off you go. Fetch Marshall.'

Chapter 25

'Right. It's his relationship with Naomi Armstrong first,' Whitney said to Clifford as, along with George, they made their way to the interview. 'Anything to do with illegal betting, the club, and the syndicate will be left until last.' The more the elements were kept separate, the more chance she had of the case not being taken from her.

'We've already established that. But there will be some overlap. We're going to have to talk about the snooker club and when the couple met.' His voice was friendly enough, but had a firmness about it. He needed to realise that she was still in charge. Nothing had changed.

'We'll see how it goes. You're not to mention his bank account initially.' She refrained from adding '*and that's an order*' even though she was tempted. 'My gut is telling me that the affair and the money are two totally separate things.'

'Gut?' George said, disbelief on her face.

'Yes.' She jutted out her chin in defiance, not prepared to elaborate. 'Brian informed me that Marshall didn't mention his solicitor on the way in, so hopefully he'll be compliant.'

George headed into the observation area as Whitney and Clifford walked into the adjoining room.

'How many times do you have to speak to me?' Marshall asked, his eyes focused directly on Whitney.

'We're in the middle of a murder investigation, surely you understand that.'

'I don't appreciate being marched out of my house by two of your officers. It's upsetting for my wife and the neighbours could have seen.'

'You're being a tad melodramatic. Were you in handcuffs?'

'No.'

'Were you arrested?'

'No.'

'So, as far as anyone else is concerned you were doing your duty by helping us solve the murder of your best friend and business partner.'

He slumped in the seat. 'I suppose so.'

'Good. I'm glad we've got that sorted. Before we start, I'll set up the recording equipment.' She pressed the button. 'Interview on Friday, March the twelfth Those present: Detective Chief Inspector Walker, Detective Inspector Clifford and ... please state your name for the recording.'

'Scott Marshall.' He punched his fist into the palm of his hand. 'Before you start, I'd like to say something.'

'Go ahead,' Whitney said.

'Naomi told me that you know about us.'

Ah. Was that why he hadn't asked for a solicitor, so it could be kept low-key?

'Why didn't you mention it when we last questioned you?'

'I didn't think it was relevant.'

'You have got to be kidding. How could it not be relevant when we're investigating the murder of her husband?' She shook her head in exasperation.

'If you think Naomi killed Ryan, you're wrong. She can't have because we'd arranged to meet at the time it happened, but Sienna was sick and Naomi wouldn't leave her. I spoke to her for much of the night after I'd got home, so I'm her alibi and vice versa.'

'Are you telling me that you were talking on the phone for two hours, from one until three?'

'No. But for some of the time.'

Her jaw flexed. 'Wait a minute, the last time we spoke you said you went straight home drunk. Are you changing your story?'

'Yes.' He bowed his head. 'I was the first to leave Ryan's. I'd driven myself over there and parked a little down the road so the others couldn't see. Naomi and I had planned to meet at Wigston Park at twelve-thirty. And before you ask, no I wasn't over the limit. I only had a couple of beers. Nobody noticed, we were too busy eating and playing snooker. I went there, but Naomi didn't arrive. She called me at one to say she couldn't make it, so I went home.'

'That still allowed plenty of time for you to have arranged to meet Ryan at the club and shot him. Naomi could've been in on it, too.'

Marshall glowered at her. 'Stop with your false accusations. I didn't kill Ryan. Nor did Naomi. This is why we didn't tell you. We knew you'd try to pin the blame on us.'

'Why did you tell us Rory Clarke called you a taxi?'

'I messed up when we first talked by saying I'd got a taxi, because it wasn't in my call log, so I pretended one of the others called it for me. Then you said you thought it was Rory so I agreed. It seemed the easiest thing to do.'

'Except now we know that Rory called it for himself.'

'I might have lied about that, but everything else I've told you is the truth.'

'Let's talk about your affair with Naomi. How long has it been going on?'

She wanted to know if his version was the same as Naomi's.

'About a year.'

'When did you decide that you were going to leave your partners and set up home together?'

'Um …' He hesitated, glancing upwards.

'I'm not sure they did,' George said in her ear.

'It's a simple enough question,' Whitney pushed.

'We'd talked about it generally, but nothing had been finalised. It was more a case of it being a long-term plan.'

'That's not how Naomi explained it to us. She was quite definite you were planning to move in together, although it would be delayed now, after Ryan's death.'

'Yes, exactly.' He expelled a breath. 'We can't think about it now because of what happened to him. It's something we may consider in the future.'

'I'm getting the impression that Naomi is more committed to you living together than you are.'

'It's tricky, especially now.'

'Why is Naomi attracted to you, do you think?'

'What sort of question is that? Why wouldn't she be? Ryan was a great guy, but I think she found him boring compared with me. She likes a bit of excitement and unpredictability.'

Whitney exchanged a glance with Clifford, refraining from rolling her eyes at his arrogance.

'Have you had affairs in the past?'

'I fail to see why that has anything to do with it,' he said.

'He means yes,' George said.

'That's my call. Can I take it that as well as Naomi you have cheated on your wife at other times during your marriage?'

He threw his hands in the air. 'Yes. I admit it.'

'Did you ever considering leaving your wife for any of these other women?'

'Never.'

'Does your wife know of these affairs?'

'There were a couple of occasions when she did find out I'd been seeing someone.'

'What happened?'

'I ended it and we stayed together.'

'Do you think your wife might know about your relationship with Naomi?'

'I'm not sure. She hasn't accused me, which is what she did in the past when she found out.'

'If she had confronted you about it, what would you have done?'

'It's complicated because of the way the business is set up. My wife has a stake as it was her money I used when putting up my share.'

'Correct me if I'm wrong, but if you and your wife split up, then it would cause you financial problems, which you would want to avoid.'

'Yes,' he said nodding.

'So, we're actually getting two different stories here. One from Naomi Armstrong who believes that you were definitely going to leave your partners and set up home together. Another from you that it wasn't a foregone conclusion, and most likely not going to happen. Why do you think her understanding of the situation is so very different from yours?'

'I don't know. You know what women are like.' He looked at Clifford.

'No, I don't. You tell me,' Whitney said, leaning forward and fixing him with a cold stare.

'Women are more emotional and, you know ... Anyway, it doesn't matter whatever it is, we're not doing anything at the moment, we can't. Not now Ryan is dead.'

'Returning to your wife, how careful were you in ensuring that she didn't find out about the affair?'

'We used WhatsApp with false names when messaging each other and always deleted after reading them. But how is Jess's knowledge about the affair relevant to Ryan's murder? For which both Naomi and I have an alibi.'

'Your alibis are tenuous, to say the least. But that aside, you could have been in it together. You'd have all the money she inherits, which includes half of the snooker club and would certainly go some way towards mitigating the loss from your wife withdrawing her funding.'

'What a load of shit. You must be desperate to find the killer if you're accusing us. How many times do I have to tell you? Ryan was my business partner and my best friend. The business is doing well, in no small part because of Ryan's presence at the club. Why would I rock the boat?'

Whitney exchanged a glance with Clifford. They were going around in circles. It was time to move on. But first they needed to regroup.

'Interview suspended for the time being. We'll be back shortly.'

They left the room and met George in the corridor.

'From his mannerisms and answers, I don't believe he ever intended to leave his wife. I think this was another affair which could well have run its course if it hadn't been for the murder.'

'Let's grab a coffee and leave him to stew for a while,' Whitney said. 'Then you can question him about the money, Seb.'

Chapter 26

Seb walked a couple of steps behind Walker and Dr Cavendish. They made an odd couple, seeming total opposites, in personality, background, as well as physicality. But he'd glimpsed a closeness and mutual respect that went much further than working together. What bonded them? Her determination to remain in overall charge of the case, irrespective of what the higher-ups had to say about it, impressed him. And as for her disdain for Chief Superintendent Douglas, that amused him. The man was a sycophant of the first degree.

He was fully aware that his background caused one of two reactions. Either folks went out of their way to make sure they didn't treat him any differently from other members of the force, including merciless teasing about his accent and background. Or they put on an upper-class accent, which they couldn't maintain, and tried to make him their friend, wanting him to think that they were the same as him. Needless to say, he much preferred the former. The whole point in him joining the force was to get away from his stifling upbringing. It was bad enough when he had to attend certain events to keep his family happy. But other than those he was content to keep his distance.

DCI Walker had already poked fun at how he spoke, but he suspected that was as a result of her friendship with Dr Cavendish. He'd been surprised when she'd offered for him to take the lead in the second part of the interview, without him having to ask. He'd been expecting a modicum of resistance. He wasn't as convinced as she was that the shooting was unconnected to his operation, and that it was likely linked to the affair between Armstrong's wife and his partner. They'd learn soon enough, though. If he was right a decision had to be made. One he suspected Walker wouldn't be happy about.

He adjusted the earpiece he was wearing. If Dr Cavendish was highly rated by Walker, then he knew, without reservation, that she'd be good. He looked forward to having her input.

Dr Cavendish left them, and Walker opened the door to the interview room. Did she still expect him to sit to the right of her, or would she leave the seat opposite the interviewee for him? She did, and he flashed a smile in her direction. She gave a sharp nod in return.

'Interview resumed.' Walker said, restarting the recording.

'Why am I still here? Surely you've asked me every-thing you want to know?'

'I want to move on from your affair with Ryan Armstrong's wife, Mr Marshall. My interest is in the illegal betting that takes place at your snooker club on a regular basis, which you endorse,' Seb said.

'The what?' Marshall's brow furrowed.

'Your manager has a gambling side hustle, and he informed us that not only were you fully aware of its exis-tence, but you were happy to allow it to continue.'

'Oh, that.' He glanced to Walker a blank expression on his face. 'Look, it's harmless. Small bets on the side, nothing major. I'll make sure he doesn't do it again.' He waved his hand dismissively.

'It's illegal,' Whitney stated.

'Yeah, okay, I get it. But like I said, they were small wagers on the side. It's done all the time in clubs like ours. Why make such a big deal of it?'

He certainly played a good part when it came to acting innocent, but he'd have to try a lot harder than that to pull the wool over Seb's eyes. He'd been in the game far too long for that to happen.

'It's illegal,' Seb repeated, keeping his voice flat. 'But we'll put that to one side for the moment. Tell me about the money that's been going into your bank account from Singapore, via several other overseas financial institutions. How do you account for it?'

Marshall looked away briefly, before fixing his gaze on Seb. 'I have no idea what you're talking about. I don't know anyone in Singapore, so why would I receive money from there?'

'He's not telling the truth,' George said in his ear, causing him to start. He'd forgotten about her being there. 'His voice increased in volume when talking to you, and his feet were shuffling under the table which you wouldn't have been able to see. He's exhibiting other signs, but these are enough in themselves.'

He nodded his acknowledgement.

'I don't believe you. Are you telling me you don't know what's in your bank account?' He leant forward slightly, and Marshall tensed. One of the benefits of being a large man was he had the ability to intimidate those he was questioning.

'My wife handles all the finances.'

Seb gave a frustrated sigh, loud enough to indicate to Marshall that he didn't believe him. 'We are fully aware of the joint bank accounts you and your wife have. I'm referring to the one in your name only. Regular payments were made into it. On July the seventh last year fifteen hundred pounds. August the twenty-third, two and a half thousand. September the fifteenth, five thousand. October the twenty-first—'

'What are you, a robot? How do you know that?'

'I read your bank statement. I can go on. The latest payment to reach your account was ten days ago. Ten thousand. The biggest yet.'

'He's scared,' George said. 'Look at the micro-expressions on his face. His lower eyelids are tense, and his mouth is half-open. I suggest you take a less confrontational approach and let him know that you're there to help him.'

Again, an excellent contribution made by Dr Cavendish.

'If you're in trouble or have got yourself involved in something you'd rather not be a part of, then you can tell me and we'll help. Are you being paid to throw matches?'

Seb stared directly at Marshall, looking for some of those telltale signs Dr Cavendish had pointed out to him. He had some knowledge of body language as he studied it when looking at match throwing, but they were different signs from the ones she'd highlighted.

'I have never thrown a match in my life.'

'Try again. We can go through footage of every single match that you've played and our experts will soon be able to tell.'

'That would take you ages.' Marshall folded his arms in front of him, a belligerent expression on his face.

'Not as long as you'd think as I've got a good research team back at the Met and use the latest software on the market. Our sole purpose is to investigate fraudulent behaviour in gambling and, at the moment, we're looking into match-fixing in the snooker industry, in particular at an international level.'

Marshall sunk down in his chair. 'You can't say you heard it from me.'

Seb exhaled a satisfied breath. Now he was getting somewhere. 'Okay, let's start at the beginning. Why are they paying you?'

'I was approached by a man who knew about my affair with Naomi. He said he represented an organisation from overseas and that if I didn't do as he asked, he would blow the whistle on me and that it would ruin the business. He said they'd pay me, and that would stop me from going to the police because then I was as guilty as they were. I had no choice.'

'What did you have to do for this money?'

'Set up matches between specific players. They were friendlies and didn't have to be part of a tournament. They told me who was to win the match, and I ensured that it happened.'

'And these players were quite prepared to throw a game for money?'

'Yes. It wasn't like they were matches which mattered. What you've got to understand is, unless you're a top-level player, like Ryan, professional players don't earn enough money to live.'

'Like you?'

'I have the snooker club which supplements my income.'

'Let me get this straight,' Walker said, asking a question for the first time. 'You get paid for arranging matches that are fixed and all of you get paid. People then bet on the match and make a lot of money. Why don't you fix matches in tournaments?'

'It's harder to do because tournaments attract a lot of media coverage,' Seb said, answering for Marshall. 'Were these matches always held at your club?'

'Not always. We'd have different venues. I'd travel around the country and arrange them, often they were exhibition matches which would attract public interest.'

'How were you contacted, and by whom?'

'I don't know who contacted me. I'd get a text message instructing me what to do, and after the match the money would appear in my account.'

'Were you responsible for paying the players involved?'

'No, it was all arranged in advance.'

'How long have you been a part of this?' Seb asked.

'About nine months.'

'And did Ryan suspect?' Whitney asked.

'I don't think so.'

'Did your contact mention Ryan at all?'

'No.'

'When is the next match you've got set up?' Seb asked.

'Four weeks' time. In Birmingham.'

'Have all the arrangements been made?'

'Yes, everything's in place. Do you want me to cancel the match?'

'You've got two choices. The first is that we prosecute you for what you're doing and put an end to your part in it and, yes, we would cancel the forthcoming match in Birmingham. Alternatively, you can work with me and my officers so we can track down the nucleus of this particular overseas organisation and put a halt to their operation, which might take a little longer.'

It could work. If Marshall was being watched by their men, they wouldn't suspect he was there discussing the syndicate. They'd think he was being questioned about the shooting.

'Do I have a choice?' Marshall asked, resignation clouding his face.

'Everyone has a choice, but my advice is that you work with me and avoid a prison sentence.'

Not counting the death of Ryan Armstrong, which still played heavily on his mind, this was turning out to be most fortuitous. The information Marshall would be able to provide would most likely give them a breakthrough.

'I'll do it. But I want some guarantees.'

'Which are?'

'Protection for my family. If these people find out what I'm doing, there'll be a price to pay. I can't risk their lives.'

'Your family's security would be a priority. Trust me. We'll make sure they don't find out.'

He wouldn't make the same mistake he had with Ryan and have their meetings discovered. He still had no idea why they'd been targeting Ryan. Did Marshall know?

'Before we end this session, we suspect that the organisation you're working for was keeping tabs on Ryan for a couple of weeks before his death. Do you know why?'

'I've no idea. Unless they wanted to recruit him. Or had already recruited him.' He shook his head. 'That's not likely though, when you consider how squeaky clean he was.'

Could they have been following Armstrong as part of a regular check up on Marshall?

'I want you to continue with your normal behaviour. Don't make any changes and I'll be in touch.'

Walker arranged for Marshall to be taken to the snooker club as that's where he'd been heading when he was brought in for questioning, and then Seb met up with her and Dr Cavendish.

'He could be a useful informant,' Walker said.

'Yes. And more help than Ryan, who was reporting on what he'd seen but, as he wasn't a part of the match-fixing, his information was limited. Marshall, on the other hand, can give us a way in. But it's still unclear as to why Ryan was being followed by Palmer. What prompted that?' He turned to George. 'Thanks for your input by the way, it was extremely useful.'

'I told you,' Walker said. 'You may not agree, and we have more digging to do, but I'm even more convinced that this affair might be at the heart of Armstrong's killing and not your syndicate.'

'Not one of your *gut feelings*?' Dr Cavendish said, shaking her head.

'I take it you don't believe in that,' he said.

'Do you?' Dr Cavendish said.

'No.'

'You two would stick together,' Walker said.

'Why's that?'

'Whitney, leave it,' the doctor warned. 'The DCI and I don't agree on certain things, this being one of them.'

He looked from Walker to Dr Cavendish and shook his head. Whatever he was missing, he could live with, especially as it appeared he'd now got himself a way into the syndicate.

Chapter 27

'Now you've enlisted Marshall to help with infiltrating the syndicate, does that mean you're going to leave and return to London?' Whitney asked Clifford, after George and she had met him heading towards the incident room the following morning.

Despite his intrusion not turning out to be as bad as she'd imagined it could have done, she'd still be happy to see the back of him, so she didn't have to consider anything other than her team solving Armstrong's murder. Not to mention his link to Douglas. Even if Clifford didn't like him, it wouldn't stop *Dickhead* sticking his nose in the incident room again to suck up to Clifford because of who he was.

'Not yet. I'll run my plans for Marshall's input into my operation past my boss and get her approval. Without it, it's a non-starter. Plus I'd rather we were further down the track with discovering Ryan's killer before totally dismissing the syndicate's involvement.'

She tutted. 'If you'd let us interview Jad Tan, it might help move things forward.'

'You already know that's not possible as it could jeopardise everything I've worked on so far.' He gave a frustrated sigh. 'This is why it's so much easier working alone.'

'Well, we're a team, and I think you're being overcautious. It stands to reason that during our investigation we would have spotted anyone following Armstrong and pulled them in for questioning. Palmer could have told the syndicate we'd questioned him.'

'I doubt he'd do that,' George said. 'He wouldn't want them to know his fake identity had been compromised in case of repercussions.'

'You're not helping,' Whitney said scowling in George's direction.

'Palmer could also be a useful contact for you, DI Clifford,' George said.

Was she totally oblivious to Whitney's annoyance?

'Agreed. I may interview the PI again at sometime,' Clifford said.

They reached the incident room, and he held open the door for Whitney and George to enter.

'Guv,' Frank called out the second she was in there. 'Perfect timing. While I was going through some CCTV footage looking at Marshall's and Mrs Armstrong's cars, to see if I could work out the times when they'd met, I spotted a car following Marshall on a couple of occasions.'

Was it this Jad Tan? Had he been following Marshall as well as Armstrong? Where would that leave Clifford's plans?

'Good work. Have you been able to identify the car?'

'Yep. It's a Range Rover Evoque and belongs to Jessica Marshall. Scott's wife.'

What? She hadn't expected that. 'Did she know about the affair and had been following him? Or maybe she'd *suspected* he was having an affair and wanted to find out who the woman was. Either way, we need to look into her background. Ellie—'

'I started digging as soon as Frank discovered the car, guv.'

'But why would she kill Armstrong?' Frank said. 'It makes no sense. Surely if she was going to kill anyone, it would be Marshall or Mrs Armstrong.'

'One step at a time. We don't even know if she was involved. Have we found out when the victim's phone was last used?'

Whitney drew a line between Scott Marshall and Naomi Armstrong's names on the board. 'Let's recap. We have an affair and the wife possibly knew about it. But did the victim know too? Could there have been an altercation between Ryan Armstrong and Scott Marshall? Was Naomi there? Could Marshall and Mrs Armstrong have been in cahoots and shot him? All this needs considering. But before we make further assumptions, we'll pay Jessica Marshall a visit. George, you can come with me.' She turned to Clifford 'There's no need for you to be with us as this line of enquiry clearly has nothing to do with your operation.'

'Agreed.' Clifford nodded. 'I'll settle down over there.' He nodded at the desk he'd been using since being there, then tilted his head to one side. 'Would you mind if I used your office? I have some private calls to make and would rather do it inside as it's raining.'

'Arranging an assignation, are you?'

Why did she ask that? She couldn't care less about his private life.

'There are a few things going on at work that I want to know more about. If it's a problem, then—'

'It's not. I was joking. Help yourself. And if you feel the

urge to tackle the piles of admin on my desk, then knock yourself out. There could be a drink in it for you.'

'I'm not sure that's appropriate …' He paused and looked at her. 'Another joke?'

'Yeah.'

~

'Clifford seems to have lost some of his laissez-faire attitude. Do you agree?' Whitney asked George as they were driving out to the Marshall house.

'I think he's frustrated that after finally making some headway with the syndicate his informant could be our murderer.'

'Don't you find him being a viscount and a copper weird?'

'As I keep saying, he's only the son of a viscount. He doesn't have a title or family money to fall back on. People from the aristocracy still have to work and earn a living.'

'I get that. But as a copper? Surely, he'd be more suited to owning an art gallery, or working for a charity.'

'You have stereotypical views. However, it's unusual for an aristocrat to be a police officer, I'll grant you that.'

'Do you like him?'

'I don't know him well enough to form an opinion. From what I've seen, he is measured and takes pride in his work. Traits I admire.'

'Is he married, do you know?'

'I've no idea. Why are you asking?'

'We don't know anything about him, other than he has a dog called Elsa. Actually, he can't be married, because he leaves the dog with a neighbour. In which case does he have a partner?'

'I neither know, nor care,' she said, glancing at the satnav. 'We're almost here.'

She turned into Favell Drive and three houses down on the right stopped at number seven, a large Victorian detached house with wrought-iron gates that were open. She parked on the street and they walked up the short drive.

'Nice house,' Whitney said. 'Purchased by Daddy. Some people don't know they're born.'

Whitney rang the bell, and the door was opened by a woman in her thirties, dressed in jogging gear, with her blonde highlighted hair pulled back into a ponytail. Her face was flushed and there were beads of sweat along her forehead.

'Jessica Marshall?' Whitney asked.

'Yes.'

'I'm Detective Chief Inspector Walker and this is Dr Cavendish. We'd like to come in and have a word with you about the shooting of Ryan Armstrong.'

'I've been on my exercise bike, do you mind if I have a quick wash and get changed, I'll only be five minutes?' She opened the door and ushered them inside.

'We'll wait here,' Whitney said.

Mrs Marshall ran up the large staircase which dominated the hall.

'She could be hiding something,' George said.

'We don't have a search warrant, and she clearly had been exercising, so I'm not concerned. If she takes longer than five minutes, I'll go upstairs to find her. It's not like she can escape from up there, unless she's going to throw herself out of the window.'

'She didn't appear to be a person with tendencies towards defenestration.'

'What?' Whitney said, a blank look on her face.

'Defenestration is the action of throwing someone out of the window. Although having said that, does it relate to oneself, or just the act of another? I need to check.' She was distracted by the sound of Mrs Marshall coming down the stairs. She'd changed into a pair of slim fit jeans with a pale blue, mohair jumper over the top. On her feet were a pair of white tennis shoes.

'Sorry to have kept you,' the woman said. 'We'll go into the kitchen and I'll make us a coffee, if you'd like one.'

'Yes, please,' Whitney said.

They followed her through to a large open-plan modern kitchen, with chrome fittings, white cupboards and light-grey granite worktops. Not something George would like to have. She much preferred something in keeping with the age of the house.

'What happened to Ryan was such a shock. I couldn't believe it.' She took three white china mugs from the cupboard and filled them with coffee from the jug sitting on the coffee machine. 'This is fresh, made only a short while ago.'

'We understand that on the night of the shooting you were staying with your parents. Is that correct?'

'Yes. Scott had gone over to meet up with the boys, and I knew he was going to come in drunk. I didn't want him waking Leo, so we went over there. My parents love to see him, he's their only grandson. They spoil him rotten.'

'Where's your son now?' George asked.

'He's out with the nanny, they've gone to a local play-group. He enjoys mixing with the other children, and I enjoy some time to myself. It's true what they say about the terrible twos. As lovable as Leo is, he's also quite a handful at times.'

'Where do your parents live?' Whitney asked.

'In Hampshire Close.'

'And they can vouch for you being there Sunday morning, between the hours of one and three.'

'Yes, of course. Why do you ask?'

'It's a routine question. We ask everybody we interview what they were doing on the night of the shooting, in order to eliminate them from our enquiries.'

'I understand. I left here at four on Saturday afternoon and went straight to my parents, to give them time to play with Leo before he had his tea and went to bed. Once he was asleep, we had dinner and then watched the telly. We all went to bed around the same time, I think it was half-past ten. My parents don't stay up late. I can give you their number if you'd like to check my story with them.'

'Thank you,' Whitney said, as she handed over her notebook and pen. 'Please jot it down for me.'

'I've written down the landline and also my mum's mobile,' Jessica said, handing back the notebook which Whitney returned to her pocket.

George scanned the room and noticed a certificate on the wall with an embossed silver gun in the top corner. She got up and walked over. 'First prize in the East Midlands targeting shooting contest. You shoot?'

Jessica cleared her throat. 'Yes. I've been shooting since I was a child. My father used to go, and occasionally he took me with him to the club. One day he let me have a go and I didn't miss a target. I was instantly hooked. My school also had a shooting club, which I joined, and we won the junior national shooting contest for three consecutive years. At fourteen, I was selected for England's junior team. I'm still a member of the same club, and so is my father. It's the Lenchester Shooting Centre and was where I met Scott.'

She stared at Whitney, witnessing the surprise on her face. They hadn't realised Scott Marshall shot.

'Do you own guns?'

'No. We use the club's.'

'What about your father? Does he own any?'

'No,' she said, biting down on her bottom lip.

'How often do you go to the shooting club?'

'Not as often as I'd like as there are always so many other things to do.'

'What about Scott? Does he still go?'

'Sometimes. He's a very good shot, not in my league, but better than the average club shooter.'

'Do you still shoot competitively?'

'Occasionally, I'll enter a tournament, like that one.' She pointed to the certificate on the wall. But I don't have time to practice. Having children changes things.'

'During our enquiries we discovered several instances where you'd been following Scott in your car. Why?'

The woman blushed. 'I-I … I don't trust him.'

'In what respect?' Whitney asked, her voice gentle.

'My husband hasn't always been faithful. I was checking up on him. You probably think that's stupid. But I'd rather know what he's up to than be kept in the dark.'

'What did you discover?'

'Nothing. The times when I followed him he went where he said he was going. Maybe I was wrong this time.'

'Had Scott been acting differently recently?'

'Yes. More secretive. That's why I thought he was seeing someone, but as I've just said, I didn't find any evidence of that. I wondered if there was a problem with the business, but when I asked him, he said it would sort itself out soon. I didn't push him on it.'

'Do you have any idea what the problem could have been?'

'Not really, but I got the feeling it was something to do with the tournament they're hosting this week. He'd been on edge for a while, because it was such a big deal. But … he could be extremely secretive at times, so I could be completely wrong. Is there anything else I can help you with?'

'Nothing further. Thank you for your time,' Whitney said.

They left the house and returned to George's car.

'Was this issue Scott referred to related to the syndicate blackmailing him, do you think?' George said. 'Except that had been going on for months, so why would it suddenly become an issue.

'It could be the fact that Ryan Armstrong would soon be dead and things would change. Let's go to the Lenchester Shooting Centre, they could have access to handguns. Then we'll visit the snooker club.'

'Should we let Clifford know we're going to interview Marshall?' George asked.

'He doesn't need to know. I don't want him interfering and saying we can't speak to him because he's going to be an informant. The less he knows the better until I decide otherwise.'

Chapter 28

Lenchester Shooting Centre was situated on the edge of the city. Surrounded by trees, the club comprised two large warehouses and a brick-built building, looking as though it was built in the seventies, with *Reception and Clubhouse* sign-written on the door.

'Have you ever been shooting?' Whitney asked George.

'Many years ago, but it wasn't something I wished to pursue. You?'

'I keep up my firearms training as part of my job. I do enjoy target shooting, it's a great stress relief, especially if you imagine the face of someone who annoys the heck out of you on the target.' She grinned. 'And I'm sure you know who I mean.'

'Indeed, I do.'

A man in his early forties, wearing a green polo shirt with the club logo embroidered on it, was sitting behind the reception desk. He glanced up and smiled as they approached.

Whitney held out her warrant card. 'Is the manager here?'

'That's me. Aiden Black.'

'We're investigating the shooting of Ryan Armstrong and would like to speak to you about his partner and wife, Scott and Jessica Marshall, who are members.'

'Yeah. Sure. We'll go through to the clubroom where we can talk undisturbed.' He came out from behind the desk. 'It's through here, we finished refurbishing it this week.'

He led them down a short corridor and pushed open the double doors into a well-lit area with floor to ceiling windows running along the back. There was a stage area at one end and the tables were a light wood, with matching chairs.

'Very nice,' Whitney said, as he stopped at one of the tables and pulled out the chairs for them to sit down.

'We have a licensed bar, a restaurant where you can order snacks or a meal and over in the corner a pool table. We encourage social visits as well as people using the shooting ranges.'

'Where do they actually shoot?'

'We have two indoor ranges with ten firing points in each, you'd have seen the buildings on your way in. To the rear of this building, unseen from outside, we have two outdoor ranges.'

'When was the last time you saw the Marshalls?'

'Off the top of my head, a few weeks ago but I can check the records to confirm. They're not regulars. Jessica's an excellent shot and has been a member since she was a child when she came shooting with her dad, Gordon Elliott. He's still very active here and donated a large sum of money towards the refurbishment which we appreciated as we wouldn't have been able to have afforded it other-wise. We're going to name the clubroom after him and have an official ceremony.'

And no doubt he was able to write it off against his taxes, which they already knew he managed to avoid paying. Not that she was going down that avenue now. It wasn't relevant.

'How long has the club been going?'

'My father opened it twenty-five years ago.'

'Is he here?'

His eyes clouded over. 'He died last year. I'm in charge now.'

'Sorry to hear that. Is Scott Marshall a good shot?' Whitney asked, wanting to confirm what they'd already been told.

'Not as good as Jessica, but he's okay. He's a typical sportsman, competitive and better than average at whatever he attempts. But …' He hesitated. 'I'm not sure whether I should mention this.'

'Yes, you should. This is a murder investigation and any piece of information you have, however inconsequential you might think it is, could help us.'

He nodded. 'Scott has caused *issues* here over the years.'

'What sort of issues?'

'Let's just say he has a wandering eye. There was one time when I caught him in a compromising position with a female trainer we had working here. And if that wasn't bad enough, his wife was here shooting on one of the ranges.'

'What did you do?'

'Told my father, and he changed the trainer's shifts so she wasn't around at times when we thought Jessica and Scott would be here. They were more regular visitors then, so it was easy to organise. We didn't want to lose Jessica as a patron in case her father decided to withdraw from the club also.'

'Did Jessica suspect anything between Scott and this woman?'

'If she did, we didn't hear about it.'

'Is this trainer still here?'

'No, she left a few years ago.'

'Ryan Armstrong was killed with a .22 calibre handgun. Would you be able to get your hands on one, if asked?'

'They're illegal.'

'That's not what I asked,' Whitney said.

'I would have an idea where to get one.'

'Has anyone asked you about acquiring one recently?'

'No, they haven't.'

'Did Ryan Armstrong ever visit the range with Scott or Jessica?' Whitney asked.

'I saw him a couple of times with Scott. Not recently, though. He was a good shot, too. Like I said about Scott, good sportsmen can turn their hand to anything.' His phone rang, and he looked at the screen. 'Sorry, I have to get this.'

Aiden walked away, leaving them alone.

'Scott can handle a gun. Is that relevant? It's too much of a coincidence for it not to be.'

Chapter 29

When they arrived at the Palace Snooker Club Whitney spotted Glen Tibbs standing by the bar talking to one of the staff. She hurried over and interrupted his conversation.

'Is Scott Marshall here?'

Tibbs looked at his watch. 'He went to the gym an hour ago.'

'In the middle of a tournament?'

'He said he had to do something to let off steam. We didn't need him here as he doesn't have anything to do with the day-to-day running of the place. If anything, it's easier when he's not around as I can get on with the job of having everything in place, instead of having him following me around questioning what I'm doing.'

'Which gym does he use?'

'The one in Giles Street. You might just catch him there as he's usually gone for an hour and a half.'

'Does he go regularly?'

'As clockwork. He's there most days.'

'I know the gym,' she said to George as they left the

club. 'I went to a couple of aerobics sessions there a few years ago.'

'Only a couple?'

'Work got in the way, as usual. I keep meaning to start going to classes again, but it's never the right time. And now with the baby on the way there's no chance.'

'You should try to make time. You'll benefit from it.'

'I know, but it's not going to happen.'

'It could if you were determined. We could go together if you like,' George offered.

'Let me think about it. But I can't promise.' She had enough on her plate without adding the need to exercise more.

When they arrived at the gym, Whitney held out her warrant card for the girl behind the reception desk to see.

'I'm Detective Chief Inspector Walker. Can you point me in the direction of Scott Marshall, please?'

'I'm sorry you've just missed him. He left about five minutes ago to grab a coffee and then head back to his snooker club where there's a tournament going on.'

'Damn,' she muttered. They'd have to go back to the snooker club and catch him there.

'Does he have a locker?' George asked.

She hadn't thought about that. Although how likely was it that the murder weapon would be in there?

'Yes, in the male changing rooms.'

'Where are they, and which one is his?' Whitney asked.

'Down there.' She pointed down the corridor. 'I'll check the locker list for his number.' She picked up a folder on the desk and opened it. 'Scott's is 431.'

'Is the manager here? We need permission to go into it?'

'I'll call her.' She pulled over a microphone and pressed

the button. 'Hallie York to reception, please. Hallie York to reception.'

'Don't you need Marshall's permission?' George asked.

'No. The manager's will suffice as the gym owns the lockers.'

'Here she is.' The receptionist said, as the double doors to the right of reception opened and a woman in gym gear headed towards them.

'What is it, Kylie?'

'The police.'

'DCI Walker,' Whitney said, stepping forward and holding our her warrant card. 'We'd like permission to take a look in Scott Marshall's locker. I'm assuming that when people hire lockers they sign an agreement allowing you to open them at any time.'

'That's right, they do. What are you looking for?'

'It's part of an ongoing enquiry.'

'Kylie, pass me the locker master key.' She took the key from the receptionist. 'Each locker owner sets their own keypad code. This will override it.'

They followed her down the corridor and to the changing rooms.

'Is anyone in here?' Hallie called out, pushing the door open a few inches. After waiting a couple of seconds and there being no reply, she opened the door fully, and they entered the large changing room, which had wooden benches along three of the walls and one going down the middle. The showers were on the left and there was a bank of lockers to the rear. 'This is Scott's. I'll open it for you.'

'Thanks. You can leave us now,' Whitney said, once the locker was open. 'Please make sure that no one comes in here until we've finished.'

Whitney waited until she'd left, pulled on some dispos-able gloves, gave a pair to George, and then opened the door fully. 'What a mess,' she said, looking at everything piled high. She took out her phone and photographed each item in situ. 'Hold out your hands so I can pass some things over. He's got two fitness training manuals, a sponge bag with razor, shampoo, shower gel, deodorant, and aftershave.' She zipped up the bag and gave it to George. 'Two pairs of trainers. Why? Surely he'd only need one.'

'Can I put these things on the bench as my arms are full?'

'Yes, okay. What's this?' she said standing on tiptoe and feeling towards the back of the locker. It was a towel with something wrapped up inside it. She turned to George. 'There's something at the back which I can't see. Can you take a photo of it before I pull it out.' She held out her phone and stepped out of the way while George approached.

'How many photos do you need?'

'Take one from each angle.'

Whitney waited while George took several.

'Done. Do you want me to take the item out of the locker, or do you have to?' George asked.

'You can.' She waited while George extracted it and handed it to her. She opened the towel. 'Bloody hell. A handgun. I've got an evidence bag in my right-hand jacket pocket. Can you reach it?'

'Yes,' George said, pulling it out.

'Good. Open it up and let me drop this towel and gun in there. I'll keep it wrapped so the gym staff can't see what we've found. We need to get back to the station pronto and get this to forensics.' She piled everything back into the locker, pushed the door shut, which automatically locked, and then returned to reception, where the manager was stationed. 'The changing rooms are to be locked. No one is allowed in there. I'll be arranging for forensics to go in there.'

'Why?'

'I'm not at liberty to explain, other than to say they are now part of an investigation.'

'How long will they be closed for?'

'At least for the rest of the day, maybe longer. Please ensure no one is told of our visit here.' She looked from the manager to the receptionist. 'We'll be in touch if we need anything further from you.' They walked away, and once out of earshot she turned to George. 'Once we get back to the station, I'll instruct uniform to bring Marshall in again for questioning. This could be the murder weapon, but we need confirmation from forensics.'

'It's a bit convenient if it is,' George said, shaking her head.

'Is it? He wasn't to know we'd be tracking him down at the gym. He probably stashed it there before getting rid of it.'

'Maybe,' George said.

'You're not convinced.'

'I don't doubt that we've found the weapon. My hesitation is around Scott Marshall being the murderer. I'd like more concrete evidence because, at the moment, it feels like we're being led in that direction.'

'Who do you think it is then?'

'I'm not prepared to comment without further evidence.'

'You can be most infuriating. I'm going to phone Claire to let her know that we've found the gun.' She pulled out her phone and pressed speed dial for the pathologist.

'Dexter.'

'It's Whitney. We've located a handgun which might be the murder weapon in the shooting of Ryan Armstrong.

Do you want to see it first before it gets dropped off at forensics?'

'I can't do anything with it here, so take it straight there. Ballistics will look at the gun and check the markings on the bullet and those found in the body. They'll also fire the gun into some cloth and take a look at the residue patterns to see if they match the ones on the clothing belonging to the victim. If all of this matches, it's the weapon.'

'Okay, we'll do that. Thanks.' Whitney ended the call. 'Claire just explained to me the process they go through for identifying whether the gun was used in the shooting. I know all of that, as we've had shootings before, so why do it now?'

'Could be the result of that meeting she went to with the Chief Constable about improving relationships?' George suggested.

'Maybe. But it's still weird.'

Chapter 30

Once Whitney was back at the station, after George had dropped her off, she took the gun to forensics, went to the incident room and updated the team on their discoveries. She'd hoped that Clifford would be there so he could hear the latest, but he wasn't at the desk where he usually sat.

'Brian, contact uniform and ask them to bring in Scott Marshall for questioning. He should be back at the snooker club by now. Meena, I'll forward photos of the gun we found. Print off several copies. Frank, did you see Marshall's car?'

'Yes, guv, I tracked him as far as I could and he was heading in the direction of his house, and nowhere near the club.'

'Damn. But that doesn't mean he didn't go out again.'

'Nothing showed on the cameras, but there are routes he could take where he could avoid them, if he knows the area well. Or he could've used a different car, or phoned for a taxi.'

'Okay. I'm going to let the super know what's going on.'

The super's door was open when she arrived, and she knocked gently and stuck her head around.

'Come in, Whitney. Good news, I hope.'

'Yes, ma'am. We're closing in on the murderer. A handgun was found in Scott Marshall's gym locker, and forensics are currently examining it to confirm whether it's the murder weapon. We'll need a search warrant for the Marshall house and the Palace Snooker Club.'

'Excellent work. Leave it with me, I'll make sure the warrants are expedited. Solving this case can't come soon enough. Do we have a motive? How does it fit in with DI Clifford's case?'

'We've yet to learn the motive, although it is pointing to being linked to the affair between Scott Marshall and the victim's wife. If that's the case, it's unlikely to be anything to do with the syndicate being investigated by Clifford. That means he'll return to the Met. Which I'm not unhappy about.'

'Has there been a problem?' The super scrutinised her face.

Whitney squirmed in her seat. She hated that the woman could do that to her. 'Not at all, ma'am. If anything, we've developed a good working relationship. But that doesn't alter the fact that having two potential bosses, you and Clifford's superior, is a recipe for disaster.'

'As long as I don't hear from the Met that we've been obstructive, that's fine. I'll let you know once the warrants arrive.'

As all they had to do was wait, she decided to pop down to the canteen and buy a coffee. It seemed ages since her last caffeine fix, and she was desperate for one. She took the lift to the ground floor and as she pushed open the canteen door, she spotted Clifford near the front of the queue. She'd break the news about Marshall to him now, to save doing it upstairs in front of everyone.

'Coffee and a chocolate muffin for me,' she said as she approached him.

'Okay, guv.'

'I'll find us a table and we can have a chat.'

She headed to the corner, away from prying ears, as she was still conscious of the need to keep the Met operation secret from everyone.

'You have something to tell me?' Clifford said, when he arrived at the table carrying a tray with coffee and muffins.

'I have good news and bad news.'

'Start with the good.'

'We've recovered what we believe is the murder weapon and should be arresting the killer shortly.'

'And the bad?'

'It's Scott Marshall, so you've lost your informant.'

'Damn. Are you sure about this?'

'The gun was found in his locker at the gym.'

'It could have been planted.'

'Yes, that's correct, so it's not a slam dunk. We're waiting for a search warrant to go through his house and the club. Uniform are being instructed to bring him in as we speak.'

'I'd like to interview with you because, as yet, we don't know the motive. What he told us in his previous interview could have been a pack of lies. The fact he's agreed to work for me could be a double bluff. The syndicate might have authorised him to work with me, so they have a plant. They could have murdered Armstrong to get Marshall in with the special squad.'

'That's stretching it, but as we don't know for certain then yes, I agree for us to interview him together.'

'Do you have an alternative suggested motive to mine?' he asked.

'To get Armstrong out of the way so he could be with Naomi. Saves the bother of a messy divorce for her.'

'Except that *he* would end up with one instead, as his wife invested in the club. And don't forget, Naomi was the one who mentioned them moving in together. I got the feeling from Marshall that it probably wasn't going to happen. There's got to be something else. This doesn't sit right.'

'If you're talking about having a gut feeling, then make sure not to mention it to George.'

He laughed, it was deep and warm. 'My lips are sealed. Will Dr Cavendish be with us for the interview?'

'No, her day job beckoned.'

'Day job?'

'Just a joke. She sometimes spends more time here than she does at the university. We'll manage fine without her.'

'I don't doubt that. I must admit I found it exceptionally useful having her whispering in my ear, so to speak. It's not something I've done before, but will see about introducing it.'

'Good luck finding someone.' She picked up her mug and took a large swallow of coffee, enjoying the warmth as it travelled down her throat. Then she took a large bite of her muffin and just about managed not to groan as the chocolate liquid centre oozed into her mouth. Her phone rang, and she picked it up. 'Walker.'

'Marshall's in interview room three, guv,' Meena said.

'Thanks. Bring down a brown folder with a photo of the weapon inside. We'll meet you there in five minutes.'

They finished their coffees and left for the interview room, where Meena was waiting.

Armed with the folder, Whitney and Clifford went in to confront Marshall, who jumped up when they walked in.

'What the hell's going on? Why was I brought in by officers in uniform so everyone at the club could see?' He looked at Clifford. 'And you want my help? Well, you're going a funny way about it.'

'Sit down,' Whitney snapped, with such force that the man immediately dropped back down onto his chair. She pressed the recording equipment. 'Mr Marshall, we're—'

'Oh, suddenly you're calling me *Mr Marshall*. What's going on? Do I need a solicitor?'

'You're entitled to have one, if you wish. At the moment, we just want to question you about certain aspects of our investigation.'

'Am I under arrest?'

'You're helping us with our enquiries. But, if you attempt to leave, I may be forced to arrest you.'

'For what?'

'The murder of Ryan Armstrong.'

'But that's ridiculous. I didn't do it. We've had this conversation already and you know that I was at home after going to meet Naomi and her not turning up.'

'According to you, but there's nobody to vouch for you.'

'Has something else happened? Is there a reason for me being brought back in?' His voice slowed, uncertainty in his eyes.

Whitney opened the folder and took out the photo of the gun. She slid it across the table. 'Do you recognise this?'

He pulled it forward. 'It's a photo of a gun.'

'Do you recognise which gun?'

His brow furrowed as he continued staring at the photo. 'I think so.'

'Guess where we found it?'

He didn't appear concerned. Was it an act, so he could pretend he had no knowledge of how the gun got in his locker?

'In my father-in-law's gun cabinet?'

What the …

'Explain?'

'It looks like the gun my father-in-law owns. It's a family heirloom and belonged to Jess's grandfather. It's hers now, but she keeps it with her father because it's illegal to own one and she was worried about being found with it.'

Was that why Jessica said that neither she nor her father owned a gun?

'This handgun was placed at the back of your locker at the gym, wrapped in a towel.'

'Why were you looking in my locker?'

'We went to the gym to find you and took a look while we were there. We had permission from the manager. We're awaiting confirmation from forensics that this gun is the murder weapon.' A slight exaggeration, but he wasn't to know.

Colour drained from his face and his body went rigid. 'B-but … it can't be. How … I mean … it … No. This is … I didn't shoot Ryan. I swear on my son's life. It …' His voice faded away.

Whitney glanced at Clifford whose expression was unreadable. Was he being taken in by Marshall's denial?

'How do you account for it being in your locker?'

'It must have been planted. Do you really think I'd leave it there if it was me? I'm being framed, I tell you. You have to believe me.'

'By whom?' Clifford asked.

'I don't know. Someone who knew about the gun and

thought they'd use me as a scapegoat by stealing it and using it to kill Ryan.'

'That demands a huge stretch of the imagination. It's an illegal weapon that nobody knew about. Unless you're suggesting it was your wife? Or her father,' Whitney said.

'Of course I'm not. She was at her parents' house when he was killed. And why would she shoot Ryan? We were all friends. It makes no sense … I don't know …' He threw his hands up in despair. 'I need my solicitor.'

'Yes. I think maybe you do. But, in the meantime, Scott Marshall, I'm arresting you on suspicion of murdering Ryan Armstrong. You do not have to say anything, but it may harm your defence if you do not mention when questioned something which you later rely on in court. Anything you do say may be given in evidence. Do you understand?'

'This is ridiculous.'

'Do you understand?' she repeated.

'Yes, I understand. I'm not stupid. But you are if you think that I'd shoot my best friend. Instead of accusing me you should be out there finding the real killer. It's …' His voice fell away, and he slumped forward, resting his head on his hands.

'You may phone your solicitor and then you'll be taken to one of the cells until they arrive and we'll resume this interview.'

She escorted Marshall to the custody suite and went back to find Clifford who was waiting for her.

'There's something we're missing,' Clifford said, a puzzled expression in his dark eyes.

'If there is, then we'll find it. That's what we're good at. Let's see if the super has managed to fast track the search warrants.'

Chapter 31

'Guv, the warrants have arrived,' Brian said, as soon as she walked into the incident room with Clifford.

'Wow, that was quick. The super's certainly excelled herself today.'

'They've also called from the custody suite to say that Marshall's solicitor won't be here for another three hours.'

'Perfect, that gives us time to look around the house. Doug and Meena you can come with me. We'll go shortly, I've got a call to make. Brian, I want you to take Frank and pay a visit to Gordon Elliott, Marshall's father-in-law. Ask him to check his gun cabinet for the handgun he has. He might try to deny having it because it's illegal, but explain that we know he has it and that we believe it's been stolen and used in the murder of Ryan Armstrong. That should ensure he cooperates with us. I want to know when he last saw it and who has access to the cabinet.'

'Yes, guv.'

She turned, intending to go to her office when Clifford stepped towards her.

'What about me? I'd like to be a part of the search,' he said, in a low voice.

Damn. She'd forgotten about him. Though, the more the merrier and he could be useful.

'Sure, if you want to. I'll be back in a minute.'

She hurried to her office and pulled out the phone from her pocket. The call she had to make wasn't for work. Martin had left her a voicemail. He wanted to take her and Tiffany out for dinner on Saturday and, with the case virtually solved, she couldn't see there would be a problem. She'd texted Tiffany to ask what she thought, and she was very keen.

'Whitney,' he said. 'Thanks for getting back to me. Is Saturday okay?'

'Yes, we'd love to go out with you. I do have a message from Tiffany, though. She asked for it not to be anywhere too fancy as she's got nothing to wear.'

'I was thinking of The Swan pub between Lenchester and Long Buckby, if that's okay. I found it online, and the menu looks good.'

'Yes, I'm sure that would be perfect.'

'Shall I pick you both up at six?'

'Yes. The only thing …' She paused.

'What?'

'Nothing.' She didn't want to jinx it. She ended the call and returned to the incident room. 'Everyone ready?' she called.

Clifford came over to her. 'Whose car are we going in?'

'Not mine. What do you drive?'

'A BMW 6 Series.'

'That'll do nicely.' She glanced across at the others. 'Doug, take Meena, I'm going with DI Clifford.'

'Okay, guv. We'll see you there.'

'You don't like to drive?' Clifford asked as they left the incident room for the station car park.

'I don't mind driving, but I like to be in comfort and as I'm surrounded by people with nice cars I take advantage. You'd understand if you saw the sorry state of my old banger.'

'I've had my fair share of those.'

She found that hard to believe but didn't pursue it. George would have been proud of her restraint.

It took twenty minutes to reach Favell Drive, and Clifford parked outside behind Doug, who was already there. Whitney headed up the path, with the others close behind her, and rang the doorbell. Jessica Marshall answered within a few seconds.

'Mrs Marshall, we have a warrant to search your house.' She held it out for the woman to see, but all she took was a cursory look.

'Why? You've already been here.'

Clearly Scott's solicitor hadn't contacted her to inform her of what was happening. Whitney would have to do that herself.

'Things have progressed since we saw you last, and we have your husband in custody. He's been charged with the murder of Ryan Armstrong.'

Jessica grabbed hold of the door frame, terror in her eyes. 'What? It can't be true. He wouldn't. I know him. I can't believe it. You must have got it wrong. Why do you think it's Scott?'

'Sorry, there's nothing more I can tell you at this stage.' She rested her hand on Jessica's arm, wanting to calm her. 'We're going to be here for a while. Is there somewhere you and your son can go, like your parents' house, and we can let you know when we've finished here?'

'Yes,' she nodded. 'They won't mind us going there.'

Damn. She'd sent Brian there. It had briefly slipped her mind.

'Actually is there anywhere closer, in case we need to speak to you?'

'My sister, Jackie, lives in the next street. I'm sure she won't mind me calling round.'

'Perfect. The nanny should go with you, too.'

'She's not here. I gave her the day off.'

'I'd like her contact details before you go. She's to be questioned because she lives with you. We'll be interviewing you again, later, too.'

Jessica took out her phone. 'Her name's Susan Bedford, and this is her number,' she said, showing it to Whitney, who wrote it down in her notebook. 'Will everything be left in a mess?'

'We'll make sure to put things back as we go through. I'll come with you while you grab whatever you need.'

'Okay.'

Whitney walked into the house with the woman, leaving the others outside. They first went into the lounge where the little boy was playing in a playpen. Jessica picked up her handbag from the side and then took hold of her son. 'Come on, Leo. We're going to see Auntie Jackie.' The little boy grinned and clapped his hands.

'He's a cutie,' Whitney said, smiling.

'Thanks. He's my life,' she said, stroking the top of her son's head. 'When can I see my husband?'

'Not yet. He's waiting for his solicitor before we resume interviewing him.'

'Okay. I understand.'

Whitney escorted Jessica to her car, which was parked in the garage, and waited until she had driven away before ushering the others in to do their search. 'Right, let's spread out and see what we can find. Anything to confirm we have the right person in custody. Don't make a mess, if at all possible.'

After looking through the study, and discovering nothing incriminating, Whitney headed upstairs and into the son's bedroom. It was white with a life-sized Spider-Man painted on the wall opposite the small bed. Clifford was standing beside the white chest of drawers, holding a dark brown teddy bear.

'I didn't have you down as a stuffed animal lover.'

'Appearances can be deceptive. Just like this is. It's a nanny cam. People put them in their houses so they can check up on what their nannies or babysitters are doing.'

'Good find. I am aware of what they are.'

'In which case you know that, most likely, there will be others in the house, if they're keeping an eye on the nanny.'

'We can use them to look for evidence against Scott Marshall. Where do the recordings go to?'

'Usually a phone, tablet, or laptop, through an app.'

She hurried down the stairs and called out to the others. 'Stop what you're doing and turn your attention to finding hidden cameras. There was one in the son's bedroom in a teddy bear.'

After half an hour of concerted effort, they'd found cameras in the lounge, dining room, kitchen and hall.

'Now what?' Doug asked.

'We look for a laptop or tablet, to which the recordings could be downloaded,' Clifford said.

'There's an iPad in the kitchen on the table,' Meena said. 'That was the only electronic device I came across.'

'We'll get that back to the station now. You two stay and finish the search,' she said to Doug and Meena.

Clifford drove them back, and she headed straight over to Ellie.

'We're looking for recordings from nanny cams on here. I know it's an iPad, but can you get into it using the self-service kiosk? Does it work the same as a phone?'

'Sorry, guv. I can only get into mobiles. I'll get it over to Mac in forensics and see if he can start working on it straight away.'

'Thanks. Please stress the urgency. We're hoping the recordings from the cameras will show Marshall with the gun. If anyone can get him to do it quickly, you can.'

'Leave it with me.'

'I'm going to contact the Marshalls' nanny and get her in for an interview. She might have witnessed something.'

She went into her office, took her notepad from her pocket and called the number she'd written down.

'Hello, Sue speaking.'

'This is DCI Walker from Lenchester CID. We'd like to talk to you as soon as possible about the Marshall family. It's urgent. Where are you at the moment?'

'I'm in a café with my friend. I can be with you in forty minutes, or so, if that's okay?'

'I'll let the front desk know to expect you. Please don't mention to anyone that you're coming here.'

After ending the call, she decided to contact George.

'Whitney, is there a problem?' the psychologist said, dispensing with any pleasantries.

'I was hoping you could get back here. We've arrested Scott Marshall, and the interview has been halted until his solicitor arrives. I'd value your input.'

'I'll see what I can do, but no promises.'

Chapter 32

'Gordon Elliott's gun's missing, guv,' Brian said, when he arrived back at the incident room, and had come over to where she was standing by the board. 'He kept it in a locked cabinet in the garage and couldn't remember the last time he'd looked at it. It took a while for him to admit to having it.'

'Where did he keep the key?'

'In his desk drawer. Unlocked. Would you believe.' He shook his head. 'It means that anyone could've taken it. I've arranged for SOCO to go there to fingerprint the gun cabinet and the desk. Marshall often visits so he could've easily found a way to take the weapon without being discovered.'

'Did he mention that he'd given the gun to his daughter as a keepsake?'

She wrote the name *Elliott* on the board with an arrow to the word *gun*.

'No, but I did, and he said it wasn't true. That the gun was his. Probably to protect her because it's an illegal weapon. Not that we can prove otherwise.'

'Did you inform him that it was the murder weapon and ask for an alibi?'

'Yes, I did. He was in bed at the time of the murder with his wife. His daughter was there also, as we already know.'

'Guv, Susan Bedford has arrived,' Meena called over. 'They've put her in interview room one.'

'Thanks. She's the Marshalls' nanny,' she said to Brian. 'Let's go and speak to her,'

'Wouldn't you rather take DI Clifford?' Brian nodded over to the far corner where Clifford was seated looking at the computer screen.

'Don't you want to interview with me?'

'Yes, of course I do, it just … It doesn't matter, I'll grab my jacket.'

They headed out the office and once out of earshot she turned to him.

'Have you felt excluded during this investigation?'

'Not left out intentionally, but I know how difficult it is having DI Clifford here. I have first-hand knowledge of how the Met guys view themselves.'

Ah. So that was it. She'd thought Brian of all people wouldn't have let that bother him.

'DI Clifford isn't too bad, to be honest. I've known a lot worse. He has to be included in parts of the enquiry, but I don't think questioning the nanny is going to make any difference to his syndicate operation. The whole point in this interview is to learn more about what goes on in the Marshall household. In particular, what she's seen between Scott and Jessica that might assist in our interview with Scott once his solicitor arrives.'

'But didn't you take DI Clifford with you to interview him?'

'Yes, I did.'

'So shouldn't he come with you now?'

'Stop trying to talk yourself out of being part of the investigation. I took Clifford to the earlier interview because Scott Marshall might have had information on the syndicate. As I've just explained, speaking to the nanny is different.'

This sensitive side of her sergeant was unnerving. It wasn't how she'd expected him to act.

'Okay, guv. I'll just be glad when the Met is well away from us and we can get back to life as normal.'

'You can say that again.'

'I'll just be glad when …' He laughed.

'Don't you start. You've been spending too much time with Frank and Doug.' She shook her head in exasperation.

'Guilty as charged,' he said, holding up both hands.

They reached the interview room, where seated behind the table there was a young woman in her early twenties, with short red hair in a pixie cut. She was fiddling nervously with the edge of her blue and white striped cardigan.

'Susan Bedford?' Whitney said.

'Yes. Everyone calls me Sue.'

'Thank you for coming in.' Whitney pressed the button on the recording equipment. 'Interview with Detective Chief Inspector Walker and Detective Sergeant Chapman. And … please state your full name.

'Susan Bedford.'

'We'd like to talk to you about the Marshall family. How long have you been working for them?'

The young woman sat upright in her seat and stared directly at Whitney. 'I've been with them for twelve months as nanny for Leo.'

'Was this your first nannying job?'

'Yes, as a private nanny. After training as a nursery nurse, I worked in a nursery for five years in Leamington Spa.'

'Why did you move to Lenchester?'

'I saw the job advertised when I was looking to get away after splitting up with my boyfriend. The Marshalls asked me over for an interview and offered me the job on the spot, subject to references. I couldn't believe my luck. Leo's a lovely little boy and Mr and Mrs Marshall seemed nice, so I accepted. They also provided accommodation as it was a live-in position, so it was perfect.'

'How do you find working with Mrs Marshall? Do you get on well with her? Are there any arguments?'

'I have no complaints. She's very fair and gives me time off every week. I get paid regularly and always on time. You do hear stories from other nannies, but I've got no complaints in that respect.'

'Were you informed about the nanny cams in the rooms?'

Sue's mouth dropped open. 'No, I didn't know they had them.'

'Does that bother you?'

'No. Well, maybe. Sort of. I should have been told they were going to check up on me.'

'Wouldn't that defeat the object of the cameras?'

'In a way. But it's still an invasion of my privacy.'

Whitney could see her point. Even if she was behaving appropriately and not doing anything wrong, there were still things that a person wouldn't want others to see them doing.

'How do you get on with Mr Marshall?'

'Um … He …' She averted her eyes and stared at the table.

'Anything you say will be between us.'

'I don't want to risk losing my job, but to be honest he gives me the creeps. I don't like being left alone in the house with him. He's got this funny way about him where he invades your space. You know, gets in your bubble. I spend all my time stepping away from him.' She shuddered.

Not again. Was there any woman out there who was safe in his vicinity?

'Has he tried it on with you?'

'Not exactly. It's difficult to explain, but I get the feeling that if I made a move, he wouldn't refuse.'

'Does he act in the same way when Mrs Marshall's around?'

Whitney needed to find out if he was like that all the time without it meaning anything. It wouldn't excuse the behaviour but it would give her some perspective.

'When they're together, he doesn't get close to me at all. If anything, he's always touching Mrs Marshall. Taking hold of her hand. Stroking her shoulder. It was a bit over the top, if you ask me.'

Interesting.

'I'd like to ask you about Ryan Armstrong, Scott's friend and business partner, who was recently shot. Did you ever meet him?'

'Yes, he'd often come to the house. He was really nice and always took the time to speak to me. It was such a shock to hear he'd been killed. I really liked him.'

'Did you witness any arguments at all between him and Mr Marshall?'

She bit down on her bottom lip and glanced upwards. 'Not arguments as such.'

'What do you mean?'

'One time when he was over, I did overhear them having a disagreement over the staff at the snooker club.

Mr Armstrong accused Mr Marshall of being too friendly with them and said that some of them didn't like it.'

'Did it sound as though Mr Marshall was acting towards them in the same way he did with you?'

'It did seem sort of similar, now I come to think of it.'

'Do you know whether Mr Marshall has had any affairs in the past?'

'Recently, I suspected that he was seeing someone when I heard him on the phone. He didn't realise he could be heard because he was in the garden. But sometimes, if the wind is in the right direction, a voice travels. He was telling this person he'd try to get away and then said he loved them. I knew it couldn't be Mrs Marshall because she was upstairs working out on her treadmill.'

'Did you tell Mrs Marshall what you'd heard?'

'No way would I do that. It was nothing to do with me. Plus, I didn't want to risk losing my job, especially as I didn't know for certain. I could've been mistaken.'

'Where were you the early hours of Sunday, March the seventh, the night that Mr Armstrong was shot?'

'I can tell you exactly. I went back to Leamington Spa to see my family. Mrs Marshall went to stay with her parents and I had a weekend off because she didn't need me.'

'Can anyone vouch for you?'

'My parents can. I can give you their number. I took the train on Friday evening, arriving at seven, and then came back first thing Monday morning. My dad picked me up from the station and took me back there.'

'Don't you have a car?'

'Not one of my own. For work, I use one of the Marshalls' cars.'

'Is there anything you can think of which might assist in our enquiries into Ryan Armstrong's shooting?'

'Nothing. I'm sorry. But why are you asking me? Do you suspect Mr Marshall? I couldn't imagine him doing something like that. They were friends.'

'We're just covering all bases. Thank you for coming in to see us, you've been very helpful. Please remember to keep this interview confidential.'

Chapter 33

'George, over here.' She scanned the area and saw Whitney beckoning her over to the station's front desk, where she was standing with Brian and Clifford.

'Sorry I couldn't make it any sooner. Have I missed the interview?' she said as she approached them.

'No, we're on our way. I wanted to wait a few minutes to see if you made it. You can join Seb in the observation area.'

Whitney's phone rang. She pulled it from her pocket and held it to her ear. 'Walker.' She nodded. 'Thanks.' She ended the call. 'That was Ellie. She said forensics have been in touch and the gun we found is the murder weapon.'

'That was quick,' George said.

'They rushed it through. It had been wiped clean, so no prints. That would be too much to expect, but not crucial.'

Brian pushed open the doors, and they all headed down the corridor to the interview room. George and Clifford split off and went to observe.

'I'm surprised you didn't ask to interview with Whitney, rather than observing with me,' she said to Clifford once they were seated on the stools looking through the one-way mirror.

'She wanted Brian in with her. Do you think it would have made a difference if I'd asked to be included?'

'Probably not. Once Whitney has made up her mind, it takes a lot to change it. She's always believed this shooting isn't connected to your operation, and it appears she might be right.'

He shrugged. 'We'll see. What do you make of the suspect?'

'Look at the tight lines around his eyes and the way he's pressing his thumbs together in his lap. He's worried. Extremely so. Whether that's because he's guilty, or innocent and scared no one will believe him, is a different matter.'

'But—'

'Stop talking, I want to listen to the interview.' She turned her head away from him and focused on the scene in front of her. She much preferred being on her own so she could concentrate.

'Interview with Scott Marshall resumed,' Whitney said, after starting the recording equipment. 'DS Chapman replacing DI Clifford. In addition, we have …' She nodded at the solicitor.

'Beatrice Bloom, solicitor for Scott Marshall.'

'Mr Marshall, we'd like to discuss in more detail your relationship with Ryan Armstrong.'

'He was my friend and business partner.'

'Would you say that you got on well?'

'Yes, of course we did. We've been friends and practice partners for years, which is why we decided to buy the snooker club together. When he was shot … it was like … like losing my right arm.' His eyes went glassy.

'The truth?' Clifford asked her.

'I'm not seeing anything to dispute it.'

'Can you remember the last time you had a disagreement?' Whitney asked.

'What are you trying to say? That I shot him because of a falling out?' He banged both fists on the table. 'I've already told you I don't know how that gun got into my locker. It was planted by someone. You have to believe me.' He turned to his solicitor. 'It's the truth.'

She rested her hand on his arm. 'I know.'

'We'll come back to the gun shortly. Let's return to you and Ryan. Would you say it was a volatile relationship?'

'No, we never argued.'

'You were overheard arguing at your house about your relationship with the staff at the snooker club. How do you account for that?'

'Who told you? My wife?'

'Mr Marshall, please answer the question.'

He leant in and exchanged words with his solicitor.

'No comment.'

Whitney let out an exasperated sigh. 'You're not helping your case. I'll ask you again, did you and Ryan Armstrong argue?'

'Sometimes we had disagreements, but we were no different from any other business partnership, especially when regarding the direction to take a business.'

'Were your disagreements to do with your manager and the bets he was taking on the side?'

'We didn't ever discuss that. It was things like me buying beer from another source and breaking our contract with the brewery. He was worried it would get us in trouble. When he played snooker, he'd take plenty of risks, but away from the table he was so risk-averse it wasn't funny.'

'Did Ryan know about your affair with his wife and that she was going to leave him for you?'

'Nothing was definite about us moving in together and, no, he wasn't aware of the affair because we were careful.'

'You mentioned in our previous interview that you'd had relationships with other women over the years?'

He coloured. 'What's that got to do with Ryan being shot?'

'Who were these women?'

'They were in the past and nothing to do with Ryan's shooting, or my affair with Naomi. If that's all you're going to ask me then take me back to the cell because I'm done talking.'

'She needs to end this line of questioning,' Clifford said, running his fingers through his hair.

'Be patient and wait for a moment. She knows what she's doing,' George replied.

'I'd like to discuss the gun which you say was planted. Who would do that to you?' Whitney leant forward slightly.

George approved of the manoeuvre, as it gave her the upper hand.

'You were right,' Clifford acknowledged.

'How the hell do I know?' Marshall said. 'That's your job to find out, not mine.'

'Who knows which gym you use and how often you go there?'

'Lots of people. Friends, family, employees. Everyone at the gym. It's not a secret.'

'And your wife's *family heirloom*. Is anyone aware that Jessica owns it and her father looks after it?'

'I don't know. My father-in-law might have told people about it.' He shrugged.

'Why would someone want to frame you?'

'How the hell do I know?'

'You must have thought about it and come up with some suspects.'

'Why don't you do your job properly and find out, because I don't know. All I can tell you is it's not me who shot Ryan.'

'When did you last handle the handgun?'

'The gun belongs to Jess and her father. I don't *handle* it.'

'Are you saying you've never touched it?'

'I don't remember. Maybe a few years ago. But not recently. You have to believe me.'

'The murder weapon was found in your locker.'

'Were my fingerprints on it?'

'No.'

'So that's proof it wasn't me.'

'There were no prints on there at all as it had been wiped clean.'

'What do I have to say to get you to believe me?'

'Try the truth,' Brian said. 'Because you're facing a very long prison sentence. And it won't be like Butlins, either. Maximum security prison. Locked up for most of the day. Limited fresh air. You'd love it, it'll be just like a walk in the park.'

His eyebrows drew in together. 'This is ridiculous. You've made up your mind and won't listen to anything I say.'

'You have no alibi for the time during which the shooting took place,' Whitney said.

'I was at home. How many times do I have to tell you?'

'But conveniently no one can vouch for you. The

nanny was away for the weekend and your wife and son were with her parents. You can see that it's not looking good. Why don't you admit to killing Ryan Armstrong and make it easier on yourself? It will go in your favour. You're already facing a long prison sentence, it could be even longer if you don't cooperate.'

'I. Didn't. Do. It.' He folded his arms tightly across his chest, his eyes narrow slits as he stared in their direction.

Whitney's body stiffened. 'Interview suspended. DS Chapman will escort you back to your cell.'

'What about bail?'

'That's for the judge to decide.'

Whitney came into the observation room.

'Your view?' George asked.

'It would be nice if, just for once, a culprit would fess up once they were caught, without us having to go through all this crap to nail them.'

'You don't believe he was framed?' Clifford asked.

'George?'

'He was certainly in a state of shock after Brian explained what was likely to happen to him.'

'Maybe the shock was over being caught. Armstrong could have found out about the affair with his wife and confronted Marshall. It turned nasty and, believing he was about to lose everything, Marshall went to the in-laws' house, under some pretext or other, took the handgun, called Armstrong and asked him to meet at the club to sort it out once and for all. Except how could he have got into the garage to take the gun without anyone knowing? Especially as he'd need to get hold of the key first. We need to go back over the CCTV footage. There's got to be something.'

'We should also check taxis and Uber. If it was Marshall, he could have left his car at his house, so it looked like he was there,' George said, as they walked into the incident room.

'Stop what you're doing and listen,' Whitney called to her team. 'We've just reinterviewed Marshall, who continues to claim he's been set up, despite us finding the weapon in his locker,' Whitney said. 'Frank, go back over all the CCTV footage again and check the comings and goings at the Armstrong and Marshall houses. Like you said earlier, he could have sneaked out on foot and called a taxi to take him to the club to meet the victim.'

'Yes, guv,' said Frank. 'But I don't think I missed anything.'

'Someone needs to get onto taxi companies and Uber, to see if they had a passenger fitting his description.'

'I'll do that, guv,' Meena said.

'Okay.' Whitney looked at her watch. 'It's getting late. We'll finish now and I want everyone in early so we can get cracking on nailing Marshall. The clock's ticking, and he'll have to be released without charge in thirty-six hours if we can't find something more concrete to nail him.'

'Like the gun found in his locker isn't enough,' Frank said, letting out an infuriated sigh.

'You know how this works, Frank. Reasonable doubt. Was the gun planted … blah, blah, blah,'

'Yeah, I know, guv.'

'Do you want me, too?' George asked.

'Yes, please, if you can make it.'

'I can stay late tonight if you want,' Frank said.

'Okay, own up,' Doug said. 'Who's stolen Frank and replaced him with some form of AI?'

Frank frowned. 'AI?'

'Artificial intelligence. Come on, Frank, you're not that old. Even you should know what that means.'

'Fuck off.' He stared daggers at Doug.

'No, you fuck off.'

'For goodness' sake, will the two of you please give it a rest. We do have a visitor here, in case you'd forgotten.' Whitney nodded at Clifford.

'Don't mind me,' Clifford said. 'I'm thoroughly enjoying the floor show.'

'Believe it or not, they are the best of friends. And, Frank, I'm sort of with Doug on this. Won't your wife mind you staying late?'

'She's going out with a friend for the evening.'

'And poor Frank doesn't want to be on his own in the house.' Doug laughed.

'It's up to you if you want to start having a look,' Whitney said. 'But I still want you here early tomorrow morning.'

Chapter 34

George looked up from her book when she heard the front door open. Ross walked into the kitchen holding a large bunch of yellow, pink and red tulips.

'I bought these for you,' he said, smiling.

'Thank you. What's the occasion?' She took them from him, placed them on the draining board, and went to the cupboard, taking out a Stuart crystal barrel-shaped vase that had once belonged to her grandmother.

'Only you would ask that. Aren't I allowed to buy you flowers?' He tilted his head to one side.

'For no reason?'

Was she being over-analytical?

'Well, there is something I'd like to discuss.' He rolled his shoulders.

She froze. What was he anxious about?

Three months ago he'd asked her to move in with him, so they could be together all the time. She'd agreed. The time they'd spent apart after she'd ended their relationship had made her realise that she would be unhappy without him. She wasn't going to make the same mistake twice.

The only problem they'd faced was work. She needed to be close to the university and the police station, and, as a sculptor, he needed a studio large enough to work in. They'd ended up splitting their time. During the week they stayed at her house and at the weekend they were at his.

Ross didn't mind commuting, he said it helped clear his head.

It was the perfect arrangement and nothing like when she'd previously lived with someone. Ross gave her space when she needed it, and didn't insist on the TV blaring all the time. Nor did he get annoyed when she had to work. She had no regrets. Did he? Or was she overthinking? Would a person bring flowers if they were discontented?

'Would you like some wine before you start?' she suggested, as she filled the vase with water and arranged the flowers, enjoying their apple-like aroma.

'That would be nice.'

She poured them both a glass of red, from the bottle they'd opened the other night, and sucked in an anticipatory breath.

'I have a suggestion. Please hear me out and don't say no straightaway.'

He pulled out a chair and sat at the table. She sat opposite, so she could see his face to gauge his reaction to whatever she said in response to his suggestion.

'I'm not impulsive, I will give your idea some thought before making a decision.'

This wasn't what she'd been expecting.

'I know that.' He took a sip of wine. 'Living together has been great and we've managed very well considering our busy lives, don't you agree?'

'Yes.' She nodded in agreement. 'It has been satisfactory. Apart from the travelling which, at times, has been arduous. More so than I'd first imagined.'

'My point exactly. So, I've come up with an idea.' An eager face stared back at her. 'Why don't you sell this house, and I'll sell mine and we'll buy somewhere together, maybe a barn conversion, on the outskirts of Lenchester. I've been searching online and seen several which might be suitable. More than suitable, in fact. As long as I have a studio, I can work anywhere. It's the perfect solution for both of us.'

She stiffened. 'You want us to buy something together?' That thought hadn't crossed her mind. Was she ready to sell the Victorian terraced house that she loved so much? The first house she'd ever owned and had bought thanks to an inheritance from her grandmother. She'd looked at countless other houses before settling on this one, and had spent hours and hours decorating and searching for perfect pieces of furniture, to make sure everything was in keeping with its history. 'I'm not sure.'

'I understand. Take as much time as you need to think about it. No pressure. Right now, how about we finish our wine and then go out for a drink? We'll go to your favourite pub for some real ale.'

'That's a lovely idea,' she said anxious to put thoughts of selling to the back of her mind for a short while. She picked up her glass and was about to take a sip as her phone rang. 'It's Whitney,' she said after glancing at the screen.

'That woman has impeccable timing,' Ross said, laughing. 'She always seems to phone during something important.'

'Hello, Whitney.'

'I wanted to talk through today's interview and next steps, if you've got time. Are you working?'

'Ross and I were about to go out for a drink.'

'Sorry, I always seem to interrupt you.'

'That's what he said.'

'It's not intentional, I promise. Not something important, is it?'

How did she do that? It was like the woman had a hotline to her mind.

'We'll talk tomorrow.'

'Oh, I get it. I'm looking forward to hearing whatever it is. And remember, you can't keep any secrets from me, so don't even think of trying.'

'I'll see you in the morning,' she said, ignoring the comment, not wanting Ross to guess what the conversation had been about.

Chapter 35

When George arrived at the station, Whitney was standing by the board, with her hands on her hips, talking with Clifford. She'd intended to be there earlier, but sleep had evaded her, owing to all that was on her mind. Finally, at five, she'd drifted off for a couple of hours. She didn't even hear Ross leave, instead saw the note he'd left for her on the pillow. He hadn't wanted to disturb her. She appreciated his consideration.

'Morning,' she said.

'You've made it just in time,' Whitney said. 'We're about to have a run through of where we are and what we intend to do moving forward.'

'I'm glad not to have missed anything.'

'Attention, everyone,' Whitney said. 'We've got to get this nailed once and for all, not least because the media are being a thorn in PR's side, constantly pestering them, wanting to know how the investigation is progressing. And PR, in turn, is bothering the super daily for updates. Frank, did you by any chance come across anything that you'd previously missed?'

'I stayed late last night and went through the footage from cameras near the Marshall house again, to double-check. His car is sighted going in the direction of his home and there was definitely no indication of him having left his house on foot, or in his car after he'd arrived. But we do have to remember that there are many areas where there aren't cameras, so he could have taken back roads and not been spotted. I also—'

'Guv,' Ellie called out, a sense of urgency in her voice. 'You'll want to see this straight away. Mac's sent everything over.' George, Clifford and Whitney hurried to her desk, with Brian following close behind. 'I've got the footage from all of the nanny cams. This is from the hall camera and shows the wife leaving on Saturday afternoon with the child.' She fast-forwarded the recording. 'And here is Scott Marshall in the kitchen making a sandwich and having a beer. He leaves at seven. Now look when it gets to one-fifteen in the morning, he walks in the front door.' She moved the footage on for them to see.

'After being stood up by the victim's wife,' Whitney said. 'Which they'd both told us about. He said she called at one to say she wasn't going to meet him at the park and then he went home.'

'What time did he leave the house again to go to the club?' Clifford said.

'That's just it. He didn't.'

'What?' Whitney spluttered. 'Are you sure?'

'Yes. It's all on here. He goes into the lounge and falls asleep in the chair, and doesn't move until four in the morning, which is after the killing took place.'

'Crap. It puts him in the clear. He claimed to have been framed and it looks like he was right. Unless he orchestrated the murder but didn't actually pull the trigger.'

'From my observations of him, it's a stretch to believe that,' George said.

'Shall we release him from custody?' Brian asked.

'We'll keep him a while longer. I know what you're saying, George. But we can't discount that he was involved until we're one hundred per cent sure. He may have stolen the gun from Gordon Elliott and given it to the killer.'

'I suggest you look further into Marshall's wife as she also has easy access to the gun,' George said.

'But what would her motive be?' Clifford asked.

'Motives are complex things. Just because we can't immediately discern one, doesn't mean it's not there,' George said.

'Alternatively, Naomi Armstrong could have crept out of her parents' home and done it herself,' Brian suggested.

'With a sick child? How likely is that?' Whitney said. 'Let's take this logically. First, we'll interview Jessica Marshall's parents. I want to know more about who had access to the gun and also want to confirm their daughter was there all night. George, you can come with me.'

'Now we know Scott Marshall's in the clear, I might speak to him about our arrangement,' Clifford said quietly so only Whitney and George could hear.

'Not yet. As we've already discussed, he might have orchestrated it even if he didn't do it himself. It's not going to affect anything if you wait a while longer, is it?'

'As long as it's not for too long, I've got—'

'Trust me, you'll get your chance to speak with Marshall as soon as it's possible.'

They headed to the car park and George's car. Once they were in traffic on the way to the Elliotts' house, George turned to Whitney. 'I've got something to tell you.'

'I gathered as much. I'm impressed that you volunteered, and I didn't have to ask. That's got to say something for our relationship.'

Was Whitney correct? It wasn't something she'd given much thought to.

'Ross has come up with a suggestion regarding our living arrangements, and I'm conflicted. I would value your input. He wants us both to sell our houses and buy somewhere close to Lenchester, with a studio. He mentioned a barn conversion.'

'That's an inspired idea.'

'Is it? I love my house. It took me a long time to find and decorate it.'

'But it's just a house, George. Houses are replaceable. People aren't. You want to be with Ross, and that has to be better than being stuck on your own with nothing to look at but four walls. However nicely decorated they are.'

'It's not that simple.'

'He's not pressuring you to make a decision immediately, is he?'

'No, he's not. But he's been checking out the estate agents and said there are some suitable places out there. I'll have to make a decision soon.'

'You know, you could always keep your house and rent it out. The rent would cover the cost of a mortgage on your new property.'

She had enough money in the bank to cover her half of a new property, but Whitney didn't know that.

'That's an option, but I don't know whether I'd want anyone in there because it's my house with my belongings.'

'You take all your possessions to the new place and rent it unfurnished. If it wasn't for the fact I own my place, I'd be tempted.' George frowned. 'What? Oh, I know what you're thinking … I'm too messy and untidy and I wouldn't take care of your garden.'

'The thought didn't cross my mind.'

'Good. Think about what I said, and we can discuss it later if you wish. Ross isn't going to rush you. Take your time. We're almost here, so let's get our minds back on the case.'

Chapter 36

Whitney glanced over at George as they pulled into Hampshire Close where Jessica Marshall's parents lived. Her face was set hard, clearly worried about the decision she had to make. Whitney had been so pleased when her friend got back with Ross and hoped she'd come to realise that his idea of buying together was a good one. But she couldn't say any more. George would come to her own decision soon enough. Whitney knew from experience that her friend wouldn't appreciate being pushed into deciding before she was ready.

'Number sixty-three is the next on the left,' she said, as they got close. 'Another mansion. Let's hope they're in.'

She rang the bell, and the door was opened by a woman who was clearly Jessica's mother as there was a marked family resemblance, the angular jaw and the same green oval-shaped eyes.

'Mrs Elliott, I'm Detective Chief Inspector Walker, and this is Dr Cavendish. We'd like to come in and have a word, if we may?'

'Jessica told me that you've arrested Scott for Ryan's

murder. It was such a shock, I had no idea things were so bad between them. Is that why you're here?' She ushered them inside and they followed her into a sitting room. 'Your forensics men were here yesterday and left such a mess. There was powder everywhere and my cleaner had a dreadful job getting rid of it.'

'I'm sorry about that. Is Mr Elliott home?'

'He's at work. I doubt he'll be back much before eight. He never is, even though he's meant to be taking it easy because of his health.'

'Jessica informed us that she stayed overnight with you on Saturday the seventh of March. Is that correct?'

'Yes, it is.'

'What time did she leave?'

'In the morning about eleven-thirty after we'd all had a late breakfast.'

'Are you sure she didn't go out at all during the night?'

'Not that I know of, but we were all asleep.'

'Did Jessica usually stay with you when Ryan Armstrong had a boys' night at his house?'

'Yes, because she didn't want Leo being woken up when his father came in a bit the worse for wear. Leo isn't a good sleeper, and if he does wake up, it's almost impossible to get him back to sleep. I can't begin to tell you the number of times I've wandered up and down his bedroom with him in my arms, trying to rock him back to sleep.'

'Does Jessica sleep in the same bedroom as Leo when they're here?' George asked.

'She sleeps in our guest room. Leo has his own bedroom that we had decorated especially for him. He often stays with us if they go out.'

'What can you tell us about the relationship between Scott and Ryan Armstrong?'

'Not much, I'm afraid. They had a good business and

travelled a lot together. But that's all I know. Ryan was so nice and the last person I'd have expected to be murdered. Knowing it's Scott who did it. I've got to tell you, it's totally floored me.' She sighed.

'Do you and Mr Elliott get on well with Scott?'

The woman moved from foot to foot and Whitney noticed that she had the same dolphin tattoo on her ankle that Jessica had. 'We know what he's like, if that's what you mean.'

'Could you be more explicit?'

'He has an *eye for the ladies*, as Gordon would say.'

'Have either of you ever approached Scott about this?'

'It's Jess's business and she wouldn't thank us for getting involved. To be honest, we rarely see him. I'm sure he suspects that we know what he's up to, so he keeps away.'

'We arrested Scott because the gun was found in his possession. Do you think he could've stolen the gun from the cabinet? Does he know where the key's kept?'

She wasn't going to let them know that he now had an alibi, especially as he hadn't yet been released.

'Everyone knows where it's kept. Family. Friends. Household staff. Gordon wasn't very secretive about it.'

'Mr Elliott informed my sergeant that he rarely takes out the gun and he couldn't remember the last time he saw it so doesn't know exactly when it was stolen. Can you remember seeing it recently?'

'Um …' She glanced up towards the ceiling. What was she hiding?

'Mrs Elliott, this is a murder enquiry. You must tell us everything you know, or you could be charged with obstructing the course of justice,' Whitney said.

'I do remember a couple of weeks ago Jess and I were talking about the gun because it's now hers. But please don't tell Gordon I told you that. Jess loves guns. She took it out of the cabinet and went into the garden and shot at a target for a while.'

Was Jessica the murderer? Was she practicing? All guns are different. If she wanted to make sure to kill Ryan instantly, then it would help to be familiar with the weapon.

But why? What would be her motive?

'Did you see Jessica replace the gun?'

She bit down on her bottom lip. 'I believe so.'

'Only *believe*?'

'You're confusing me. I have to think.' She paused. 'Yes. She put it back. I remember now.'

'Where are the bullets kept?'

'In the locked cabinet. They weren't there either when your officer and Gordon looked.'

'Are you sure Jessica replaced the gun? Do you think she could have taken the gun away with her?' Whitney pushed.

'What are you saying? That Jessica took the gun and gave it to Scott to shoot Ryan? No way would my daughter do anything like that. She might have inherited her father's ruthlessness but also his moral compass.'

Whitney bit back a retort. The man managed to get away without paying his taxes. What sort of *moral compass* was that?

'Before we go, is there anything else you can think of that might help us?'

'Nothing. Except that Jessica had nothing to do with it, I'd stake my life on it. She wouldn't have given Scott the gun.'

They left the house and headed towards the car.

'If Jessica's our killer, we need proof that she left the house during the time of the murder,' Whitney said.

'Look, there's a camera.' George pointed to the opposite side of the road. 'Suppose Jessica did go out without her parents knowing. It might have been captured.'

They crossed the road, walked up the drive and knocked on the door. An older woman, in her sixties, answered.

'I'm Detective Chief Inspector Walker and this is Dr Cavendish,' Whitney said as she held out her warrant card for the woman to check. 'We noticed you've got a camera focussed on the road. Does it capture right across to the houses on the opposite side?'

'Yes, it does. We had it set up so my husband can keep an eye on what's going on. We were burgled once while we were upstairs in bed.'

'We'd like to take a look at your footage from Saturday night, the sixth of March, through into the early hours of Sunday morning, the seventh, if that's possible.'

'Yes. Come on in. I'll need to access my husband's laptop.'

She took them into a study and sat at the desk where she called up the recording from the time Whitney had asked.

'An Audi four-wheel drive left the house opposite at fourteen minutes to one.'

'Do you recognise that car?' Whitney asked, walking around the desk and peering over the woman's shoulder.

'Yes. It belongs to Mr Elliott.'

'Can you enlarge the image so we can see who's driving?'

'I don't think so.'

'Please could you email me the footage and I'll get one of my officers to take a look.' Whitney pulled out a card and handed it to the woman.

'I'm not sure how to do it,' she said, her hands twitching.

'I'll do it,' George said.

The woman gave a sigh of relief and got up from her seat. George sat down and quickly sent the footage to Whitney.

'Thank you for assisting us,' Whitney said to the woman as she saw them out. 'We really appreciate it.'

'I'm glad to help.'

They walked back over the road to where George had parked.

'I'll send this to Ellie so she can take a look while we're on our way back.'

Chapter 37

'Have you had time to look through the footage from the neighbour's CCTV?' Whitney asked Ellie once they'd arrived back at the station.

'Yes, and I've identified the driver.' The officer smiled. 'It was Jessica Marshall, driving her father's car.'

'She must have sneaked out without them knowing. Did you follow the car to see where it was heading?' Whitney asked.

'There are no other CCTV cameras on their street, but I picked her up as she headed onto the main road. She was driving in the direction of the city centre. I tracked her until she turned into Sherwood Road, where there are no cameras. It's a side road five minutes' walk from the snooker club. I'm about to check the time she returned to her parents' house and the route she took.'

'Okay, keep going.' She called the team to attention. 'Jessica Marshall is now our prime suspect. But when did she put the gun into Scott's gym locker? We need to know before we question her. Let's get it watertight. Jessica doesn't know we suspect her as she believes Scott has been charged. We can use that to our advantage.'

'What's her motive?' Doug asked.

'We don't know that yet, but we'll find out soon enough. I'm going back to the gym.'

'Do you need me? I have some errands to do,' George said.

'I'll take Brian. I'd like you here when we bring her in to interview. Is that okay?'

'Yes. Give me a call and I'll come straight back.'

'Brian, we're off to the gym. Your car.'

'No need to keep saying, guv. I know.'

Whitney laughed. He sounded just like George.

When they arrived at the gym, she went up to reception and held out her warrant card, as it was a different person on duty from the last time.

'Is Hallie here?'

'It's her day off. I'll fetch the duty manager,' the young man said.

After a few minutes, a man in a tracksuit came over to them. 'I'm Jon Gifford.'

'Detective Chief Inspector Walker and this is Detective Sergeant Chapman. Do you recognise this woman?' She held out her phone on which she had a photo of Jessica.

'No, sorry, I don't.'

'We'd like to find out if she was here recently, specifically from early Sunday morning the seventh of March onwards.'

'I wasn't on duty last weekend, but I can ask one of the trainers, if you give me a moment.' He walked through some double doors into the gym and after a few minutes came back with another man following. 'This is Sam, he was working all weekend on the date you mentioned.'

'Do you recognise this woman?' Whitney asked, holding out her phone.

He stared at it for a couple of seconds and nodded. 'Yes, she's the wife of Scott Marshall.'

'Did you see her on the weekend of the seventh?'

'I don't remember her coming in.'

Damn.

'Could she have come into the gym without you noticing?'

'Yes, I suppose so. I don't spend all my time in reception.'

'Thank you.' Whitney turned to Jon. 'Can we look at your camera footage for twenty-four hours from one in the morning on Sunday the seventh?'

If Jessica did plant the gun it would have to be soon after the murder took place to ensure that Scott was put in the frame.

'The recordings are in the office if you'd like to come through.' They followed him to his office and watched while he called up the footage and went through it. 'It doesn't look like she came in.'

'Hang on a minute, what's that?' She pointed to a shadow close to the wall. 'Could it be someone keeping out of sight of the camera?'

'Yes, it looks like it,' Brian said.

'Can you zoom in?'

'A little.' Jon enlarged it but they still couldn't see who it was.

'What about when this person comes back through reception towards the door.'

Jon fast-forwarded the footage and stopped when the shadow reappeared. 'They're back again and not sticking so close to the wall this time. I'll zoom in again.'

Although the face and upper body was hidden, they

had a much better look at the bottom half of the person. It was a woman, wearing three-quarter length leggings.

'We've got her,' Whitney said, pointing at the footage. 'The tattoo of a dolphin on her ankle. Both Jessica and her mum have one.'

'And that can't be her mum because she's not so slim,' Brian said.

'Exactly.' Whitney pulled a card out of her pocket and gave it to Jon. 'Can you email me the footage, please?'

'Sure.' His fingers slowly pressed the keys. 'Done.'

They left the gym, and she turned to Brian. 'Okay, we've nailed her. Now let's bring her in for questioning. She wasn't at her parents' house earlier, so we'll try her house.'

On the way she called George and arranged for her to meet them at the station.

Chapter 38

They drove straight to the house, adrenaline coursing through Whitney's body.

'There's her car,' she said, as they pulled up behind it in the drive. 'It looks like she's in.'

They approached the front door and rang the bell. After a short while the nanny answered.

'Hello, Sue, we've come to see Mrs Marshall.'

'You've just missed her.'

'Isn't that her car?' Whitney nodded towards it.

'Yes, but for some reason she took the one I usually use.'

So she wouldn't be spotted?

'Did she say where she was going?'

'Can we talk inside, Leo's on his own in the playroom and I don't like leaving him.'

'Of course.'

They followed as Sue hurried down the hall and into a room on the right. The little boy was placing a pile of multi-coloured bricks on top of each other.

'I'm back, Leo,' Sue said, going over to him and

scooping him up in her arms. 'Say hello to the inspector.' He hid his face in her shoulder. 'He's shy.'

'Mrs Marshall?' Whitney reminded her.'

'She'd been acting strange all morning. It's not surprising, I suppose, with Mr Marshall arrested.'

'Did she talk about it?'

'After I mentioned speaking to you at the station, she—'

'I asked you to keep it confidential.'

'I didn't intend to, it slipped out during breakfast. After that she went all distant and seemed preoccupied. Twenty minutes ago she said she was going to see Naomi Armstrong.'

'Did she say why?'

'She muttered something about unfinished business, but I might have misheard because Leo had tripped and banged his head on the floor. I was taking care of him and didn't double-check.'

'Did Mrs Marshall take anything with her?'

'Her handbag. She carries a tan coloured Mulberry tote.'

Large enough for a weapon. Had she got her hands on another gun?

Whitney exchanged a look with Brian and nodded towards the door.

'I want you to stay here, speak to no one and I'll arrange for an officer to be with you shortly.'

'B-but …'

'No buts, Sue. This is important, I need you to do exactly as I've said.'

'Okay,' she nodded.

They rushed back to Brian's car and Whitney picked up the radio. 'DCI Walker here. I want an officer at 7 Favell Drive immediately'

'Yes, guv.'

She then phoned the incident room.

'DC Baines.'

'Doug. Get Frank and Meena and meet me and Brian at the victim's house. Jessica Marshall is there and we've no idea if she has a weapon. Naomi Armstrong could be in danger. Park a little way up the road so you're not spotted and make sure you're all carrying Tasers.'

'What about DI Clifford, as he's here?'

Did she want him muscling in on it? An extra body may come in handy.

'Okay bring him with you, unless he doesn't want to.' She ended the call. 'Let's get motoring.'

'What makes you think she has a weapon?' Brian asked.

'*Unfinished business*. I take that to mean that she wants to harm Naomi. We can't take any risks.'

The drive to Marsden House didn't take long and Whitney impatiently strummed her fingers on her leg while waiting for the others to arrive.

'Doug has just turned into the road, with DI Clifford following,' Brian said after they'd been waiting almost twenty minutes.

'About time.' She jumped out of the car and ran to where Doug had parked. 'What kept you?' she asked as he rolled down the window.

'You wanted Tasers and we had to sign them out, which took a while.'

'Okay. This is what we'll do,' she said once they were all out of the car and Brian had joined them. 'We don't want to alarm them, in case Jessica tries anything stupid. We have no idea whether or not she's got a weapon or what she's intending to do, apart from she said she had unfinished business. It could just be a chat with Naomi and she's going to tell her she knows about the affair, but we're not taking any risks. Doug and Seb, you come with me. Do you both have Tasers?'

'Only me,' Doug said.

'The three of us will go around the back and see if we can get in that way. If we stick close to the trees we won't be seen. Brian, I want you to take Meena and go to the front door. On my instruction, you can knock on the door. If Jessica answers she won't recognise you. Frank, stay by the gate, so if she does try to escape you can go after her.'

'In his condition?' Doug said.

Whitney glared at him. 'Come on.'

They stayed on the opposite side of the road until level with the house, and then split up. Whitney, Seb and Doug kept close to the trees and out of eye sight from the house. When they reached the end Whitney ran over to the side of the house and peered through the window. Jessica and Naomi were standing in the kitchen, their backs to her.

She beckoned for Seb and Doug to join her.

'They're both in the kitchen. Brian,' she said into her radio. 'Ring the bell.'

'Okay, guv.'

As the bell rang, both Jessica and Naomi's heads turned towards the sound. Naomi went to walk away, and Jessica blocked her way.

'Jessica's stopping her from answering. Is the door open?'

'No, it's locked,' Brian said.

Seb tapped her on the shoulder. 'The conservatory door is open. We can get in that way.'

'Did you hear that, Brian?'

'Yes, guv.'

'Stand by.'

'They crept past the kitchen window, all the time

keeping their eye on Jessica who stood in front of Naomi, and they ran through the conservatory, turning right and heading towards the kitchen. She gestured for Seb to let the others in through the front door and tapped Brian on the shoulder, counting down from three to one before opening the kitchen door and charging in.

'Jessica,' she called out, wanting to distract her.

The woman turned and, on seeing Whitney and Brian, with one hand she grabbed a knife from the block standing on the centre island and with the other made a grab for Naomi, who ducked and managed to escape.

'Keep away,' Jessica shouted, holding the knife to her wrist. 'Or I'll kill myself.'

'Jessica, don't do anything stupid,' Whitney said, taking a step towards her. 'Put the knife down. Let's talk about this.'

'There's nothing to talk about. My life's ruined thanks to this bitch.'

'That doesn't mean you have to end it.'

'Yes it does. I'm not—'

The knife dropped from her hand as two wires embedded themselves in her chest. She dropped to the floor.

Whitney turned to see Brian's Taser pointing in Jessica's direction.

Chapter 39

After receiving medical attention, and the doctor confirming she was able to be questioned, Whitney was informed that Jessica Marshall had been taken to interview room one with her solicitor.

'Brian, I want to show Jessica the recordings of the car and also her at the gym. Can you set that up for me?'

'Yep, no problem.'

Whitney wandered over to Clifford who was sitting at the desk he'd been using, staring into space.

'Brian and I are about to interview Jessica Marshall.'

'When are you releasing Scott? I'd like to speak to him again.'

'After we've charged Jessica he's all yours.'

'Good.'

'Will you be going back to London?'

'Once we've discovered her motive.'

'Don't tell me you're now thinking that she was paid by the syndicate to murder Armstrong and frame her husband, because that's plain ridiculous.'

'I'm not making any assumptions one way or the other.'

'George is going to observe. If you'd like to stand with her you're perfectly welcome.'

'Thank you. I will.'

The four of them headed downstairs and parted company as Whitney and Brian entered the interview room. Jessica didn't acknowledge their presence and continued staring ahead.

'Interview on the fifteenth of March. Those present: Detective Chief Inspector Walker, Detective Sergeant Chapman. And ... please state your names for the recording.'

'Andrew Hart, solicitor.' There was silence, until he nudged the accused.

'Jessica Marshall,' she said, finally looking up and making eye contact with Whitney.

'We'd like to speak to you about the shooting of Ryan Armstrong.'

'Ask my husband.'

'We have evidence indicating that he wasn't responsible for the shooting. It was you. You sneaked out of your parents' house, drove to the car park adjacent to the snooker club and shot Ryan with your father's handgun. The next morning you took the gun and placed it in your husband's locker at the gym.'

'That's crazy. Why would I do that?'

'Brian, the first piece of evidence, please.' She waited until the footage was on the screen. 'This is you coming out of your parents' house in the early hours of Sunday morning, the seventh of March, driving your father's car.'

'How do you know that's me?'

'We enlarged the image and were able to identify you. The CCTV cameras picked you up going in the direction of the snooker club. You parked in Sherwood Road and walked to the car park where you met Ryan Armstrong and shot him.'

'What proof do you have? All you know is that I went out in the car.'

'Where did you go?'

'I couldn't sleep so went out for a drive. I wasn't going anywhere in particular.'

'The next morning, you visited the gym and went to your husband's locker. Here's the recording.' She nodded to Brian to put up the next piece of footage.

'I can't see anything.'

'That shadow is you heading for the locker room.'

'Rubbish. That could be anyone.'

'Brian.' Whitney waited until the next piece of footage came up. 'Stop there,' she said when they could see the legs.

'Those legs could belong to anyone.'

'Except they don't. Zoom in please, Brian.' She waited until there was a clear view of the leg. 'That's your tattoo.'

'Lots of people have them, including my mother.'

'True, although we know it's not her as you're smaller. We believe you planted the gun in Scott's locker to incriminate him.'

She ran her fingers through her hair. 'It's not like that at all. It's—'

'Don't say anything further,' the solicitor said, interrupting. He leant in and whispered something which Whitney couldn't make out. Did that mean they were now going to get the *no comment* treatment?

'Okay, I'll tell you everything,' Jessica said.

Whitney jerked her head back. She wasn't expecting that.

'But …' the solicitor said.

'I know what you said, but they need to know the truth,' Jessica continued. 'Scott made me go out to meet him. He'd already killed Ryan and he forced me to take the gun and put it in his locker so it couldn't be traced.'

'Why did you do what he asked? You could have called the police.'

'I was scared of him. You don't know what he's like. He threatened to harm Leo, so I had to do as he asked. I didn't shoot Ryan, he did. You have to believe me …' A sob escaped her lips. 'Please … You have to believe me.'

'We would, except for one thing,' Whitney said. 'We know for certain that your husband couldn't have committed the murder as he has an alibi.'

Jessica gasped. 'What? That woman. Naomi. Was he with her? She would give him an alibi. They probably planned the whole thing together.'

'She's not the alibi.'

'Who is then?'

'It's not a person. You have nanny cams in your house, yes?'

'Yes.'

'We've looked at all the footage on the iPad and the exact time when Ryan Armstrong was shot, Scott was home. Jessica Marshall, I'm arresting you on suspicion of the murder of Ryan Armstrong. You do not have to say anything, but it may harm your defence if you do not mention when questioned something which you later rely on in court. Anything you do say may be given in evidence. Do you understand?'

'Yes,' she said. 'But you don't understand. You'd have done the same in my position.'

'Would I? Tell me why.' The more she told them now, the harder it would be for her barrister to get her off.

'You don't know what it's like living with someone like

270

Scott. Never faithful, always going after women he comes in contact with. He thinks I don't know, but I do. I know about every single affair he's had, including the one he's been having with Naomi.'

'But why kill Ryan?'

'To set up Scott.'

'Are you admitting that you did shoot him?'

'You've got all the evidence, what's the point in denying it.' She stared back at Whitney, her eyes empty.

'You could have shot Scott,' Brian said.

'No because I wanted him to suffer for a long time. Prison would've destroyed him. It's what he deserved. Ryan was collateral damage.'

Whitney swallowed hard, forcing herself not to reach over and slap the girl. *Collateral damage.* Was Ryan's life worth so little?'

'How did you persuade Ryan to meet you at the club car park?'

'That was easy enough, the man was so gullible. I phoned and begged him to meet me because I'd had a fight with Scott and he'd hit me. I told him that I'd taken a taxi to the club but it was locked and I didn't know who else to call. He was there in a shot. The rest was easy. I got into his car, took out the gun and shot him.'

'What happened to your clothes? There must have been blood on them.'

'I'd brought some spare clothes with me and I changed behind the car. I then put them into a carrier bag, along with Ryan's phone and went home via the river where I dumped everything.'

'Why did you choose the early hours of Sunday morning?'

'I knew that Scott had arranged to meet Naomi at the

park and was out at the time of the murder. I was hoping they might both have been done for the murder.'

'How did you know about the meeting?'

'I subscribe to a mobile phone tracker which I put on his phone. I can track all of his messages, emails and phone calls. It was a foolproof plan, except it's only updated every thirty minutes and I hadn't realised that Naomi couldn't get out to meet him. By then it was too late and Ryan was already dead.'

'What about Naomi? Were you intending to kill her, too?'

'No. Once I knew that it was unlikely she'd be charged, I wanted her to know that I was going to financially screw her. I was going to withdraw any funding for the club and insist it was sold.'

The solicitor leant in and whispered in her ear.

'That's it. You get nothing more from me.'

'You'll be escorted back to your cell, where you'll remain until your bail hearing, which we'll be opposing.'

Epilogue

Whitney and George headed to the pub where they'd agreed to meet with the team, and Clifford, to have their celebratory drinks. They were all congregated at the back of the room standing around a tall bar table.

'Okay, the drinks are on me,' she said as they approached, interrupting the high spirits.

'No, let me get them,' Clifford offered. 'It's the least I can do.'

'That works for me,' Whitney said. 'I'll go with you to help.'

'Much appreciated,' he said, flashing a smile.

They left the others and made their way to the bar, skirting around the throng of customers, most of them from the force, as it was their local.

'I expect you'll be glad to get back to the high-flying Met and leave the sticks behind.'

'I'd hardly call Lenchester the sticks. It's not in the middle of nowhere.'

'It's not London, either.'

'I've enjoyed my time here. You certainly operate a

very effective team, and I was impressed with the way you worked. And Dr Cavendish as well. She's a useful asset.'

'We couldn't do it without her. Shame you didn't get any further with your investigation into the syndicate.'

'I wouldn't say that. I've now got Scott Marshall working for me, and his input will be invaluable.'

'When are you going back?'

'The day after tomorrow. The Northampton Saints are playing the Leicester Tigers tomorrow night. Rugby.'

'I do know who the rugby teams are around here,' she said rolling her eyes. 'Women do support rugby as well, you know.'

'That wasn't what I meant. So, you're a fan?'

'No,' she admitted. 'My dad used to love rugby, but he died over twelve years ago now. Do you play?' she asked, realising that apart from him being an aristocrat with a photographic memory, or whatever it was George said he had, she knew very little about him.

'Yes. I sometimes play for a local team, when work doesn't get in the way. I'm a flanker.'

'I pity anyone being tackled by you.'

'I'm not the largest on the team.'

'Seriously? Bloody hell.'

They ordered the drinks and headed back to the rest of them. Clifford stood with Frank and Doug, laughing, and George and Whitney were a little way away.

'Have you thought any more about selling your house?' she asked.

'No.'

'Let me guess, you're compartmentalising it,' Whitney said.

'For the moment, yes I am. How are Tiffany and Martin, anything further on that front?'

'We're all going out for a meal on Saturday, and he

texted me the other day to say that he was going to ask her to accompany him to a concert next week, and was it okay.'

'It was good of him to ask you in advance. Do you mind them going out together?'

'I think it's good for them to get to know each other. Hopefully, he's going to be around when she has the baby. Two grandparents are better than one. Well, providing ...'

'Guv,' Frank called over interrupting them. He nodded at Clifford who was standing away from the rest of the team deep in conversation with Chief Superintendent Douglas.

'What the hell's that all about?' she muttered.

'Maybe they'd arranged to meet for a drink,' George said.

'Here? Now? No way. This is a celebration and Seb knows my views on Dickhead. He wouldn't invite him.'

'It certainly doesn't appear like they're celebrating. The body language, the expressions on their faces ... it's something serious.'

'You're right. Douglas doesn't even have a drink in his hand.'

She tried not to stare but her eyes were drawn to the pair of them. Finally after a few minutes, Douglas marched off.

She hurried over to Clifford, who was staring at his phone.

'Seb, what's going on? What did Douglas want?'

He glanced up; his face set hard. 'I've got to get back to London, now.'

'Why?'

'The shit's hit the fan. I'll be lucky to get out of it unscathed.'

The End

∽

Book 11 - Whitney and George return in *Dark Secrets* when they investigate the deaths of a family in their own home. Was it a murder suicide, or was someone else involved?
Tap here to buy

∽

Would you like to know more about **Sebastian Clifford**? He returns in his own series, in the book *Web of Lies* when, alongside DC Bird from Market Harborough police force, he investigates a high-profile death that had been recorded as a suicide.

Tap here to buy

HERE'S THE FIRST CHAPTER

11 April

'For goodness' sake,' Jenny Johnson said, turning to look in the back seat of the car where her two sons were squabbling, as usual, this time over a toy truck. 'The plan was for a nice day out, so stop arguing.' Her body tensed. Was it going to be like this for the entire day? If so, she'd sooner go back home and get on with the pile of ironing waiting for her.

It was late Sunday morning on a beautiful spring day, with the sky a soft pale blue and an array of yellows and oranges from the wild daffodils in bloom growing on the side of the lane as they drove through the countryside. She loved this time of year. It was perfect for a trip to Foxton Locks, their favourite place to visit. Though she suspected lots of other people would be there, too. Weather could be so hit-and-miss it was best to take advantage of it when you could.

'Are we there yet?' Lucas, the younger of her two boys, asked, fidgeting excitedly in his seat. 'I hope we see a boat coming through.'

'Yeah, that would be great, wouldn't it?' Tyler said.

At least it had stopped their latest argument.

She'd wanted the day to be special because it was the first time in ages since her husband, Kyle, had a day off. He'd been working seven days a week to get a big order shipped out. They were glad of the overtime, but it meant she'd had sole responsibility for the boys, who could be a handful, and that was putting it mildly.

'Boys, I've got a surprise for you,' Kyle said. 'But only if you're good.'

'We're good, aren't we, Tyler?' Lucas said. 'What is it, Dad?'

'Do you promise?'

'Yes,' Lucas said.

'Me, too,' Tyler agreed.

'Okay. I've booked us on a narrowboat for a trip down the canal after lunch. But if you keep fighting, I'm going to cancel it.'

'Yay. We're going on a boat. Thanks, Dad,' Tyler said. 'We'll be nice to each other. You can have the truck, Lucas,' he said handing it over to his younger brother.

Jenny smiled to herself and turned back to face the front of the car. 'Nice one,' she whispered to her husband.

He glanced at her and winked. Even though the boat

trip had been her idea, she didn't resent him taking the credit if it gave her some peace and quiet. There were times when she could cheerfully take herself off and never come back. But those moments were few and far between. She loved her kids. And her life. It wasn't like every other family didn't have their share of problems. She saw the state of some of her friends' marriages and knew that she was luckier than most.

'There's the prison,' Tyler said, as they drove past it on the left. 'Do prisoners escape from there?'

'No. It's perfectly safe,' his mother said.

'If they do, I'll smash myself into them and knock 'em over. Then I'll kick and …'

'Tyler, no one's going to escape from the prison.'

'But what if they did?' Lucas, who wasn't as fearless as his older brother, asked.

'They won't. Look out the window, boys. We're nearly there. There's the signpost for the Foxton Locks top car park,' Kyle said.

'Can't we get any closer? Let's try the lower car park, especially as we've got the picnic and blankets to carry,' Jenny said, not fancying the fifteen-minute walk with the boys in tow.

She'd been looking forward to having lunch at the picnic tables close to the lock and the gift shop, which she loved to look around.

'Okay, but at this time of day it's bound to be full. So don't blame me if we end up having to turn around and come back.' Kyle took a right turn and after driving for a few minutes, they came to the lower car park. It was full. People were milling around, heading straight to the canal staircase lock and the museum. And, of course, the pub.

'Sorry. Should have listened to you,' Jenny said, hoping it wouldn't set the boys off again, although judging by their shrieks of glee in the back they were so excited about the boat trip she suspected they wouldn't much care.

Kyle turned the car around and headed back along Gumley Road towards the top car park, joining a steady flow of traffic. 'Let's hope there's still somewhere in the overspill section.'

She sensed the frustration in his voice.

Luckily, there were still some spaces, although Kyle had to drive right to the far side where it backed onto some overgrown wasteland.

'Can we have lunch at the pub?' Tyler asked. 'I want some beer.'

Jenny laughed. 'First of all, no. We've brought a picnic. And second of all, you're only eleven and much too young for beer.'

'Henry's dad lets him have some.'

'Well, we're not Henry's parents and the answer's still no. It's a lovely day and we'll enjoy having our lunch outside watching the boats go by.'

'Can we get out now?' Lucas asked as the car came to a standstill.

'Yes, but stay close while we're sorting everything out.'

'Can I take the football?'

'Okay, but don't kick it close to the cars or you might do some damage. Go over there and stay where we can see you.' Jenny pointed at the piece of wasteland directly in front of them. 'And make sure to come back when I call, or there'll be no boat trip.'

For once it would be nice not to be the disciplinarian, but that seemed to be the role she'd adopted. Kyle was much more laid-back than she was. It made a good balance, though. It would be no good if they were both the same.

'Yes, Mum,' they both said in unison.

'Come on, Tyler, I'll race you,' Lucas said to his older brother, holding the ball and running off.

Jenny leant against the car and watched them. 'That's far enough,' she called. 'We're not going to be long, and I don't want to waste time waiting for you.'

The sun's rays beat down on her back and she breathed in the fresh country air. Market Harborough, where they lived, was a lovely small town, and they were happy there, but escaping to the country was still a perfect way to relax.

'You mollycoddle them too much,' Kyle said, cutting into her thoughts, as he came around the front of the car, stopping beside her. 'You know, they're ten and eleven and need to find their feet so they can manage on their own. You've got to stop being so protective. You're not going to be there for them all the time and it's not like they're going to run away or do anything stupid over there. Let them enjoy themselves. They're in no danger.'

She sighed. 'It's easy for you to say because you grew up in a rough and tumble house with three brothers. I was an only child, and only had to catch my breath and my parents would whisk me off to the doctor. But you're right. What harm can they come to over there?'

She headed to the back of the car, determined to relax a little, and pulled out the two cool bags which contained their lunch, and placed them on the ground. She then took hold of two blankets and closed the boot. She listened. There was silence. 'I can't hear anything. Where have they gone? I'm going to have a look.'

'I keep telling you, they'll be fine,' Kyle said. 'Leave them to play.'

Ignoring her husband, she headed to the spot where the boys had run in to the wasteland. The grass was over-grown, but not so much that they'd be hidden. 'Tyler.

Lucas,' she called, scanning the area, willing them to appear. There was no reply.

'Kyle, they're not here and they're not answering,' she called out, swallowing back the panic.

Her husband strolled over. 'They're probably hiding in the bushes. Or one of them kicked the ball too far. They'll be back soon, you'll—'

'Daaaaaad.'

Jenny's heart pounded in her chest at the sound of the terrifying yell from Tyler. She ran in the direction of his voice and crashed into him. 'Are you okay? Where's Lucas? What's happened?' She wrapped her arms tightly around him.

'He-he's …'

'Muuum,' Lucas came charging through the bushes over to where they were standing, his face ashen and his body shaking.

Kyle grabbed hold of him, picking him up and holding him close. 'It's okay, son. I've got you. Take some deep breaths and tell us what you saw. It was probably nothing.'

Jenny glanced at him. How did he know that? The pair of them were clearly shaken. Sometimes Kyle's attitude was too laid-back.

'A b-body. Dead,' Tyler said, pulling out of Jenny's hold and trying to pull himself together.

'You saw a body?' Kyle asked, looking at Jenny and pulling a disbelieving face over the top of Lucas's head.

'A man lying on the ground. He's dead,' Tyler said.

'It's true,' Lucas said, as Kyle placed him on the ground so he could stand on his own.

'Are you sure he isn't asleep?' Jenny asked.

'No, Mum. He's dead. Half his head is missing,' Tyler said. 'The flies were …' Tears rolled down his cheeks and Jenny pulled him back into her arms.

She'd never even seen a dead body herself, and now her two little boys had … this could affect them forever.

'Kyle, go and see and I'll stay here with the boys.'

Lucas ran over to her, and she stayed hugging the pair of them, while Kyle headed in the direction the boys had come from. Lucas was shaking, and Tyler was ramrod straight, although she could feel his tears seeping through her T-shirt.

After a minute or two, Kyle came running back from through the trees, shaking his head. His face was devoid of colour.

'It's true. I've just seen the body.' He pulled out a phone from the back pocket of his jeans. 'Take the boys back to the car and I'll call 999. We'll have to wait for the police to arrive.'

Tap here to buy

❧

Read more about Cavendish & Walker

DEADLY GAMES - Cavendish & Walker Book 1

A killer is playing cat and mouse……. and winning.

DCI Whitney Walker wants to save her career. Forensic psychologist, Dr Georgina Cavendish, wants to avenge the death of her student.

Sparks fly when real world policing meets academic theory, and it's not a pretty sight.

When two more bodies are discovered, Walker and Cavendish form an uneasy alliance. But are they in time to save the next victim?

Deadly Games is the first book in the Cavendish and Walker crime fiction series. If you like serial killer thrillers and psychological intrigue, then you'll love Sally Rigby's page-turning book.

Pick up *Deadly Games* today to read Cavendish & Walker's first case.

FATAL JUSTICE - Cavendish & Walker Book 2

A vigilante's on the loose, dishing out their kind of justice…

A string of mutilated bodies sees Detective Chief Inspector Whitney Walker back in action. But when she discovers the victims have all been grooming young girls, she fears a vigilante is on the loose. And while she understands the motive, no one is above the law.

Once again, she turns to forensic psychologist, Dr Georgina Cavendish, to unravel the cryptic clues. But will they be able to save the next victim from a gruesome death?

Fatal Justice is the second book in the Cavendish & Walker crime fiction series. If you like your mysteries dark, and with a twist, pick up a copy of Sally Rigby's book today.

~

DEATH TRACK - Cavendish & Walker Book 3

Catch the train if you dare...

After a teenage boy is found dead on a Lenchester train, Detective Chief Inspector Whitney Walker believes they're being targeted by the notorious Carriage Killer, who chooses a local rail network, commits four murders, and moves on.

Against her wishes, Walker's boss brings in officers from another force to help the investigation and prevent more deaths, but she's forced to defend her team against this outside interference.

Forensic psychologist, Dr Georgina Cavendish, is by her side in an attempt to bring to an end this killing spree. But how can they get into the mind of a killer who has already killed twelve times in two years without leaving a single clue behind?

For fans of Rachel Abbott, L J Ross and Angela Marsons, *Death Track* is the third in the Cavendish & Walker series. A gripping serial killer thriller that will have you hooked.

LETHAL SECRET - Cavendish & Walker Book 4

Someone has a secret. A secret worth killing for....

When a series of suicides, linked to the Wellness Spirit Centre, turn out to be murder, it brings together DCI Whitney Walker and forensic psychologist Dr Georgina Cavendish for another investigation. But as they delve deeper, they come across a tangle of secrets and the very real risk that the killer will strike again.

As the clock ticks down, the only way forward is to infiltrate the centre. But the outcome is disastrous, in more ways than one.

For fans of Angela Marsons, Rachel Abbott and M A Comley, *Lethal Secret* is the fourth book in the Cavendish & Walker crime fiction series.

LAST BREATH - Cavendish & Walker Book 5

Has the Lenchester Strangler returned?

When a murderer leaves a familiar pink scarf as his calling card, Detective Chief Inspector Whitney Walker is forced to dig into a cold case, not sure if she's looking for a killer or a copycat.

With a growing pile of bodies, and no clues, she turns to forensic psychologist, Dr Georgina Cavendish, despite their relationship being at an all-time low.

Can they overcome the bad blood between them to solve the

unsolvable?

For fans of Rachel Abbott, Angela Marsons and M A Comley, *Last Breath* is the fifth book in the Cavendish & Walker crime fiction series.

～

FINAL VERDICT - Cavendish & Walker Book 6

The judge has spoken......everyone must die.

When a killer starts murdering lawyers in a prestigious law firm, and every lead takes them to a dead end, DCI Whitney Walker finds herself grappling for a motive.

What links these deaths, and why use a lethal injection?

Alongside forensic psychologist, Dr Georgina Cavendish, they close in on the killer, while all the time trying to not let their personal lives get in the way of the investigation.

For fans of Rachel Abbott, Mark Dawson and M A Comley, Final Verdict is the sixth in the Cavendish & Walker series. A fast paced murder mystery which will keep you guessing.

～

RITUAL DEMISE - Cavendish & Walker Book 7

Someone is watching.... No one is safe

The once tranquil woods in a picturesque part of Lenchester have become the bloody stage to a series of ritualistic murders. With no suspects, Detective Chief Inspector Whitney Walker is once again forced to call on the services of forensic psychologist Dr Georgina Cavendish.

But this murderer isn't like any they've faced before. The murders are highly elaborate, but different in their own way and, with the clock ticking, they need to get inside the killer's head before it's too late.

For fans of Angela Marsons, Rachel Abbott and L J Ross. Ritual Demise is the seventh book in the Cavendish & Walker crime fiction series.

MORTAL REMAINS - Cavendish & Walker Book 8

Someone's playing with fire.... There's no escape.

A serial arsonist is on the loose and as the death toll continues to mount DCI Whitney Walker calls on forensic psychologist Dr Georgina Cavendish for help.

But Lenchester isn't the only thing burning. There are monumental changes taking place within the police force and there's a chance Whitney might lose the job she loves. She has to find the killer before that happens. Before any more lives are lost.

Mortal Remains is the eighth book in the acclaimed Cavendish & Walker series. Perfect for fans of Angela Marsons, Rachel Abbott and L J Ross.

SILENT GRAVES - Cavendish & Walker Book 9

Nothing remains buried forever...

When the bodies of two teenage girls are discovered on a building site, DCI Whitney Walker knows she's on the hunt for a killer. The problem is the murders happened in 1980 and this is her first case with the new team. What makes it even tougher is that with budgetary restrictions in place, she only has two weeks to solve it.

Once again, she enlists the help of forensic psychologist Dr Georgina Cavendish, but as she digs deeper into the past, she uncovers hidden truths that reverberate through the decades and into the present.

Silent Graves is the ninth book in the acclaimed Cavendish & Walker series. Perfect for fans of L J Ross, J M Dalgleish and Rachel Abbott.

∼

KILL SHOT - Cavendish & Walker Book 10

The game is over.....there's nowhere to hide.

When Lenchester's most famous sportsman is shot dead, DCI Whitney Walker and her team are thrown into the world of snooker.

She calls on forensic psychologist Dr Georgina Cavendish to assist, but the investigation takes them in a direction which has far-reaching, international ramifications.

Much to Whitney's annoyance, an officer from one of the Met's special squads is sent to assist.

But as everyone knows…three's a crowd.

Kill Shot is the tenth book in the acclaimed Cavendish & Walker series. Perfect for fans of Simon McCleave, J M Dalgleish, J R Ellis and Faith Martin.

∽

DARK SECRETS - Cavendish & Walker Book 11

An uninvited guest...a deadly secret....and a terrible crime.

When a well-loved family of five are found dead sitting around their dining table with an untouched meal in front of them, it sends shockwaves throughout the community.

Was it a murder suicide, or was someone else involved?

It's one of DCI Whitney Walker's most baffling cases, and even with the help of forensic psychologist Dr Georgina Cavendish, they struggle to find any clues or motives to help them catch the killer.

But with a community in mourning and growing pressure to get answers, Cavendish and Walker are forced to go deeper into a murderer's mind than they've ever gone before.

Dark Secrets is the eleventh book in the Cavendish & Walker series. Perfect for fans of Angela Marsons, Joy Ellis and Rachel McLean.

Read more about Sebastian Clifford

WEB OF LIES: A Midlands Crime Thriller (Detective Sebastian Clifford - Book 1)

A trail of secrets. A dangerous discovery. A deadly turn.

Police officer Sebastian Clifford never planned on becoming a private investigator. But when a scandal leads to the disbandment of his London based special squad, he finds himself out of a job. That is, until his cousin calls on him to investigate her husband's high-profile death, and prove that it wasn't a suicide.

Clifford's reluctant to get involved, but the more he digs, the more evidence he finds. With his ability to remember everything he's ever seen, he's the perfect person to untangle the layers of deceit.

He meets Detective Constable Bird, an underutilised detective at Market Harborough's police force, who refuses to give him access to the records he's requested unless he allows her to help with the investigation. Clifford isn't thrilled. The last time he worked as part of a team it ended his career.

But with time running out, Clifford is out of options. Together they must wade through the web of lies in the hope that they'll find the truth before it kills them.

Web of Lies is the first in the new Detective Sebastian Clifford series. Perfect for readers of Joy Ellis, Robert Galbraith and Mark Dawson.

~

SPEAK NO EVIL: A Midlands Crime Thriller (Detective Sebastian Clifford - Book 2)

What happens when someone's too scared to speak?

Ex-police officer Sebastian Clifford had decided to limit his work as a private investigator, until Detective Constable Bird, aka Birdie, asks for his help.

Twelve months ago a young girl was abandoned on the streets of Market Harborough in shocking circumstances. Since then the child has barely spoken and with the police unable to trace her identity, they've given up.

The social services team in charge of the case worry that the child has an intellectual disability but Birdie and her aunt, who's fostering the little girl, disagree and believe she's gifted and intelligent, but something bad happened and she's living in constant fear.

Clifford trusts Birdie's instinct and together they work to find out who the girl is, so she can be freed from the past. But as secrets are uncovered, the pair realise it's not just the child who's in danger.

Speak No Evil is the second in the Detective Sebastian Clifford series. Perfect for readers of Faith Martin, Matt Brolly and Joy Ellis.

Acknowledgments

As always, first and foremost I'd like to thank my writing friends, Amanda Ashby and Christina Phillips, who have been with me every step of the way.

Thanks, to Emma Mitchell, whose edits are incredibly insightful and help me produce the best book I can. Thanks, also, to Kate Noble for her brilliant proofreading and patience as the same errors appear time and time again.

To Stuart Bache… what can I say. Thanks for such an amazing cover, I've had so many comments about it.

To my family, Garry, Alicia and Marcus, thank you for your continuing love and support which does not go unnoticed.

About the Author

Sally Rigby was born in Northampton, in the UK. She has always had the travel bug, and after living in both Manchester and London, eventually moved overseas. From 2001 she has lived with her family in New Zealand, which she considers to be the most beautiful place in the world. During this time she also lived for five years in Australia.

Sally has always loved crime fiction books, films and TV programmes, and has a particular fascination with the psychology of serial killers.

Sally loves to hear from her readers, so do feel free to get in touch via her website www.sallyrigby.com

Made in United States
North Haven, CT
30 July 2022

22058061R00182